Hrolf the Viking

Book 1 in the Norman Genesis Series

By

Griff Hosker

Contents

Hrolf the Viking i
Prologue 1
Chapter 1 3
Chapter 2 16
Chapter 3 27
Chapter 4 41
Chapter 5 50
Chapter 6 66
Chapter 7 78
Chapter 8 87
Winter Interlude 97
Chapter 9 101
Chapter 10 114
Chapter 11 123
Chapter 12 139
Chapter 13 149
Chapter 14 158
Chapter 15 168
Chapter 16 181
Epilogue 194
Glossary 195
Historical note 200

Published by Sword Books Ltd 2016

Copyright ©Griff Hosker

The author has asserted their moral right under the Copyright, Designs and Patents Act, 1988, to be identified as the author of this work.

All Rights reserved. No part of this publication may be reproduced, copied, stored in a retrieval system, or transmitted, in any form or by any means, without the prior written consent of the copyright holder, nor be otherwise circulated in any form of binding or cover other than that in which it is published and without a similar condition being imposed on the subsequent purchaser.
A CIP catalogue record for this title is available from the British Library.
Cover by Design for Writers
Thanks to Simon Walpole for the Artwork.

Prologue

I am Hrólfr Son of Gerloc. Until I was rescued by the legend that is Dragonheart I was a slave of the Franks. We had lived in the land they call Neustria on the banks of the river which winds all the way to the heart of the Empire. That time burned a brand in my heart. From then on, I hated all Franks. I was treated badly. That is the way with most slaves. Dragonheart was different. He treated slaves better than most. My life might have ended there as a thrall had not Dragonheart freed me and taken me to his home at Cyninges-tūn. The time I spent with him there made me a man. Men have often asked me why I did not stay with him. It is known that those who sail with Dragonheart have riches beyond their wildest dreams and are protected by the gods. He is a legend amongst the Norse. In truth, I did not wish to leave him but my destiny was not decided by the Dragonheart but by the Weird Sisters. A witch, I believe she was a servant of the Weird Sisters, told me that I had a different path to follow. I remember as clearly as if she spoke them now, her words to Dragonheart as we left her lonely island, *'**His family will be remembered long after you are dead, Jarl Dragonheart, but they will not know that they would have been nothing without the Viking slave who changed the world.**'* The Dragonheart had understood and he had given his blessing to my decision to find my own destiny.

I had chosen to sail with Gunnar Thorfinnson. He was a fine leader and wished to raid Neustria. The Dragonheart looked closer to home. *Wyrd*. I chose Jarl Gunnar as it gave me the chance to hurt the Franks who had slain my parents and made my young life such a misery. I could not bring myself to forgive them. They had worked my mother to death. The followers of the White Christ could forgive; I was Viking and we neither forgot nor forgave.

I had not left Cyninges-tūn empty-handed. Dragonheart had his smith, Bjorn Bagsecgson, make me a sword. It was a shorter sword than Ragnar's Spirit, Jarl Dragonheart's blade, but it had been made by the finest smith in the world of the Vikings. It had been Bjorn Bagsecgson who had made the sword touched by the gods. Heart of Ice was a magical weapon and I was lucky to have it. I also had my wolf cloak. I had killed the wolf and I had done so in the presence of the Ulfheonar. They were the wolf warriors. They were the most feared warriors and they followed only the Dragonheart. I had learned much from them. I was not Ulfheonar nor could even dream of such an honour but they had made me welcome in their company. Along with my helmet, shield and leather byrnie, I left feeling that I was the richest man in the world.

The sister of Dragonheart, Kara, was a volva, a powerful witch, and on the day I left, she and her husband Aiden, the Galdramenn, took me to one side. Their words are still in my head. I remember everything they said and I will never forget one word nor one act. She took the sword and she and her husband held it between them. They spoke words I did not understand and she sprinkled a fine power upon the blade. When they placed it over the flames of the fire in their hearth the sword burned with a blue flame and yet their hands were not harmed. I had been rendered speechless. When the flames had died, they had given me the sword. I had been fearful but Kara had told me that it was cold and it was, as cold as ice. Her words still resonate in my head, *'You have been brought to us by the Norns and they have decreed that you shall leave. You have Heart of Ice as your weapon and we have made it powerful. It will never break and it will never let you down. It is a connection to Aiden and to me. The sword connects you to the heart of the Dragon and the land of the wolf. Use it well. Be as the blade; be ice. You must be cold and dispassionate. If your heart is hot, then your actions will become flawed. We may never see you again but we will never forget you. Your people will rule this land when we are but dust. They will rule the Middle Sea and all of this comes from within you, Hrólfr son of Gerloc.'*

Two witches had predicted my future. I would not argue with them nor would I seek the opinion of a third. The three Norns were jealous creatures!

And then I had left and marched down the road to Úlfarrston and a future sailing with Gunnar Thorfinnson and his drekar *'Raven Wing'*. One life ended that day and another one began. What I did not know was that it was like a stone being thrown into a pond; the ripples spread further and further. Long after I was dead the fruit of my loins would rule vast lands and be known as the most powerful warriors. Before then I had to become worthy and I had to endure trials. My life would not be easy; the Weird Sisters and the Allfather wished to harden me into a weapon as cold and deadly as my sword.

Chapter 1

Bourde 820

That had all been two years ago. Since then I had been on many raids. We sailed around the coast of Northumbria to attack Frisia, Neustria and Austrasia. It was a long journey there and sometimes an even longer one back. The Jarl had us spend our winters in Ljoðhús where his father, Thorfinn Blue Scar, ruled. I would not be speaking the truth if I said my time there was happy. It was not. The crew of the Jarl's ship were, by and large, protective of me but others in the warrior hall resented my association with the Dragonheart. They were envious of him and his success. I was treated by some as though I was still a slave. It did not help that I looked younger than my years; I had down for a beard! Each time we left that island I felt a sense of relief. *'Raven Wing'* was my real home. The chest upon which I sat contained all that I had collected. I did not waste coins as many of my shipmates did. I didn't throw them away on whores and gambling; I saved them. One day I would have my own drekar and I would be jarl. Gunnar Thorfinnson understood that. My dream and that of the Dragonheart had saved Gunnar off Dyflin and he owed me a life. So long as he was captain then my life was bearable. Others took reluctance to whore and to gamble as a weakness.

I rowed three oars from the bow and the raven prow. I sat next to Siggi White Hair. The Jarl had placed me under his wing when I had joined the crew and he had looked after me. He was the oldest warrior on board but not as old as his white hair might suggest. It was said that he went berserk once and his hair became white overnight. For that reason, many men would not share an oar with him. They feared that he would go berserk again. A berserker could kill a friend as easily as a foe. I did not mind for I had fought with the Ulfheonar and knew that such men would not harm me. I had a magical sword. I told no one of the powers of my sword. I had seen, at first hand, what envy can do. Many men had tried to take the sword which was touched by the gods from the Dragonheart. I did not need such envy.

As we rowed towards the land they called Aquitaine I wondered when the Weird Sisters would interfere in my life again. We had raided up and down the coast of Charlemagne's empire for two years. We had brought home treasure but not enough for me to buy a mail byrnie. The men we had fought had not possessed such armour. I received a share of the booty but to get a good mail suit you either killed for it or took enough gold to buy one. I knew that I would need such mail if I was to achieve my ambition and become jarl. At least I had swollen my purse. My chest had two bags of coins and jewels hidden in the wolf cloak.

"You are quiet, Hrólfr. That is most unusual." Siggi was very observant.

We were lucky for the wind was from our quarter and rowing was easy. We could speak. "I just wonder where we will raid this time. That is all." I kept my ambitions and dreams to myself. I liked Siggi and I trusted him but speaking of what I desired might make the Weird Sisters become awkward. I kept those thoughts and dreams within my head.

"The same as we always raid. The coast of the Franks. The Danes have taken the best of the land of the Angles and the Franks are like sheep. We shear them."

"We should stay."

"Stay?"

"Each winter we sail all the way north to Ljoðhús. It takes us a month to sail north. Then, in spring, we have a month to sail south. Why?"

"We are safe in Ljoðhús," I said nothing. "Ah, I remember, Harald Black Teeth makes your life a misery when we are in the warrior hall."

Harald Black Teeth was a warrior who served another jarl in Ljoðhús. He had filed his teeth and stained them. For some reason, he did not like me. He would have challenged me to combat had he been able but Thorfinn had rules about that and no warrior wished to be exiled from his home. Harold just made my life hard. It was another reason I rarely strayed from the hall. There I was safe. Siggi and my crewmates offered me protection but when they were not around he was cruel.

"Perhaps but why do we not stay the winter here? The climate is better and there are many places we could claim for our own. There are those islands north of Neustria. They have a couple of farmers on them and no soldiers. We could make those our stronghold."

"Soldiers would come and besides what about women? Perhaps Harald Black Teeth makes your life a misery because you do not seek the company of women."

"I do like women. It is just those of Ljoðhús whom I do not find attractive."

Siggi laughed, "You are too choosy. Harold thinks you like men."

"Well, he is wrong!"

"Stop rowing, ship oars!"

The Jarl's voice carried to us. I glanced over the side. It was getting dark and we were approaching the low-lying shores of Aquitaine and the estuary of the river the Franks called the Garonne. We had not been here before but I knew why we had come. The Jarl knew from his time with the Dragonheart that this land was rich. They made fine wine which was highly valued. It meant they were able to afford golden ornaments for their churches and spices for their food. Both were light to transport and easy for us to take. What I knew, but the rest of the crew did not, was that there were other enemies here too. It was not the Franks only who were a danger. There were Arabs and Moors.

As we stored our oars the captain edged us into the shore. We were heading for the northern shore of the river. The sail was reefed and was barely visible. The sun was setting behind us and we would soon be invisible. I stood and stretched. The first months of rowing had been hard but my body had grown and my muscles with it. I could now row as long as any but I still found the seated position hard. I was not a natural sailor.

None of us needed instruction. We were enemies to all ashore and they to us. We each took our shield from the sheerstrake and then went to our chest to take out our helmets. Mine was well made and better than most. Bjorn Bagsecgson had made it for me. It was not welded but made of one piece and the nasal had three rivets holding it. Beneath it, I had a leather cap. Haaken One Eye had recommended one. He had tapped his own head when he had done so. Aiden the Galdramenn had put a plate in his head because of a head wound. The leather cap might make the difference. I knew that I needed mail. At the very least I needed an aventail to protect the back of my neck.

The last thing I did was to unwrap Heart of Ice from its sheepskin and fasten the baldric around my waist. I looked after the sword for it would protect me. I felt the sand under our hull as the ship's boys leapt over the side to secure us to the land. I had done that for one voyage. Luckily, I had grown so much that on the next voyage I had been promoted to the oars.

Gunnar walked down the centreboard. He nodded as he passed me. Kara had told Gunnar that I brought luck to him and his ship. He treated me well. Some of the crew resented that. I could do nothing about the resentment. I had not asked for special treatment. I suffered their snide comments. I suppose I could have challenged them but that might have upset the harmony of the drekar. My time would come. The Jarl dropped over the side and we followed. The Jarl led, that was our way.

The water came up to my thighs. It was much warmer than the seas further north. It almost felt like the hot springs in the lands of the fjords. Once we reached the beach Jarl Gunnar waved away the scouts. Ulf Big Nose led the way; he was half dog half warrior. The ship's boys began to set up the camp having first tied us to the shore. We gathered in a defensive half circle at the head of the beach. It was doubtful that there were any enemies close by but this was a good practice. We had seen no lights and felt safe.

The scouts came back. Ulf Big Nose said, "There is no one close by, Jarl. We are safe."

"Good, then we eat and rest. We leave at moonrise. Siggi, you and Hrólfr have the first watch."

Neither of us grumbled for the Jarl was fair. There was no favouritism on his drekar. Perhaps that was because we were not a large one such as *'Heart of the Dragon'*. We had a crew of forty-five only; forty rowers, a helmsman, three ship's boys and the Jarl. The *'Heart of the Dragon'* had a crew of up to eighty! If we had to do a duty now it meant that we would not be called on again for some time.

After leaving our shields by the fire which had been just been started, we headed for the top of the river bank. There were a few trees and we found one and settled down beneath its branches. We wished to be invisible. Pressing our backs into the bole we sat in silence to grow accustomed to this new land. There were different smells and sounds. It was only when we were in the rhythm of the land that Siggi spoke. We did so quietly and were sparing with our words. Even when we spoke our eyes never left the land to the east of us. We had a duty to watch and protect the others.

"Have you been here before with the Dragonheart?"

"No. I joined him when he was raiding Neustria. I know that he has raided here and gained great quantities of riches. The wine he took sold for a great profit. The people of Cyninges-tūn were grateful."

"His words impressed the Jarl. He has been desperate to raid here." I nodded. "It is too warm for me. Even now at night, it is warm. During the day, we will bake."

I tapped the mail shirt he wore. It covered just his chest and his back; his arms were bare but it gave good protection against arrows and sword thrusts. "Then take off your iron."

He shook his head. "I will sweat. There is danger all around us and I wish to live a little longer. I do not mind the smell and you have little say in the matter. You have yet to kill your first man." I hung my head and he said, quietly, "It is one of the reasons that you are not totally accepted yet."

"Our raids have gone too well. Our enemies have fled before us. Only four have been killed by the whole crew. I have tried to be at the fore."

"I know but you are the only new crew member. Do not get me wrong. I do not think you have been given a fair chance by some of the clan. There are some who hate you; I know not why. They are the ones who are close to the steering board. It is why the jarl puts us by the bow. Many of the clan think that your presence brings us good luck. I do. Your luck guides the raven at the prow. Since you joined us we have not had a man wounded nor a sheet snap. They say it is because you touched the sword which was touched by God!"

"Perhaps." I remained silent about my own weapon. I did not want to risk losing its magic."I cannot judge. I am just me."

When the moon began to rise, we returned to the fire. Jarl Gunnar Thorfinnson had not slept. He began to ladle out some fish stew. The rest of the crew had eaten before they slept. "Here. You have earned it."

"Thank you, Jarl."

As we ate he went around to wake the crew. As they stood to make water and to stretch their legs the Jarl returned to us. He came and sat next to me and spoke quietly. "I know that you have had problems with some of the crew, Hrólfr, but I am sure that this raid will change that. You have brought us good fortune. We are all richer. I believe it is you. The Gods like you."

"Do not worry, lord, I was a thrall. I am used to such treatment. I have thick skin and I know how to make myself inconspicuous."

I saw Siggi shake his head and the Jarl smiled, "You should not have to. I owe my life to you. Things will change."

Siggi said, "Tell the Jarl your idea, Hrólfr."

"He will not want to hear it, Siggi White Hair."

"Let me be the judge of that, Hrólfr."

I sighed, "I just thought that we could be more profitable if we overwintered in the land of the Angles or the Franks. We could save ourselves a long journey back to Ljoðhús."

He nodded and gave me a wry smile, "And that way you would be far from the tongue of Harald Black Teeth."

Shaking my head I said, "That was not the reason. I am not afraid of him. The smell of his breath perhaps but him? No."

They both laughed at that. Then Jarl Gunnar said, "It is not such a bad idea. The coast close to home is often storm-ridden. I fear that one day we will be swept over the edge of the world." He clapped me on the back. "I like the idea. We will look for such a place while we raid this summer. When the leaves fall, we will decide then what we need to do." He smiled, "You see you do bring us luck! Jarl Dragonheart said you were the brightest youth he had ever seen. That shows how much he thought of you. Now let us get aboard! Time is wasting."

It took far less time to break camp than it did to set it up and we were soon rowing up the river. For the first mile or so we had the incoming tide with us but then we fought the current. We could not use a chant to help us for we wished to be silent. It made rowing that bit harder. The whole crew were in the Jarl's hands. He had to find us a target which we could attack. I know that Jarl Dragonheart was aided by the maps of Aiden, his galdramenn. Jarl Gunnar had made copies of a couple but they had not been added to since we had left Cyninges-tūn. Who knew how much the land and its people had changed?

Slowly we began to edge towards the southern bank. The moon shone brightly. The ship's boys, the helmsman and the Jarl could see what we could not. They could see ahead. No shouts were made and orders were whispered by the ship's boys who ran up the middle. Inevitably, being at the bow, we were the last to hear the orders. We pulled in the oars and laid them silently in the middle. The helmsman, Sven, and the Jarl were both fine sailors and they used the river itself to bring us to a halt on the southern bank. As we did so I smelled the smoke from the settlement. I could not see it but I guessed that the Jarl had. As I waited for the order to leave I tightened the straps on my leather jerkin. There were a dozen metal studs on it. When I had the chance, I would add more to it. The studs could catch a blade and stop it slicing into the leather of my byrnie. I fastened the leather long under my helmet. It was not a well-made helmet. It was little more than a pot on my head. When I had money, I would buy one with a nasal, or even, if I had enough money, a face mask.

The ship's boys were over the side in an instant. As I took my shield, wolf cloak and sword I prayed to the Allfather that I would not be left to guard the drekar. As a relatively new member of the crew that had been my task too many times. I breathed a sigh of relief when I saw the Jarl speaking quietly to Erik and Olaf. Sven, the helmsman, handed each of us a spear. The Jarl was taking no chances. Ulf Big Nose was our scout. He had gained the nickname not because of the size of his nose but the fact that he had the ability to sniff out enemies. He loped off alone. He could move faster that way.

I was relegated to the rear. Siggi was often the last man. That was because he was dependable but I was next to last because I was young and unproven. We were moving through scrub and stunted trees. It was a well-worn track. It would not be long before dawn. The Jarl liked to attack just as the first rays of the sun rose in the east. We attacked from the west where it was normally still dark. I liked to think that was the reason for our success rather than any luck which I might have brought.

The smell of the settlement grew stronger. It was a mixture of smoke, animal dung and the smell of people. These people smelled differently to those at home and those in the land of the Angles. It was a more exotic smell and, to my nose, a more pungent smell. Arne Four Toes, in front of me, stopped suddenly. When I bundled into him he turned around angrily. I shrugged apologetically. We began to move again and we reached Beorn Beornsson. He was standing at the top of the trail. We could see the wooden walls of the village. I spied a cross and a tower. Beorn pushed Arne, me and Siggi to the right and pointed. We nodded and began to move around the scrubby patch of grapevines. I doubted that this would make good wine for there were few flowers upon it.

We crept towards the wall. The moon had now set and it was dark. Soon the sun would appear. We had to be quick. I held my spear above my shoulder. I preferred my sword but the Jarl wished us to use spears. Siggi shook his head and laid his spear down. Arne shrugged and did the same. Who was I to argue? I was the newest member of the clan. I did so too. And, like the other two, drew my sword. Each time I grasped it I felt more confident as though I could face any foe. I had yet to sink it into the flesh of an enemy. Perhaps this would be the day.

Arne and I followed Siggi. He had been with the Jarl longer than any. When we reached the wall, I glanced up and saw a watchman some twenty paces from us. He was looking west. I was the youngest and Arne and Siggi put their hands together. They wanted me to dispose of the watchman. I sheathed my sword for I would need both hands. I slid my shield around my back. Putting my right foot in their cupped hands I pushed hard and found myself thrust upwards. I used the top of the wooden wall to steady myself as I landed lightly on the wooden walkway.

The watchman must have felt the vibration from my feet for he slowly turned. I drew my sword and raced towards him, even as he opened his mouth to begin to shout. He would have been better drawing a weapon for I hurled myself, like a spear and impaled his throat with my sword. I fell on top of him. His warm blood spilt over my hands, my sword and my armour. I stood and withdrew my blade. It had embedded itself in the wooden walkway. I could not help smiling. I had killed my first warrior. I had been blooded. The rest of the clan would have to accept me.

I went back to the others and, reaching down, helped Arne pull himself up. We both then helped Siggi. Siggi grinned when he saw the blood on my face and patted my back. He waved Arne forward towards the gate. We crouched as we ran. I saw other figures on the wall. We were no longer alone. I saw, below us, the small town. It was coming awake. The thin light of dawn was to the east and soon there would be people about. We had almost reached the gate when we heard a cry from the east wall. Someone had been discovered. Arne threw caution to the wind and ran as fast as he could towards the gate.

Siggi shouted, "Arne, secure the tower. Hrólfr, down the steps and we will open the gate."

I was faster than Siggi and I slid down the ladder ignoring the wood burning my hands. Landing on my feet at the bottom I turned as I heard shouts. Two of the villagers ran at me. Both held weapons: one had a hand axe and the other a bill hook. I quickly slipped my shield around to my front. I did the only thing I could think of; I charged at them as I shouted. "Raven Wing!" I must have looked more frightening than I felt for the one with the hand axe hesitated. The billhook came towards me but I only had one weapon to worry about. My shield was well made, Snorri the Scout had helped me to make it. I deflected the billhook and stabbed at the man with Heart of Ice. He wore no mail and my sword was sharp. It tore through him and I twisted as I pulled it out. The second man finally reacted and he swung his axe at my shield. It was a hard blow. I brought my sword over my head and swung down, blindly. It hit something and stuck. When I lowered my shield, I saw that it was embedded in the dead skull of the axeman.

I had no time to ponder what I had achieved; Siggi shouted, "Arne, Hrólfr! The gate!"

I turned and saw that Siggi was battling with four villagers. Like those I had killed, they were armed, albeit with poor weapons. I hurled myself at them as they slashed and hacked at Siggi. I smashed my sword through the upper arm of a man with a poleaxe. It grated on the bone. Pushing my shield hard into the face of a second I stood next to Siggi and guarded his right side. As soon as Arne arrived the last three were despatched.

Siggi White Hair turned and gave orders, "Arne, open the gate. Our wolverine here will guard your back!" He nodded towards my sword. "You are blooded now! Let Harald Black Teeth speak against you and you have shipmates who will have words with him."

I heard a crash as the bar holding the gate was thrown to the ground. "Watch out!"

We stepped aside as the Jarl led the rest of the crew through the gates. I wondered what had happened to the three Beorn had sent to the east gate. Siggi smacked me on the back. "Don't stand there daydreaming! We have a town to sack!"

The sun had finally broken and the streets were filled with the screams and shouts of the townspeople as they woke to their worst nightmare; raiders. I knew that we would not have long. We had to take as much loot and booty as we could. The Jarl headed up towards the church. Siggi White Hair led us to some prosperous-looking houses on the opposite side of the town square. Siggi led and I brought up the rear. Suddenly a black giant emerged from a doorway behind Arne. In his hand, he had a huge curved scimitar. I had never seen such a giant before. His black body glistened with sweat. I ran at him and plunged my sword through his side. He roared and switched his attention from Arne to me. Arne turned at the shout and looked in horror at the giant Moor.

The scimitar scythed down towards me. I barely managed to get my shield up in time. Even though I blocked the blow I could not keep my feet and I was knocked to the ground. With an exultant roar, he lifted his arm to deliver the killer blow. I swiped sideways with my sword. It was a desperate act. I connected with the back of his ankle and bit into flesh. He dropped to one knee and Siggi and Arne both hacked and chopped at his neck and his back. I know not whose blow it was but one of them took his head. Arne reached down to help me to my feet. "I owe you a life runt. Come. We have riches to gather!"

The door of the house was solid and it was barred. Arne ran back to pick up the axe he had seen and he smashed at the side of the door. It took two blows and we were in. There were screams from those within. A man ran up to Siggi brandishing a short sword. Siggi's sword took him in the stomach.

I recognised some of the words they were speaking. They were similar to the language I had been forced to speak as a thrall. I shouted, in Frankish, "Do not resist and you shall live. Your lives are worth more than your ornaments!"

Surprisingly they stopped. Siggi looked at me and shook his head, "What did you say?"

"I told them they would not be harmed if they obeyed us."

Arne said, "They can keep their women. They are too dark-skinned for me."

I went upstairs, for it was a two-storied building. This was indeed a rich house. I remembered that the rich who lived in Neustria had kept their precious goods hidden away close to their beds. When an older woman tried to stop me then I knew that the treasure would be upstairs. I pushed her away. The stairs were narrow and I had to sling my shield around my back to allow me to climb them. A candle burned on a table and I saw that those who had been in there had left quickly. The bed was made of wood and I picked it up. There was a small trap door in the floor. I put my seax under the edge and prised it up. It was a small chest the length of two of my hands and one hand wide. It felt heavy. The candlestick was also made of metal. I guessed it was lead. I took that too.

When I reached the bottom Siggi and Arne had collected the good pots and linens. The woman's shoulders sagged when I emerged. I held up the chest. "This feels like it was worth the effort!"

We reached the square and the Jarl was organising the men. He spied the chest immediately. "You have done well. You and Arne take them back to the drekar and then return here. We are still collecting."

"Aye Jarl."

As we made our way back through the gates and down the trail to the river Arne said, "How did you know there would be a chest of treasure?"

"It was a rich-looking house. How many two-storied houses do you see? That was why Siggi chose it. There are few such houses in any town. When I was a slave I served people who lived in such a house. That was where they kept their chests and riches."

"You might be a useful addition to the crew after all."

I was silent for a while and then I asked, "Why would I not be useful?"

Arne turned and gave me a sad smile, "Hermund the Bent said that Dragonheart's galdramenn had enchanted the Jarl so that he would get rid of you. He said the Dragonheart wished you gone. Hermund the Bent said you brought bad luck."

"Why would he say that?"

"Why else would anyone leave the service of Dragonheart? He is the richest Jarl this side of Miklagård."

We had reached the drekar. I turned to him. "We met a witch and she told me that my destiny lay with Jarl Gunnar Thorfinnson. Jarl Dragonheart understood."

Arne nodded, "*Wyrd*. I have misjudged you. I did not know that and to be truthful I now see that Hermund the Bent lied. We have lost no warriors since you joined us. We will start anew."

We handed the treasures to the ship's boys and set off back up the trail. The sun was warm now and I regretted wearing my wolf cloak. I knew why I had chosen to wear it. It made me feel like one of the oathsworn of the Dragonheart. Those who served him had to kill their own wolf unaided. I had managed that feat. The cloak was, like my sword, a link with my past. As we crested the rise close to the town walls my eyes were drawn to the south.

"Arne!" I pointed south as he turned. "Riders!" There were horsemen a mile or more away. They had spears and helmets. Horsemen could hunt us down.

"You go and get the spears. We will need them. I will tell the Jarl."

I ran as fast as I could over the hard ground to the place we had discarded our spears. I was fortunate this was not the land of the Angles. There it was so verdant and lush that a man risked tripping over long grass and snaking bushes. Here it was sparse vegetation and hard-baked soil. The horsemen were riding quickly and it would be a race to see if I could reach the spears before they were close enough to catch me. I heard a shout as they saw me. It spurred me on and I reached the three spears and ran down the wall. I heard the hooves closing with me. Glancing over my shoulder I saw that they would catch me. A warrior holding a long spear and with a plumed helmet pulled back his weapon as he prepared to kill me. There was but one solution. I threw myself to the ground. Haaken One Eye had once told me that a horse will not deliberately step on a man. That may be true normally but this warrior's horse stepped on me. Luckily its hoof struck the boss of my shield. The shallow ditch which surrounded the town was next to us and the horse and rider slipped down the bank. I heard a cry as the rider's head smashed into the stone wall.

I lay still as hooves clattered past me. The other riders thought I was dead. I heard shouts as the crew emerged from the walls, alerted no doubt by Arne, and met the horsemen. I stood. The horse lay in the ditch. It was dying. The black-faced horseman was dead already. I lay the spears down and went to the horse. Taking my sword, I slit its throat, "Go to the Allfather." I grabbed the warrior's spear and his curved sword. Around his neck, he wore a golden necklace. I grabbed it. The warrior's spear was longer than the other three and might be useful.

As I clambered out of the ditch I grabbed the three spears. The noise of battle was ahead of me. The horsemen were driving the crew towards the river. I hurried after them. I was now isolated. I had to tread warily. When I reached the track, which led down to the river I spied a white head. It was Siggi White Hair. I put down my spears and the curved sword and clambered down the slope. His body was lying against a tree. It had stopped him from falling down the bank to the river. As I touched his arm he moved. He was alive. I put my hands under his arms and began to drag him back up the slope.

As I flopped down at the top he opened his eyes, "Hrólfr?"

"Where are you hurt?"

He held his hand to the back of his head and it came away bloody. "One of those horsemen used a club. Where is the Jarl?"

"They have gone down the trail." I helped him to his feet and handed him two of the spears and the curved sword. His shield and his sword were gone.

He nodded, "Thank you. I owe you a life. Come we will follow but be careful."

As we descended the trail we found the bodies of Harold Svensson and Alf Alfsson. Both were clearly dead. We had no time to do anything for them save asking the Allfather to take them to Valhalla. They both had their swords in their hands. It had been a good death. As we hurried so we heard the noise of battle. I had been up and down this trail four times now and I knew we were approaching the drekar.

"What do we do Siggi?"

He grinned, "We attack whoever we meet. We are Vikings. If you stand up to a horseman, he will back off. The bastard who got me was lucky. I was slow to turn else I would have had him. Just keep running and fighting until you get to the ship. If you find it has gone quiet and you feel no pain, then do not worry. You will be in Valhalla. You are now, truly, a warrior, Hrólfr!"

We turned a bend and saw the drekar. Between it and us was a whirling mass of horses and men all fighting. There was no apparent way through. The nearest horses were twenty paces from us.

Siggi said, "We both throw one spear and then charge with the other. I will lead. You have your shield on your back; you follow. If I fall then leave me. Get to the ship!"

I nodded. We pulled back our arms and hurled our spears. The horsemen had metal shirts that covered their fronts but their backs did not. Both spears plucked their riders from their horses. Siggi roared, "Odin!" and holding the long spear ran towards the two horses.

I held my spear in two hands and shouted, "Dragonheart!" as I followed him. The two riderless horses panicked and they reared and flailed around them to escape the two monsters who were behind them. A rider turned and Siggi rammed his long spear under the nearest warrior's arm, pitching him from the back of his horse. A warrior turned his horse and raised his spear to stab down on Siggi. I just ran at him and his horse. I stabbed forward and my spear rammed into his leg and into his horse. The horse screamed as the head of my spear broke off inside him. He fell onto a second horse. Siggi was past the horsemen now. I took the broken haft of my spear and used it as a club. I felt something crack into my back but my shield took the blow.

Then, to my horror, I saw Siggi leap on board the drekar as it began to pull away from the river bank. I would not be a slave again. There were two warriors before me. I threw the broken half of the spear at one and then leapt up behind the second warrior. **'Raven's Wing'** was now thirty paces from the shore and the current was taking it downstream. I pulled out my seax and ripped it across the black warrior's throat. Hurling his body to the ground I kicked the horse hard and it leapt into the river. I felt another blow to my back but I ignored it. The horse began to struggle under my weight and so I lay flat and held on to its mane. It began to swim. Its natural inclination made it want to go to the shore but I kept pulling the mane to the right to take it towards the drekar which was drifting on the current. I would not make it. I put my face down and used my legs to kick.

"Hurry Hrólfr!" I looked up and saw that the Jarl had the oars backing water. It was no longer moving away from me. When I was ten paces from it. I let go of the horse's mane and kicked hard towards the drekar. I was lucky. I had no mail and the wolf cloak I had regretted wearing trapped enough air so that I was able to swim to the rope which snaked towards me. I was hauled unceremoniously on board and flopped like a fish they had caught on the deck. Arne Four Toes, the Jarl and Siggi White Hair stood over me.

Siggi White Hair said, "We now have a name for you! From this day, you shall be Hrólfr the Horseman!"

I smiled. Aiden had called me something similar. This was *wyrd*. The name felt right. I stood and watched the horse struggle ashore. I was glad. It had saved me and did not deserve to die.

Sven's voice came down from the steering board, "Get to your oars! We have far to go!"

I hurried to my bench, dripping river water down its length. I sat next to Siggi and we began to row. I watched the horsemen follow us for a while along the river bank but as the current and the wind caught us they soon gave up.

Arne Four-Toes said, "There must be magic in you Hrólfr the Horseman. How else could you make the horse swim? You will bear watching!"

Chapter 2

We returned to the beach on the northern bank. It had been defensible and we needed to see to our wounded. As we rowed I saw empty chests. I had only seen two bodies but there were obviously others who had fallen. When the order was given to ship our oars, I laid mine next to Siggi's and stood. I took off my cloak and Siggi laughed, "You will need a new shield, Horseman!"

I took off my shield. The horse which had stepped on me had completely dented the boss and my shield was cracked. "My cloak and my shield saved me, Siggi White Hair."

"And you saved me. Arne and I are both in your debt." He looked towards Jarl Gunnar Thorfinnson, "The Jarl and the drekar also owe you. If you had not found me then we would not have charged the horsemen. Our attack gave the crew enough time to escape." He took the curved sword I had given him. "Here this is yours."

I shook my head, "It replaces the one you lost."

"I cannot take it. You won this weapon. It will not serve another. I have an older one I will use until I can buy another." I took the sword from him. I could not see me using it but it might be worth something. I could sell it.

We went ashore. The ship's boys were lighting a fire with driftwood. We sat in the sand, exhausted. The treasure we had captured was brought to the beach. The horsemen had prevented the crew from bringing back as much as we might have wished. Even so, we were in profit. The greatest treasure was the chest I had found. We all gathered around the Jarl as he opened it. There were many coins and jewels within. He found a flat rock and began to put the coins in piles and the jewels in groups. He was jarl and he decided how it would be apportioned.

He took a large gold coin and handed it to me. "Here Hrólfr. Before we divide it up this is for you. You discovered this."

Most of the crew banged their shields but Hermund the Bent scowled and neither he nor those from his oars joined in.

"Thank you, Jarl. I am glad that I have been of service. I am honoured to be a member of this clan."

Arne had seen the look which Hermund the Bent had given me. He stood, "I am Arne Four Toes. You know that I speak true."

There were nods and 'ayes'.

"This youth saved my life and saved Siggi's life. More than that it was his eyes which not only spotted the horsemen to allow us to escape but the charge of Siggi and him was the act that ensured we would escape. I owe him a life, Siggi owes him a life," he looked pointedly at Hermund, "we all owe him a life. Those who have spoken behind his back let them know that I will take offence at further comments." He sat down.

The Jarl nodded, "I too have heard whispers and I say now that they will stop. I will have no disharmony in the drekar. Know this also, it has been suggested to me that we winter here, closer to the places where we find riches. If we can find somewhere then I do not intend to return to Ljoðhús."

This caused a bigger reaction. Erik Karlsson, who was a confederate of Hermund the Bent, stood. "What about our homes? What about women?"

Siggi laughed, "We are Vikings! Do you not know what that means? We have no home save our ship. And women? Find them."

Others joined in and Erik was shouted down.

Jarl Gunnar held up his hands for silence, "We have to find somewhere but you know my mind. If any are unhappy then when we put into port to trade, they can leave. I will have no man aboard who is not loyal." Looking around I realised that was easier said than done. With the deaths and Hermund's faction, we would be down to twenty men loyal to the Jarl. That was not enough to crew the drekar.

The Jarl then divided the treasure. He took slightly less than half and the rest was divided equally amongst us all. I saw evil looks cast my way. Hermund the Bent had taken my success as a personal affront. Far from making my life easier, it would now be harder. My hand went to my sword. I felt the power Kara had given it and I became as cold as the blade. There was little point in becoming angry.

I know not if it was deliberate but the Jarl made Hermund and Erik stand guard. On reflection, it was not the best decision the Jarl had ever made. The two of them had a watch to fuel each other's resentment of me. As we boarded the ship Karl Knutson said quietly. "Watch your back. Hermund blames you."

I turned, "For what?"

"Harald Svensson was his cousin. He died and he says you brought the bad luck with you."

"But..."

He smiled, "I know. It makes no sense. Most of the crew are behind you. We will watch you when we can but try not to be alone. He would murder." There was shock in his voice.

I could not believe that for murder was the most heinous of crimes. A murderer would be ostracised by all and forced from his own home. I had thought I would have an easier time but I was wrong and I would still need to watch my back.

We left before dawn and headed south. The Jarl had not ventured there before but he had seen the riches the Dragonheart had brought back with him. The spices and fine garments were worth the risks we took. We were heading for Olissipo in the land of the Emirate of Córdoba. The wind was with us and we did not have to row. It was a good thing for we were undercrewed. As we headed south I was questioned about this Al-Andalus for they knew that Jarl Dragonheart had raided there.

"I only know what I was told and that was by Haaken One Eye. He makes up sagas and I learned to treat his stories with some suspicion."

"I know," said Siggi White Hair, "all singers of sagas have a tendency to exaggerate but there is always a part which is true."

"You know those horsemen we met?"

"The ones with black skin? The Moors?"

"Aye, well the crew said that the land is filled with them. Some wear robes which cover them from head to foot and others fight naked."

Siggi asked, "They are berserkers?"

"I do not think so. Haaken said that many of them were so proud of their manhood they wished to display it."

Arne Four Toes laughed, "And that is a quick way to lose it."

"The men of Cyninges-tūn had sailed the Middle Sea as far as Miklagård and they say the land to the south of the sea teems with these black warriors. They are as plentiful as fishes."

Karl Knutson shook his head, "It seems to me that we are wasting our time then. What treasures can a naked man have? At least those we fought yesterday had armour and helmets. If we had managed to defeat them then we would have had some reward for our dead men."

"But they do have treasure." I felt deceitful about not disclosing my golden necklace but I wanted no more bad feeling between the crew. I made up a story, "Haaken said that many of them liked to wear gold about them and they prize jewels. The chest we found in the house was evidence of that."

Arne nodded, "Aye and it was guarded by a giant Moor. I should have searched his body!"

"We had no time. We did not know that the horsemen were coming."

That reminded them of who had seen them. "Your eyes and ears are useful, Hrólfr the Horseman."

I smiled, "Did you know the story of horses and me? Did the Jarl mention it?"

Arne looked genuinely interested in my words, "What story?"

"I grew up in Neustria. They have horses there and I learned how to ride them. I rode them when I served the Dragonheart. It is why I was able to mount and control it. I thought you knew and that was why you named me."

"No, Hrólfr. We named you thus because you defeated the horsemen almost on your own. That is something of which you can be proud."

The Norns must have been listening to our conversation for they began to spin their webs. Their thread spread out across the sea. We spied a half-sunken boat. Boats were rarely met on the seas and any who saw our raven prow would flee. The ship would be empty and of no use to us. We would have passed it by but Knut Egilsson, the ship's boy, shouted, "Captain, there are men alive in the water."

We may have been cruel warriors and hard enemies but it was an unwritten rule that you did not leave men in the water to drown. The Gods would not approve of such a callous act. Sven put the steering board over and we headed towards the wreck. We crowded along the sheerstrake. The sea was normally an empty place. A ship could travel for days without seeing another. Usually, another ship meant danger. There could be no danger in this half-sunken boat.

There were two men and a boy clinging for life to the wreck. It looked to have been a merchant vessel for the part to which they clung was too broad to be a fishing boat. I was not certain if they were alive. The ship's boy must have seen something which suggested life. Sven the Helmsman shouted, "Knut, you and the other boys go over and take ropes with you. Tie them under their arms. Be quick!" He pointed and I saw the distinctive fins of sharks. They were circling.

Siggi White Hair said, "They will have feasted already in the rest of the crew." He shuddered. That is not a good way to go!"

The three were hauled on board and, to be honest, I was not certain if any of them lived. Siggi and Sven took charge. They turned them on their front and pulled them in the middle. The two men vomited seawater and then coughed and spluttered. The ship's boy did not need any such help. He began to cough and to bring up seawater himself.

"Sven, resume course!"

The first man to recover began to babble. Jarl Gunnar shrugged and said, "Where were you bound?"

The second man spoke and this time some of the words sounded familiar. "Jarl, I think they are Franks."

"Come, Hrólfr, speak to them. Find out where they sailed from and where they sail to. What is his name?"

I nodded and approached them. It was some time since I had spoken Frankish. There were many variations and regional accents. "Your name? Where were you sailing? What were you carrying?"

I kept my words simple. Even so, the man struggled to understand. I repeated them, very slowly. He nodded and said, equally slowly. He pointed to himself and nodded. "Hunald of Bourges. We go to the Rinaz. We had spices on board." He shook his head. I did not catch all of the words but I caught the word fortune.

"Where did you come from?"

"Portucale to the south of the Kingdom of Asturias."

I told the Jarl what he had said. "Ask him what is in this place, Portucale and if it is closer than Olissipo."

I simplified it. "Where is Portucale?" Instead of pointing due south, he pointed south-west. "Closer than Olissipo, Jarl." I turned to the man. I had decided that he must have been the Captain or the Master of the ship. His clothes were well made. "Tell me, Captain, what kind of place is Portucale?" I had used too many words. He shrugged and smiled. I tried again. "Trade? Portucale?"

He understood, "Wine! Slaves!" He saw the curved sword hanging from my belt. "Swords!"

I told the Jarl what he had said. "I see a chance here. We will return these men to their homes. At the very least we can scout out the port and if the chance arrives we can make a profit." He turned to the crew. Take the shields from the side. We will go to Portucale as merchants!" He smiled at me, "And you, our lucky charm, can tell the Captain that we will take him to safety."

I smiled at the Captain, "We take you to Portucale. Good?"

The two men grinned, "Very good. Thank your captain. I reward him."

"Reward?"

"I give him gold for saving us!"

When I told Jarl Gunnar he could barely contain his good humour. Our lack of numbers limited our potential action. This way we could sail with impunity into a port and scout out possible targets. Our act of kindness was being rewarded. By the time we reached the port perched precariously on the side of steep hills which rose almost vertically from the river, we looked like merchants. We had taken off our mail and hidden our helmets. There had been few enough drekar in this part of the world to inspire fear. We were amongst the first.

I did not row but stood, at the steering board, with the Jarl and the Captain of the Frankish ship. I was not really needed for the Frank directed Sven with hand signals. Jarl Gunnar wished me to be there. The apparent favouritism did not sit well with Hermund the Bent who gave me murderous looks.

Hunald took us upstream to a wooden quay next to a large wooden hall. When servants emerged and waved to him I realised that this was his hall. He beamed at me as his men tied us to the land, "My home."

It was when the Jarl and I entered his hall that I realised that this was a rich man. He had many servants and his walls were hung with fine cloth and tapestries. "Sit. Food, drink!" He clapped his hands and spoke a language I did not understand at all. His servants scurried off. The Jarl and I were left alone.

He looked around at the hall and nodded, "That witch on her island did me a favour when she spoke to you. This is a wondrous place." He patted the finely carved chairs on which we sat. "These were not knocked up by some old carpenter and those tapestries on the wall are worth a small fortune. If we sold them in Dorestad would be rich men."

The servants came in and poured wine into metal goblets for us to drink. They put platters with cured meats and cheeses before us. After they had gone the Jarl said, "And look at these! We could take them and sell them for a fortune in Lundenwic."

"But Jarl how do we make money here? We have no coin and we cannot buy anything."

"I have yet to work that out yet, Hrólfr, but the Norns have sent us here for a purpose. I rely on you to keep your ears open and to help me to talk to this Hunald. Your language has helped us already."

Our host returned sometime later. I suspect he had bathed for we smelled him before we saw him. He smelled of roses. He had changed and was wearing a fine and brightly coloured garment. He had with him an ancient servant. "This is Odo. He speaks your language." He pointed to me.

Odo nodded, "I come from Neustria. I was a sailor. My master said that you come from the far north. He would know where for he knows you are Vikings. Do you come for trade or war?"

The man was old but his eyes were sharp. I translated for the Jarl. He nodded and gave me the answer. "Keep your face without expression when you speak, Hrólfr. Hunald is watching you. This is a test."

I nodded and forced myself to do as the Jarl had told me. I closed my eyes and remembered when I had been a slave and had had to endure blows and insults in Neustria. "We are here to trade. As you saw, Lord Hunald, we do not have a full crew we are not here for war. We have gold and we would buy spices to take back to the land of the Angles."

The mention of the land of the Angles seemed to make them both relax a little. The lord spoke quickly and pointed at us as he did so.

"Good. My master can accommodate you and make introductions to the merchants. Instead of gold would you like a reward of spices?"

I translated and the Jarl smiled. "Another test, Hrólfr. Tell him, yes."

My last answer seemed to satisfy them both. "My master asks if you wish to stay the night in the hall. There is water to bathe you and slaves to cleanse you."

Jarl Gunnar nodded and told me what to say. "My Jarl says that is kind. He will go and tell the rest of the crew." I smiled and added words of my own, "They would worry if the Jarl did not return."

When Odo translated Hunald spoke. "My master says why would they worry?"

"They are oathsworn. They would give their lives to protect him. As would I."

Hunald shook his head and said something. It did not sound complimentary. I knew that Odo did not translate exactly. I was learning to watch faces now. "My master says those are new ideas. He has not met them before."

The Jarl left and so did Lord Hunald. Odo appraised me. "You are a warrior. I recognise a fine sword when I see one. Yet you are young to have such a weapon."

I shrugged, "I have been lucky. I was a slave in Neustria when I was rescued my life changed."

"Vikings rarely travel these waters. We had some ships which traded but that was in the past and they were not the dragon ships."

There was much unsaid in his words. I was being tested. "The Jarl and I crave adventure. We have heard of exotic places like this and others, Miklagård."

"Miklagård?"

I closed my eyes as I sought the name the Franks and Romans used for it. "You call it Constantinopolis."

"Ah. We can trade there because we are under the rule of the caliphate and can pass between the Pillars of Hercules. Your ship would be taken by the Berbers if you tried it."

"Thank you for the warning."

"It is we who thank you. Our master is a kind man. Had he been taken by the sea then his wife would have sold the business and I would be left without anything. We are only suffered here because our master is rich and the Governor likes the trade he brings. Arabs can be cruel. Since our people defeated them at Roncesvalles they have been suspicious of Franks. King Alphonso of Asturias threatens the northern borders. My Lord Hunald treads a fine line. We are tolerated, nothing more."

The Jarl returned and Odo stood. "Come with me."

We were taken to a bathhouse. I had been told of them by Haaken One Eye. Jarl Gunnar had also been told of their practices but, even so, we were surprised when slaves undressed us. Odo smiled at our discomfort. "Tell your Jarl there is nothing to fear. These slaves are employed just for this purpose. I will leave you."

"But we do not speak their language!"

"Do not worry. They will let you know what you are to do."

He was correct. They led us to a warm bath and they combed out our hair. It had been some time since I had done so and I saw, in the water, nits and lice which had fled from our hair and our beards. When we were taken to the next room I saw steam rising from the water. Had Haaken's stories not told me what to expect I would have feared we were to be cooked. He had told me of such baths in Miklagård. After the initial shock, it felt quite relaxing. When we returned to the warm bath I saw that the dead wildlife had been removed.

After we had had our bodies scraped cleaned with flattened pieces of animal bone and our beards and hair plaited, our clothes were returned to us. I saw that they had been shaken and beaten clean. Even so, they still felt dirty next to my skin. We dined well. Our host gave us a small chest filled with spices. Jarl Gunnar's eyes widened for it was worth a small fortune. At the end of the meal, we were given the unwelcome news that, before we would be allowed to trade we were to be examined by the Governor. As I lay down on the incredibly soft bed I wondered if this was a trick of the Norns to put us tantalisingly close to a fortune and then snatch it away.

The crew of the drekar were gathered outside the hall when we emerged the next morning. Sven shouted, "What goes on Jarl?" He pointed to the six guards who awaited us. They were encased in mail and had the olive complexion of someone from the Middle Sea.

"We are to be questioned. Fear not." He strode over and handed the spices to Sven. "This is our reward." He lowered his voice. "Keep the men calm. We will return."

Lord Hunald was dressed in his finest clothes and he came with us. We were flanked by the six guards. I had the chance to examine the mail.

It was finally made and consisted of overlapping scales. It went down as far as the knee where it split. I guessed that these were horsemen. The helmets had a plume and a mail aventail at the back. Their swords were the same as I had had hanging from my belt. I had left it aboard the drekar. I was glad that I had done so. I did not want to answer awkward questions about how I came by it.

The Governor's Palace was in the castle which dominated the port. It was made of stone and was heavily guarded. The gate was narrow and well protected. The walls were high. We could not take this place easily. We were taken to an antechamber where we waited. It seemed like we were there for days. I suddenly realised that Odo was not with us. Who would translate?

Eventually, the door opened and we were ushered in. The Governor was a huge man and obviously aware of his own importance. He sat on a raised dais. Next to him stood two half-naked black guards. Each held a two-handed curved sword. Their muscled bodies showed that they were not there for show. These were bodyguards. Lord Hunald bowed. The Jarl nodded and we bowed too. Lord Hunald then spoke at length. The Governor questioned him and then clapped his hands.

An emaciated man was brought out. He had a slave's collar about his neck and he only had a left hand. The right was a stump. The Governor looked at him with some distaste and then spoke. The slave nodded and then spoke to us in Norse.

"The Governor asks who are you and why are you sailing in the waters of the Emir?"

Jarl Gunnar said, "You are Viking!"

The man's eyes showed panic. "Just answer the question I beg of you! I will be whipped if we displease the Governor."

The Jarl nodded and told him.

He translated and the Governor spoke. "The Governor says you are a warship. You sail a dragon ship. Are you a pirate?"

"Tell him we do not have a large crew. We are no pirates. We wish to trade only. We only came here because we fished Lord Hunald from the sea. We knew nothing of this place until Lord Hunald told us. We were heading to Miklagård."

Surprisingly that seemed to satisfy the Governor. "He says you can stay here until the morning tide. You are to do your trades today and then go. If you are here when the sun rises tomorrow your ship will be impounded and you will be enslaved."

Even the Jarl was taken aback but he smiled and nodded.

"I am to accompany you to translate." He nodded to the guards who had brought us in. "They will watch us."

As we left I saw Lord Hunald breathe a sigh of relief. He smiled at me. "I take you to the other merchants and introduce you."

Before I translated I said, "We need to get our gold from the ship."

He shook his head, "You are strangers and not allowed to trade. I will have to buy what you need and then you will pay me."

I translated for the Jarl who nodded, "That is acceptable." He nodded to Lord Hunald and then said to the slave. "What is your story?"

"I am Erik of Orkneyjar. I was in the crew of Trygg of Orkneyjar. We served the one they call Dragonheart."

The Jarl and I stopped in surprise and looked at each other. We were rudely pushed in the back by the guards. The Jarl flashed an angry look at the Arabs. I said quietly, "Patience, Jarl."

He nodded, "We both served Jarl Dragonheart. We were told that all of Trygg's crew were killed."

The slave's eyes opened in wonder, "You know the Dragonheart! *Wyrd*. When the crew were taken, I managed to escape. They caught me after the Dragonheart came and punished those who killed my shipmates. They decided to keep me and find out about Vikings. They took my hand as punishment and to stop me from escaping. They asked about Vikings and I told them. Until you came they had not used me again. I think that they were tiring of me and resented wasting food on me. Had you not come then I would have been sent to the galleys. They may still send me there."

"A one-armed rower?"

He shrugged, "Their rowers do not live long."

I felt sympathy for Erik. I had been a slave. I understood the brief flash of hope in his eyes when I said. "Where do they keep you?"

We were passing between the river and the castle. He pointed to a door in the rock. "That is where they keep the slaves at night. We are herded in and the gate locked."

"Why do you not escape is there no guard?"

"There is but one guard." He shrugged, "If I escaped where would I go? The only Frank who is allowed to trade is your Lord Hunald. All the other ships are Arab." He pointed to a galley that was tied up next to the wall. There were many guards around it. "That ship and others like it do not trade north. They trade south. Lord Hunald is charged with trading with the Empire of Charlemagne. Your host would do nothing to jeopardise his position here. No, my friend, I shall end my days here."

We were approaching the market. The Jarl said, "What is the cargo of the ship we saw? Why was it so heavily guarded?"

"It is the tax ship. It takes the taxes back to Damascus. It sails on the morning tide."

I looked at the Jarl who grinned. I could see in his eyes that he wanted the ship. For my part, I wanted to help the Viking from Orkneyjar. The Weird Sisters had sent the sunken ship our way not to make us rich but to rescue Erik from Orkneyjar.

Chapter 3

The Jarl was clever with his trades. We chose light items such as silks and spices. Lord Hunald nodded his approval. The Jarl could have spent far more had we had the coin to pay it but he only had the coins we had taken from Aquitaine. Erik from Orkneyjar was taken away and the guards escorted us back to the ship. When we returned to the drekar Lord Hunald only stayed long enough to receive his payment. I think the Governor's words must have made him wish to distance himself from us.

Once onboard, we were assailed by questions.

"We sail before dawn but I have a fancy to take that tax ship."

"It looks formidable, Jarl!"

"I know Sven but it does not look as lithe as our ship. We are warriors. We can do this. One victory and we need not trade again this year. We can go to Frankia and be rich men."

They were all eager. Siggi White Hair said, "If it takes the taxes it will have to sail south. We could wait for it!" Excitement bubbled around the ship like waves on a rocky beach.

I said, "Jarl, I would like to rescue Erik."

He shook his head, "Like you, I feel sorry for the old man but it is too risky."

"Jarl, I have been a slave and abandoned. You cannot know what that is like. He served the Dragonheart as we both did. I believe we were sent here to rescue him." I saw him wavering. "I can examine the tax ship while I rescue him. I will be able to tell you how many crew there are."

"But if you were caught?"

"Then the Norns would have meant it to be. If I am then leave me. I have served my purpose. I will go as soon as it is dark and be back here before you know it."

The Jarl pointed to the candle we used when in port. He took out his seax and put a mark on it. "We light this when you leave. If you are not back by the time it burns down to here, then we leave you."

I nodded, "And if I do not return then Siggi White Hair and Arne Four Toes can share my chest."

I went to the whetstone and sharpened my seax and my sword. Siggi and Arne came over to me. "What is this about, Hrólfr?"

I told them of Erik. "We will come with you. We owe you a life."

I shook my head, "The Jarl has few enough crew he can trust. I am but one youth. If I am lost...*wyrd*. But you two are there to protect the Jarl from the likes of Hermund the Bent."

Arne Four Toes grinned and shook his head, "You are like a shapeshifter, Hrólfr the Horseman. There is iron in you and depths that I cannot fathom. Your task seems impossible but I believe you will succeed."

I took my wolfskin from my chest. It made me harder to see at night and I believed it brought me luck. I gave Heart of Ice to Siggi for safekeeping. "Just in case I do not return."

He nodded, "I will keep it safe for you."

As I went to the gangplank Jarl Gunnar stopped me. "I will leave when the candle has burned, Hrólfr. I want to be at sea before our sheep comes to us. I would hate to leave you behind but I have a crew and a ship to think of."

"I know and if I do not make it back then I do not blame you. I have thrown the bones. Let us see how they fall."

We were but four hundred paces from the treasure ship, the castle and the slave pens. I kept to the shadows of the warehouses and halls which lined the front of the busy port. It was after dark and no one was abroad. During the day, this was a bustling and busy part of the port. At night, it was deserted. I spied a lantern at the stern of the tax ship and I pressed myself in the doorway of a large wooden warehouse. From the smell, I guessed it stored sandalwood. I saw that there were at least four men with mail and helmets on board the tax ship. Two others stood at the gangplank. There looked to be two banks of oars. I could smell the slaves who were chained to the oars. Luckily for me, it was closer to the sea than the slave pen and the guards would not see me if I kept close to the walls. I peered around the corner and saw the guard on the gate. The gate was cut into the rock above which stood the castle walls. The single sentry was thirty paces from me. He had a helmet, a spear and a curved sword. I drew my own curved sword. It had a vicious edge to it and the point was sharp. It was unlike any sword I had seen or used before.

I left the doorway and moved along the side of the building. The sentry at the gate to the slave pen had his back to me. As he turned I turned also and pressed my face against the wall. The Allfather smiled on me. The sentry just saw a shadow. After I had counted to ten I turned my face and saw that he was looking towards the tax ship. I saw men approach the gangplank. There was an altercation and raised voices. This was my chance I ran, silently towards the sentry. He continued to stare at the ship. Blows were being exchanged. The sentry obligingly stepped out to afford a better view of the fight and I seized my chance. I put my left arm around his neck as I stabbed the curved blade up through his side. His body became limp and I laid it silently on the ground.

There were now more men at the tax ship and the altercation was growing. The Weird Sisters had spun their threads and were giving me the chance to rescue Erik. I did not spurn the opportunity. There was a large lock on the chain which held the gate. Faces appeared. I said, "Sssh!" The sentry had no key on him but he did have a dagger. I put the dagger between two of the links of the chain. They were the weakest I could see. Rowing for two years had made my muscles stronger. I twisted as hard as I could. It seemed impossible that I could break it but the Allfather watched me yet or perhaps I had strengths I knew not of. Suddenly the chain sheared. I opened the door and hissed, "Erik!"

I held the dagger before me to keep the slaves at bay. Years of servitude had made them obedient and they did not come forward. Erik stepped from the crowd.

"Tell them to slip out one by one. If they do not make a noise they might escape."

He spoke to them. As he did I picked up the guard's sword. I handed the dagger to Erik and said, "Come. We must get to the drekar."

We hurried towards the drekar keeping close to the wall. Some of the escaping slaves followed us. That could not be helped. We were just thirty paces from **'Raven's Wing'** when the alarm was given. Some of the slaves must have made a noise. The men who had been sorting out the altercation now shouted and pointed to the slaves.

"Run! To the ship!"

Siggi and Arne must have been watching for they rushed to help us get aboard. Some of the slaves tried to board. Siggi White Hair pushed them away with the tip of his sword. They got the message.

Sven hissed, "Cast off!"

As we tumbled aboard I felt the current from the river take us. The Jarl did not raise the sail and he had only a dozen oars out. We would slide silently from the port. I peered over the sheerstrake. I could see horsemen pouring from the castle as they hunted the escaping slaves. That and the altercation close to the tax ship meant we drifted out of the river unseen. Our absence would be noticed but, by then, it would be too late. It was the Norns once more. I knew that they had sent us here to rescue Erik. It was *wyrd*.

As we headed south, the sail unfurled, Siggi clapped me on the back as he handed me my sword, "You are cunning, Hrólfr. Letting those slaves escape distracted the Arabs. Well done!"

The crew all banged the deck in approval. All, that is, save Hermund and his cronies. They glowered at me. I went to Erik. He sat sobbing on the deck. He had been there since we had boarded. He looked at me with gratitude, "I owe you a life. If I die now I die among my own." He held the dagger I had given him. "I die with a blade in my hand and no one will make me a slave again!"

I think I was the only one who truly understood his feelings. Sometimes we do things and know not why we do them. Sometimes we do things that make us feel better about ourselves. I was more proud of myself that morning than I had ever been. And then I realised that I was now responsible for Erik. He had but one arm and could not row. The Dragonheart had done the same for me. I would have to protect him and feed him from my share. The clan could not afford passengers.

We did not have to sail far down the coast. Sven and his boys spied an inland patch of water some thirty odd miles south of Portucale. They had sharp eyes to spot it at night. The moonlight glistening on it was the only sign of its existence. We turned the drekar around and lowered the sail. The tax ship would have to pass us to head south. We ate as we prepared for war. Some of the men did as the Ulfheonar did and donned red paint on their faces to make them look fierce. I knew that was why Harald Black Teeth had filed his teeth. He wanted to look fearsome. I just strapped on my sword. I had no shield. I would need to make a new one. Instead, I relied on my sword and a seax.

As dawn broke we saw that the water was a lagoon and quite a wide one at that. There were houses and fishing boats but they were far enough from us not to trouble us. If they tried to sail past us, then we would stop them but so long as they do not interfere then we would not harm them.

It was Karl who spotted the galley when it did appear. "I see her! The galley! She is to the northwest!"

"Oars!"

We went to our chests and seated ourselves. Sven shouted, "Row!"

Siggi White Hair began the chant,

> *'Through the waves, the oathsworn come*
> *Riding through white tipped foam*
> *Feared by all raven's wing*
> *Like a lark it does sing*
> *A song of death to all its foes*

The power of the raven grows and grows.
Through the waves the oathsworn come
Riding through white-tipped foam
Feared by all raven's wing
Like a lark it does sing
A song of death to all its foes
The power of the raven grows and grows.'

It was not a saga in the style of Haaken One Eye but it was about our drekar and our clan. Soon we would have better songs for we had finally achieved something but that would take time and thought. We would need to speak and talk of those who had fallen. Until then we used the chant to power through the sea. I put my back into the oar. I was part of the saga. I had played my part. No matter what Hermund the Bent said he could not take away my part in this raid. Even if we failed then people would remember that Hrólfr the Horseman had served Jarl Gunnar Thorfinnson.

Siggi said, quietly, "We are a crew! Do not try to do it by yourself!"

"Sorry but I..." Realising I had been rowing too hard I took up the chant again.

'Through the waves the oathsworn come
Riding through white tipped foam
Feared by all raven's wing
Like a lark it does sing
A song of death to all its foes
The power of the raven grows and grows.
Through the waves the oathsworn come
Riding through white tipped foam
Feared by all raven's wing
Like a lark it does sing
A song of death to all its foes
The power of the raven grows and grows.'

I was desperate to turn around and see how far we had to go but I knew that it would diminish our power. I had to rely upon the judgement of Sven and the Jarl. I felt my shoulders begin to burn. That would pass. I stared at the back of Arne Four Toes' helmet. I saw the tiny flaws in the metal. Bjorn had no such flaws in his helmets. I saw his hair was lank and greasy. The Jarl and I had clean hair plaited in neat pigtails. When you rowed, you did anything to take your mind off the oar in your hand and the pain in your back. It would pass soon enough. When it did then we would begin to fight. We had no idea how many men we faced save that we knew there were warriors in mail to guard the treasure. Had they been just sailors then we would have been more confident. On the other hand, warriors meant more arms and armour to claim. I thought about slaying a warrior with an aventail. I liked my helmet but an aventail would be good.

I realised that we were now heading southwest as opposed to west. I had no doubt that we would be faster; we were a better ship. On the other hand, we had fewer crewmen than we really needed. I was rowing on the side opposite the steering board. I knew we were close when Sven shouted. "Steering board! In oars"

I was new to this but even I knew that we were going to take out the oars on the side of the galley. Arrows began to shower down on us. I heard Olaf Blue Eye shout out as one struck him. He was a tough man; it would take death to stop him from rowing. I was pushed to the right as we ground against their oars and *'Raven's Wing'* crashed into the side of the galley.

"Oars in! Prepare to board." This time the Jarl spoke.

Siggi and I hauled in our oar and laid it in the centre of the drekar. I drew my sword and seax as I stood. The galley looked far bigger here at sea than it had in the port. It towered over us like a cliff. Perhaps Sven misjudged it but the raven wing prow struck the side of the galley at the same time as our hull crashed and smashed the oars. I heard the screams and shouts from the galley slaves who were injured. The jolt as we struck threw us from our feet. I was one of the first to recover. I picked up the rope and hook which Siggi White Hair had dropped and I threw it to the sheerstrake on the galley. I began to climb up. I was almost at the top when a dark-skinned sailor's face appeared. As he drew a wicked-looking knife I pulled on the rope and climbed as fast as I could. I reached out with my right hand and, grabbing his long, lank hair, pulled him towards me. He fell screaming to the sea below. I leapt over the side and drew my sword.

It was a daunting prospect. I was alone! I counted at least twelve armed men who began to move towards me purposefully. As far as I was aware I had the only rope which our men could climb. I had to guard it until they joined me. I remembered Olaf Leather Neck. He had told me that when the odds were so great that you could not win that the only thing to do was to charge. It seemed improbable but I held my weapons before me and roared a challenge, "Heart of Ice!" I ran at the warriors. The Allfather watched over me for the first three warriors held spears. They were not the best of weapons to use for they moved too much on a ship's deck. I was lithe and I was quick. I knocked aside two of the spears with my sword and seax and ran to the nearest warrior. I kicked him hard between the legs and as he doubled over stabbed him in the back of the neck with my seax.

I was in the middle of brown and black bodies. I stabbed to my right with my sword as I head-butted the short warrior before me. Then I heard a roar and Siggi and Arne leapt, slashing and stabbing to stand on either side of me. One of the enemy warriors thrust his spear at me. I barely managed to turn it and I felt it gouge a line in my leather armour. The blow took the wind from me. Before he could finish me off Siggi swung his axe at the side of his head. It took the top of his skull off. I saw, now, the berserker in Siggi. He had an axe in each hand and he swung them both before him. Arne and I had to move to the side to avoid being struck by the whirling weapons.

The enemy fell back too and Arne and I widened the part of the deck we controlled. Ahead of me, I saw Jarl Gunnar Thorfinnson leading more men from the stern of our drekar. Ulf Big Nose appeared to my left. He had two swords and he deflected a spear with one before gutting the guard with the other. As we forced the warriors back I suddenly saw the difference between us. We fought together while they fought alone. There was no coordination. Two men struck at me. I made a V with my seax and sword and stopped their striking swords. Arne and Ulf's swords darted in to kill them. As they died a large hole appeared in the enemy line.

Siggi White Hair shouted, "Go through the hole, Hrólfr!"

I leapt into the gap and saw a sailor fighting Hermund the Bent. Even as I watched the warrior's sword sliced down the helmet and cheek of Hermund. Heart of Ice stabbed upwards into the warrior's heart before he could finish off my shipmate. We had now joined forces. The handful of men who were to the left of us were quickly slain and we formed a solid wall. The deck was slippery with blood.

Siggi shouted, "Jarl! I think the galley is holed!"

I saw immediately what Siggi meant. The deck was canted at an angle. The enemy realised it too. I saw them hurl timbers and wood over the side and then leap into the sea to join them.

"Quickly! Get below decks and grab anything of value!"

The galley had slaves. It meant that the length of the galley was a mass of humanity. I turned. The valuables had to be stored beneath the steering board. I turned and ran towards the door. One solitary guard remained there. He held a curved sword and a small shield little bigger than his hand. He braced himself. I know not how but some of the slaves must have freed themselves for there was a sudden cheer from beneath my feet and then the ship lurched alarmingly to the side closest to our drekar. The movement caused the guard to spread his arms to balance himself. I darted forward. My sword flicked the curved sword to one side while my seax tore into his middle. I pulled the blade from side to side and the man fell trying to push back his entrails into his body.

I ripped open the door and saw a short flight of steps. I raced down. Alarmingly there was water there. I opened the door ahead of me. There was a small man, he looked to be a clerk of some description. He saw me and screamed. Falling to his knees he looked to be begging for his life. I ignored him. There were the boxes of taxes. Each chest had a seal from it. I picked one up and found it to be heavy. I sheathed my weapons and picked up the clerk by the hair. I put a chest in his hands and then took a second one myself. I kicked his backside as I shouted, "Up!" The gesture with my head was clear enough and he clambered up the steps. When we came on deck I saw that the enemy had fled.

"Is that the treasure, Hrólfr?"

"Aye Jarl. It is below decks but hurry for the water is already seeping in."

"Get that treasure on the drekar. Come, the rest of you. Form a line!"

I nudged the clerk towards the side of the galley. I saw that we were no longer above the drekar. We were level. I saw Erik One Hand. "Quick, pull these boxes on board. Tell this man to get aboard the drekar or he will die." I put the chest on the sheer strake and Erik pulled it down. The prisoner looked confused. Erik shouted to him and he began to clamber across. Sometimes when a man loses luck he loses life. So, it was with the poor prisoner. He slipped as he mounted the side and fell between the two hulls. A wave pushed the two together and he was crushed. I shook my head. *Wyrd.*

I turned and Siggi thrust a chest into my hand. I put it on the sheerstrake. Erik pulled it over. Suddenly there was a crack from beneath our feet. Siggi shouted, "She is going! Back to the **'Raven's Wing'**!"

Water began to rush up from the decks below as the galley succumbed to the waves. It must not have been a well-made ship for it was sinking rapidly. The men who held boxes rushed to the side. I tumbled over the sheerstrake and landed head first. Siggi and Arne followed me each carrying a chest. Only two more chests were recovered. Hermund the Bent and the Jarl carried them. Ulf Big Nose was forced to drop his as the galley turned on its side. Had he held on to it he would have been taken down. As it was he barely managed to avoid the hull which rolled towards him. I threw a rope to him and Siggi and I hauled him aboard like a fish.

We had six chests but, as I looked down the ship, I saw that we had lost eight men in the fight. We barely had enough crew for one man to an oar. We were, however, Vikings and the Jarl raised his hand and shouted, "Allfather!" We all joined in the shout. Those who had died were now in Valhalla.

"Sven, turn us around and head north!"

"Aye Jarl. Come on, show the Gods you are warriors! Get on an oar! We row!"

Even the Jarl took an oar. I had an oar to myself as did most of the crew. Erik stood by Sven and helped him to steer. I heard shouts and screams from the water. The enemy were dying. Those who could, clambered upon pieces of wreckage. Those who could not swim shouted for help and then slipped beneath the waves. The sea was a cruel mistress. We each had an oar and we chanted.

> *'Through the waves the oathsworn come*
> *Riding through white tipped foam*
> *Feared by all raven's wing*
> *Like a lark it does sing*
> *A song of death to all its foes*
> *The power of the raven grows and grows.*
> *Through the waves the oathsworn come*
> *Riding through white tipped foam*
> *Feared by all raven's wing*
> *Like a lark it does sing*
> *A song of death to all its foes*
> *The power of the raven grows and grows.'*

There were just twenty voices but we sang for the whole crew. We sang in memory of those who had fallen. I had not served with them long but others, like Siggi, Arne and Ulf, had sailed with them since they had joined the crew. The Norns had reminded us how parlous an existence we lived. We rowed steadily. The wind helped a little but we would have to sail beyond the land of Al-Andalus before we could stop. The Arabs would not be happy that their treasure ship had been taken. We needed to put as many miles between us and them as we could.

Sven sent Erik around with ale. With just one hand it took him some time. I was at the bow opposite Siggi and we were the last to be given the ale. He grinned as he sat next to us, "A rich haul and all the better for knowing we have taken it from the Moors. They are a cruel people." He shook his head. "They hate those who follow the White Christ and they think that every Frank and Viking is a Christian."

Siggi said, "That is foolish!"

"I know but to them, we all look alike. I think that is what saved you. Had they known what a Viking is really like then the Governor would have enslaved you all. You would still be rowing but in chains."

Siggi nodded and wiped his mouth with the back of his hand. He gave the beaker back to Erik and used both hands to row. "Then I do not think we will venture down here again."

"There is no need Siggi. Those chests were heavy. If they were all filled with coins, then we are rich men."

"No matter how rich we are some men will waste their coin."

He gave me a sharp look as Erik took the empty beakers back to the stern. "I have yet to see you spend your coin. What do you do with it?" He looked down at my chest; my bench. "You save it. What for?"

"I told you the witch told me that my fate lay not in Cyninges-tūn nor serving the Dragonheart but in Frankia. I will be a jarl and when I am I will need coin to pay the men who fight for me."

"You are ambitious."

I shook my head, "No I just follow the course the Norns have plotted for me and for us. The Weird Sisters put that treasure ship in our way."

"Then why did they sink it?"

I shrugged. "It must mean that this was all that we were intended to take. Had we taken more then we might be the ones others would attack."

"You are wise, Hrólfr... for one so young."

We rowed until noon and then we could row no further. Sven spied a deserted beach and we headed for it. Ulf Big Nose dragged his weary body ashore and returned an hour later with the news that we were safe; for a while at least.

While he was ashore we opened the boxes. We would not risk taking them ashore. Counting and dividing would have to wait until we reached somewhere safer than this spit of land. We all wanted to see the fruits of our labour. There was silence for every box was filled with coins. The Arabs had been organised. Each box had either gold, silver or bronze. We had been lucky for only one box of the six was bronze. Three were silver and two gold. We had been lucky.

Inevitably there were some who moaned. Hermund the Bent shook his head. "Think of the fortune had we managed to get all the gold on that galley!"

Siggi shook his head, "Be grateful for what we have. Hrólfr here said that perhaps the Norns only wished us to have these boxes."

"The Norns!" That was all he said but it was enough for those who wore them to grasp their Hammer of Thor and beg for his intervention. I gripped my sword.

The Jarl said, "Hermund the Bent! Risk the wrath of the Norns when you sail alone. While you are in my drekar give them respect!"

Even the belligerent Hermund realised that he might have gone too far and he withdrew to the safety of his friends.

Sven came ashore having secured the drekar. "Captain we need somewhere we can beach her." He waved his arms around the desolate sand dunes. "This is no good. We need wood for fires and to repair her. She was hurt."

"How far can we sail?"

"I would not wish to risk any further north than Frankia."

"And we will need supplies. We have gold and jewels but we cannot eat them."

I ventured, "Close to Neustria there are islands off the coast. Most have trees, some have water and many are without people. We could find one there."

"Then when we have rested we sail north. What of the wind, Sven?"

He seemed to sniff the air, like a dog and he nodded, "It is from the south and west. We should be able to do it without rowing."

"Then we sail until we reach there."

Oleg, one of Hermund's men, complained, "We sail at night? That is a risk!"

Siggi snorted, "Are you a woman? We are not sailing west; we sail north!"

Looking back that was probably the moment the division in the crew began to widen. With so few crew it became more obvious. Hermund and his four men were on one side and Siggi and the rest were on the other. It made for an unhappy drekar. We left after we had all eaten and slept for a couple of hours. Sven and the Jarl worked watch on watch. We all spent some time on watch. It took three days to beat up the coast. The nights were shorter for it was summer and the danger we faced was that of other hunters such as ourselves. We could not have defended ourselves against another drekar.

We passed two islands which looked to have too many people. The third, a long piece of land, some five miles long, was about the same distance from the mainland. We arrived at dusk and found a beach on the southern shore. It looked perfect and we headed inshore. Ulf Big Nose leapt ashore first and headed up the slope. We did not draw the drekar out of the water. Instead, we tethered her to two large rocks. We all took our chests from the drekar except for Sven and the Jarl. Theirs were bigger than ours.

"We will camp here until Ulf returns with news of the rest of the island. It will not take long. It is but a large rock."

Hermund said, "Do we divide the treasure now?"

The Jarl was becoming annoyed with Hermund; we could all see that. "And where would you spend it? This is a rock! You do not need it until we go to the land of the Frisians."

"We have earned it! We should have it now to do with as we wish!"

"And I am Jarl! It is my decision."

"Perhaps we should have a different Jarl!"

Arne Four Toes and Siggi White Hair stood and drew the swords. I drew Heart of Ice. Hermund and his five men stood together but the rest of the crew stood behind Jarl Gunnar. The Jarl shook his head, "When we get to Frisia you and those who support you can have your share and then leave. I will not have men serving me who do not accept my orders."

Hermund looked at his handful of men. I think he thought he would have had more support. He pointed at me, "It is you! You little runt! You have caused this problem. I will rip your heart out."

I knew this was a challenge and I stepped forward but before I could say anything Arne and Siggi pointed their own weapons at him. Siggi spat in the sand, "And you will have to come through us first!"

Erik of Orkneyjar, now Erik One Hand stood up too. "And I may only have one arm but I will fight for this youth who risked his life for me!"

Siggi White Hair held out a hand to restrain poor Erik One Hand, "Hrólfr is the reason we have this treasure. And you, Hermund the Bent, owe him a life. He saved you in the attack on the galley!"

Hermund slid his sword back into his scabbard. "He did not! I was in no danger."

Siggi said quietly, "Do not think of calling me a liar, Hermund the Bent. I know what I saw. That scar on your face is proof enough."

Siggi's single berserk act was enough to cow Hermund who was, at heart both a coward and a bully. "I will not fight an old man! We leave you in Frisia and good riddance!"

We sat in two groups both eyeing the other warily. When Ulf returned, he frowned as he sensed the atmosphere. "Well, Ulf Big Nose?"

"There is a farm on the other side of the island. A family of five live there. They did not see me. They are fishermen. They have a small boat."

The Jarl trusted Ulf and his judgement, "Are they a danger?"

"No, Jarl. Tomorrow we can visit in daylight. Hrólfr speaks their language. He can tell them that we mean them no harm. This is a good island. There is water and I saw a stand of trees. If you wished for somewhere to winter I can think of no better place than this. There are five sheltered bays like this around the island. One would be safe from any winter storm."

"Good, then tomorrow we speak with them. Sven, you can haul the drekar onto the beach tomorrow." Sven nodded and looked pointedly at Hermund. The Jarl went over to Harold Fast Sailing. He was a good helmsman too. "Harold, you and Sven can sleep aboard tonight with the ship's boys. I do not wish the drekar to be dragged out to sea. We will sleep on the beach tonight and tomorrow build a hall." He stood. "I will come with you and make sure that the ropes are tightly fastened. I do not doubt your skills but we do not want to be stranded here."

"Aye well, we need to shift the ballast too."

They were away for quite a while and the shellfish we had cooked with the last of the salted ham was ready before they returned. They carried their two large chests between the three of them. I saw that they had canted the ship over so that it lay at an angle with its keel facing to sea. Siggi frowned as they approached. "How can Sven and Harold sleep on board that?"

"They will not. When we went on board we saw that two more of the strakes had sprung. Water was pouring into the hull. We reached this berth just in time. Tomorrow we haul her out of the water completely and make a frame to hold her."

The evening was tense. We cooked the food for the crew in the large pot but there was none of the usual banter which normally accompanied our meals. There was just silence. Siggi and Arne made sure that they slept to the landward side of me while Erik took the seaward side. I felt foolish. It was as though I could not look after myself. Despite my fears of a knife in the night I managed to sleep. However, I had to get up in the night to make water. When I did so I saw that the tide had receded and there were footprints in the wet sand; many of them. They came from the northwest side of the beach. I went back and shook Siggi awake.

"What is it? Hermund?"

"No, but there are footprints in the wet sand, heading for the drekar."

"Wake Arne. I will wake the Jarl." As the Jarl and I headed to the wet sand Erik woke up. I put my fingers to my lips and he nodded. The five of us went towards the drekar. We all had weapons drawn. None spoke the words but we all thought that Hermund and his men had gone to the ship. I had no doubt that they would have gone for the treasure. What I did not know was how they had managed to get by us all.

The compartment by the steering board, where we had stored the chests was open. "The treasure! Hermund has it!"

The Jarl laughed, "No they have a chest of bronze and five chests of stones. They have the ship's ballast. Come let us find them."

As we headed back to the beach Arne said, "Where can they go?"

Siggi said, "My guess is the farm and the fishing boat."

"Then let us wake the men and hunt them down."

Siggi shouted, "To arms! To arms!"

The men were awake in an instant all that is save one. The night guard, Olaf Ill Luck lay with his throat cut.

"Murder! When I get my hands on Hermund....." Ulf Squint Eye had shared an oar with Olaf and they were close friends.

"Let us catch them and then we can try them." The Jarl turned to Sven and Erik. You two stay here and guard the treasure with the ship's boys."

Arne said, "The treasure?"

Sven said, "Aye we put it in the Jarl's chest. They have one box of bronze and the rest is ballast."

We followed Ulf Big Nose as he headed across the island. Dawn was breaking in the east and, as we crested the rise and looked north, we saw the small sail of the fishing boat. The murderers had escaped. The Jarl said, "Perhaps now would be a good time to speak with the farmer and tell him we mean them no harm. He will be annoyed to have lost his fishing boat."

As we approached the farm we saw that we would need no word of explanation. The family had all been slain. The farm had been ransacked and food taken. The joy at having deceived Hermund was now a bitter taste in our mouths for we had lost a shipmate and four innocent people had lost their lives. By the time we had buried them the sun was up and we saw that the family had built a good farm. There were fish drying on racks by the sea and the animal furs showed that there were small animals to be hunted.

We were a saddened and chastened group who headed back to the beach. We never mentioned the treasure nor the killers. Both were in our minds but we now had a priority; we had to repair the ship and then find these killers. From that moment, the farmhouse was feared by us all. The spirits of the dead would haunt it. Hermund the Bent had left us with a curse we could not lift.

Chapter 4

Half of the crew went to find the wood to replace the damaged strakes while the rest of us made a frame with the timber which was closest to the beach. We made a crude cradle for the drekar. We used the tide to do most of the work for us. All we had to do was haul at high tide. That would be the only time we would not be able to work on her. It took all of our first day on the island. With Hermund the Bent and his men gone we were even more shorthanded now. Sven took out the tools we would need, adze, side axe, breast augur, hafted wedge and moulding irons. We made a fire to melt down the lead candlesticks we had taken. We would use them to fasten together the strakes along with wooden trenails. On the second day, I was sent with Erik to find pine trees. We would need to use the resin from them to help seal the new strakes we would be replacing. We had a small supply of animal hair but we needed more. We would have to cut some of our hair as well. I did not mind but some of the clan liked their hair long.

In many ways, Hermund did us a favour. We were now a tighter clan. We were smaller but we knew that what we had was the core of a crew. It felt like the Ulfheonar. Haaken One Eye and Snorri had told me how they had begun with just eight warriors. Those eight became more but the original Ulfheonar had the closest bond of any warriors I had ever met. We were also a small number but we had heart. It took us ten days but the ship was stronger than ever by the time we were finished. We all worked on it. Part of us was in the hull. It was always nervous when you refloated a damaged drekar but she appeared to be sealed and we had no leaks.

As we bobbed in the small bay the Jarl said, "We will go to Dorestad to trade. It is far enough from the centre of the Empire for us to be safe and it is also popular with our folk. We need warriors."

"Aye Jarl but let us choose better than Hermund!"

"That was my fault, Oleg, and I am sorry that you have lost an oar brother. I promise that we will all choose the new crew."

As we sailed north Erik One Hand proved that the loss of an arm did not mean he was useless. His left arm was as strong as many men's right and although he could not row he was able to help the ship's boys haul on the sheets and tighten the stays. He confided in me that he wished to stay with the *'Raven's Wing'* but he would understand if the Jarl let him go. When I told Jarl Gunnar he seemed pleased. "I like him. I would have him stay with us. The Norns sent him our way for a purpose. Let us see this course to the end."

Dorestad was no Lundenwic. It was a wild town. Although part of the Empire it was at the far end of that Empire. It was a major port and ships from many distant ports traded there. As a result, they charged excessively high harbour fees. The Jarl did not mind. It meant we would be allowed to trade and we had coins aplenty. On our last night on our island, named Olafstad in honour of our dead comrade, we had divided the treasure. Although the Jarl kept half we all had more than enough; I had never seen as many coins. Along with the golden necklace I had taken and the coins I had already saved, I was a rich man. We saw other drekar in the harbour as well as Saxon ships and even a ship which looked as though it had sailed from the Middle Sea. Every ship came from a different part of the world. After we had paid our taxes we were divided into two watches. I went ashore with the Jarl, Siggi and Arne. We were going to find men to serve on our drekar. When we returned then Sven, Harold and the others would go to buy food and supplies needed for the ship.

"I want you all to keep your ears open when we are in Dorestad. Listen for word of Hermund. We need to know if the Empire is seeking us. Most importantly we need to know if anyone is interested in us."

"Aye Jarl."

I took some coins with me. I needed better armour and a shield but I was loath to pay a fortune. I would have preferred to have someone like Bjorn Bagsecgson make me some and until I found a smith I could trust I would just make do. As we were heading for the market I spied a knarr I recognised. It was the knarr from Úlfarrston and her captain was Raibeart ap Pasgen. He also sailed one of Dragonheart's drekar. I wondered what he was doing here.

I put him from my mind as we entered the bustling market. There was little order to be seen. Merchants set up stalls and piled their goods on them. We had nothing to sell and so we were the subject of every merchant's attention. They shouted and called their offers. The Frisians had learned not to judge a Viking by his clothes. They knew we spent well. We were really looking for men but all of us needed to buy some things. I wanted some sealskin boots. The leather ones I wore had suffered in the seawater. They were fine boots but unsuitable for life on a drekar. I spied a stall selling them. When I reached it I recognised Einar Sorenson. He was one of Raibeart's men. He smiled when he saw me. "Hrólfr! Lucky Hrólfr! You have grown. What brings you here?"

"I am with Jarl Gunnar but what are you doing selling boots? Where is Raibeart ap Pasgen?"

He tapped his nose, "We are here under Jarl Dragonheart's orders. Best not ask."

I nodded, "I understand." Raibeart was often used as a spy. I looked at the boots which were laid on the table.

"You wished to buy boots?" I nodded. "You could have them for nothing but it will look suspicious if you did so. Choose a pair and we will haggle!" He grinned, "You will pay a fair price."

I picked a pair and tried them on. There were soft and fitted well. I then haggled. The amounts of which we spoke were ridiculous and eventually, Einar charged me too high a price. I saw faces sniggering at me. When I handed over my coins he took but one silver one. It was a remarkable sleight of hand. He winked at me and said loudly, "Send more of your friends for I like to make money from young men like you!"

Arne Four Toes had seen what went on and he came to me, his face angry, "I will teach him a lesson! You are a brother and I will not have you robbed."

I shook my head and said quietly, "It was a game. I have paid a pittance for them. I will explain later."

I spied an aventail on an armourer's table. The mail hung from the back of a helmet and afforded protection to the neck. I hoped it would be cheap. "How much?"

He looked at me and weighed me up quickly. He was working out what I could afford. "A gold piece." I dropped the mail and turned away. "Ten silver pieces then. It is a fine piece of mail. The links are riveted."

"Five!"

"Seven and I will fit it to your helmet."

I put my hand out, "Repair the dents too and you have a deal!"

He laughed, "You are not as gullible as you look. It is a deal. Come back in a couple of hours."

I pointed to an alewives' house. "I will go there for a drink. I will be out in an hour."

He nodded, "Aye."

I joined the Jarl. He pointed to the alehouse, "Let us go and see if there are any Vikings looking for a berth eh?"

The alehouse was dimly lit. It looked to have been a stable originally and had been converted. Half barrels were laid around as either tables or chairs. The large woman who ladled out the beer looked as big as Olaf Leather Neck. I suspected she could handle any awkward customers. She spied the Jarl and recognised his chain. "With you in a moment, my lord."

"Whenever you are ready!"

As we waited we took the opportunity to check out those who were packed into the old stables. Suddenly the Jarl started and strode over to a warrior whose back was to us, "Raibeart ap Pasgen!"

Raibeart turned and looked worried, "Quiet, my lord. I am a Rurik here."

The Jarl was quick on the uptake and nodded, "Of course, Rurik. I thought I recognised you."

Raibeart grinned, "What brings you here, Jarl."

"We need crewmates." The alewife appeared with a younger version of herself. She had foaming horns of ale for us. She handed them to everyone and then hesitated when she saw me. "He looks to have just finished sucking on his mammy's titty!"

I blushed and Siggi White Hair laughed as he took the horn for me. "Looks can be deceiving gammer. This boy has killed a dozen men that I know of."

To my dismay, she leaned down and kissed my cheek, "Sorry sweetheart! You must have hidden depths!"

After she had gone the Jarl explained what had happened to us. He omitted the extent of the treasure but was truthful in all other respects.

"I will keep an eye out for this Hermund the Bent but I know some men who need a berth. A drekar was impounded for failure to pay the harbour taxes. Jarl Thorgeir the Clumsy objected and struck the Count of this town. His head adorns the gate. Some of the men are good lads. They helped me unload my knarr. Come and I will introduce you." He headed towards a large group of men who appeared to be sipping their ale. That was not the Viking way. They were making it last as long as possible. The warriors needed coin.

The Jarl turned to us, "Stay here while I go to speak with them. Hrólfr, keep your ears open."

I nodded. We looked around the drinkers. Some were sailors and some were warriors. The merchants were busy in the square but I had no doubt that they would use the alehouse when business was concluded. Some of the warriors were Franks. They would not be suitable for our drekar. We needed Norse or Danes. Had there been Rus then they would have done but they preferred the rivers of the east. There were more Danes than Norse in the old stables.

I heard snatches of conversation but none pertained to anything of interest to us. The Jarl came back. He came alone. Raibeart had gone back to his mission from the Dragonheart. I was intrigued but I had made my choice and left the service of that lord. *Wyrd*.

"I have fifteen men who will come to the drekar. Eight are yonder and the rest will follow."

Siggi White Hair shook his head, "Jarl you need to look into each man's heart before you hire him."

"I know Siggi and I hear your words. We will choose from the fifteen. The ones I spoke with seem to be the sort of warrior we seek. They are down on their luck. They have had to sell mail and helmets to live. They are desperate but I will only take those who satisfy you, my crew."

Siggi nodded, "I mean no disrespect, lord. I seek to serve you."

"I know Siggi. And I know that I am young. I made a mistake with Hermund. I knew him from home as I knew you. You never truly know a warrior until you have been close to disaster or great success. They show a man's worth. It is why I have decided that we keep Erik One Hand with the crew. His heart is Norse. Better a one-armed man who fights for you than a giant who turns and runs when your backs are to the wall."

I went directly to the armourer. He smiled as I approached and took the helmet and aventail. "It is ready. The Gods favour you for it went on easily and seemed made for it. I could put a piece on the front if you wish. It would cost just five silver pieces."

I saw the Jarl waiting, "I have no time now but I will when we return." I was about to turn away when I spied a shield. "That shield there, how much is that."

He shrugged, "It has been here some time. Four pieces of silver will buy it."

I handed over the coins and took the shield.

When Siggi saw me he said, "I thought you would have repaired your shield."

I showed him the front. It had a crude picture of a horse's head, "How could I leave it?"

Siggi grinned, "*Wyrd!*"

The other half of the crew went ashore and we awaited the potential crew members. I took my old, broken shield and took the boss from it. The wood would not be wasted. We would find a use for it and the boss was better than the one on my new shield. I spent the time we waited for the new men replacing it. There was satisfaction in the task. The more time I spent on the shield the better it would protect me. I looked at the horse's head when I had finished. It was faded but I would find the time to repaint it. When we had the opportunity, I would melt down the spare boss and use it to make studs for the front of the shield. I would incorporate them into the horse design. They would add protection and make the shield look better.

I was so engrossed in my work that I was startled when the new warriors arrived for inspection. The Jarl, Siggi and Arne, along with Ulf Big Nose went to the harbour road to speak with them. They would make the decision. I took the opportunity to study our new comrades. I saw that all had retained their swords and their shields. Half had had to sell their helmets and none wore mail. Two had leather armour such as I wore while the rest wore just kyrtles and trousers. They were men who had been badly treated by the Norns. I hoped they would not bring their ill luck to us. That made me think of Olaf Ill Luck. Perhaps he had been sacrificed so that these men could have a second chance of life.

Only two were not taken. They appeared to be happy about that and the Jarl gave them a coin each. When they had left, he brought the new crew aboard. "These are our new shipmates. The two who left decided that they did not want to serve on this drekar." He shrugged. "They said that it did not smell right."

Arne Four Toes laughed and pointed to Beorn Beornsson, "I said you should wash your breeks more often!"

We all laughed, even Beorn.

The Jarl continued, "I will go with them now to buy them helmets for they cannot go to war with bare heads and we will buy ale. When we return to Olafstad there will be no alewife! Siggi, you command until I return." Siggi nodded. "When Sven returns, we will need to arrange the oars. Think about the best arrangements."

"Aye Jarl."

The new crewmen deposited their meagre possessions in the centre of the drekar close to the mast fish and the mast. I felt guilty for I was much younger than most of them and I was much richer. I realised how fortunate I had been to have met the Dragonheart. He had truly changed my life.

Sven arrived back before the Jarl. The drekar was his world. The land and the town held little lure for him. He came and sat close to Siggi and me. "The Jarl said he wished to reorganise the drekar."

"Aye, we will need to. We have lost too many men."

Sven nodded, "I would be happier with you and Arne close to the steering board. You are the heart of the ship."

Siggi nodded, "I share my oar with Hrólfr here. The Norns have determined that we face the world together."

Arne nodded, "And I would be close too. Beorn Beornsson has lost his oar mate as have I. Put us together. We four will be the first oars."

Sven nodded, "It is good and Beorn has a good voice. This is *wyrd*."

Once that was done it did not take long to arrange the others. We knew not the new men but Sven and Siggi spread the old crew so that there was a spine of our original crew in the drekar. The voyage back to Olafstad would help Sven refine the arrangement. We moved our chests to their new position. I was aware that we were sitting where Hermund the Bent and his men had sat. Their chests had been left on the island. They had taken all of value with them but what they had left might come in useful for the new crew members.

It was dark by the time that the rest of the crew returned. They came back laden. The Jarl had invested some of his money in food as well as ale. Eight firkins of beer were carried aboard as well as twenty loaves, a ham and a round of cheese.

"We eat well tonight. The rest of the ale and the grain I have bought comes tomorrow!" he shook his head. "This is an expensive place. We had best hunt again soon!"

After we had eaten the Jarl introduced us to the new men. He told a little about them as he did so. In some cases, it was the reason they had their nickname. In others, it was for a deed they had done. After Erik One Arm had been introduced he spoke of me. He spent longer this time and told of my thraldom, my service to the Dragonheart and my visit to the witch. Every eye was upon me. I wondered if I had grown a third ear in the middle of my face.

Then one by one our new crew stood and gave their names. As they had lost their drekar and their jarl they were tight-lipped about their past. I guessed that the Jarl and those who had spoken with them knew their stories but, for now, we just had their names. When they spoke them Sven and Siggi assigned them their oar and their chests were moved there.

"Erik Green Eye."
"Rolf Arneson."
"Alf the Silent."
"Harold Haroldsson."
"Gunnar Stone Face."
"Einar Einarsson."
"Rurik One Ear."
"Thorir Thorsten."
"Ketil Eriksson."

"Knut Eriksson."

"Beorn Fast Feet."

"Olvir the Child Sparer."

"Gunnstein Gunnarson."

When we were all seated on our chests the Jarl addressed us all. "You are now one crew. We are the Raven's Wing clan! We are brothers. I swear to look after you as a father and you must swear to follow me."

We all shouted, "We swear!" Even though the original crew had all sworn an oath the fact that Hermund and his men had broken theirs meant we had to reaffirm ours.

We stayed aboard the drekar that night. Dorestad was not the place to throw coins around. You might end up with a slit throat. We questioned our new shipmates about their experience and they asked about ours. I confess that I attracted more attention than I would have wished. Even though the crew of *'Raven's Wing'* had sailed with Dragonheart I had been a closer companion for I had sailed aboard the *'Heart of the Dragon'*. I had touched the sword touched by the gods. I was uncomfortable but I endured the interrogation.

We were due to sail as soon as the ale and grain arrived but before it did so Imperial officials came striding down the quay to the drekar. The Jarl was suspicious and spoke to them from the sheerstrake.

"Jarl, we have come to ask you about the taxes you paid yesterday."

"It was the right amount was it not? I thought it excessive but this is the land of Louis the Pious."

"Do not speak thus! You are in enough trouble as it is."

"Why? Have we broken laws? Have we avoided paying taxes?"

Siggi said quietly to me, "Be ready. I smell trouble." I saw him catch Sven's eye and nod.

The official said, "It is only of late we have allowed your kind to use our port."

"If you are always this inhospitable then our visits will stop."

The official held up a gold coin. "You paid with this yesterday!"

"Aye. As I said I thought one gold piece was excessive."

"This is a coin from the Emirate of Cordoba."

"Aye, what of it? It is gold is it not?"

"It is but how did you come by it?"

The Jarl smiled, "We are merchants. We trade. We traded spices here yesterday and we now have Imperial coins."

"You are pirates and we believe you may have stolen this. Cordoba is now an ally of the Empire. We wish to question you further."

The Jarl spread his arms, innocently, "And we are here."

"You are forbidden to leave the port until we have investigated."

He nodded. I peered over the sheerstrake and saw the alewife marching along with the firkins of beer. "Siggi, take four men and fetch our grain. Sven, prepare to leave! I would not suffer the same fate as Thorgeir the Clumsy."

Siggi White hair tapped me, Arne and Ulf Big Nose. We grabbed our swords and headed towards the grain warehouse. We passed the officials and, worryingly, I saw them speaking to the Captain of the Guard. Siggi said, "We had best hurry. I think we have outstayed our welcome."

Our sacks, all four of them were waiting for us. We hefted them on our backs. It looked like they would be all the grain we would have until we raided. We hurried back to the drekar. The sacks disguised us somewhat and when we passed the Captain of the Guard and his men as they marched to our drekar they did not recognise us. Once we had passed them we hurried. I saw that Sven had untied us from the wooden stanchions on the quay and the two new brothers Ketil and Knut Eriksson stood holding the ship to the shore.

We hurled the sacks aboard and Siggi White Hair shouted, "Cast off! There are men coming!"

The Captain of the Guard and his men were now running towards us in an attempt to prevent us from leaving. Ketil and Knut jumped aboard still clutching the ropes. Six of our crew pushed us away from the stone quay.

"Stop in the name of the Count!"

One of the new men, Rurik One Ear, stood and put his hand to the space where his ear should have been had it not been sliced off. He mimed deafness. As we drifted with the current we all laughed. It was the first sign that we were one crew. We were unwelcome and we had been chased out of Dorestad but we were Vikings. As soon as you boarded a drekar you were feared. We headed south. We had a home to build and a future to begin.

Chapter 5

The guards had no bows and they stood impotently shaking their fists at us as we sailed out to sea. We were running out of places where we could trade. As we began to row, for the first time as a single crew, I said to Siggi, "Perhaps we could use Olafstad as somewhere that people could come to trade."

He shook his head, "It would not work. You need a place with families. We are warriors. Your Dragonheart is lucky to have Úlfarrston and to have knarr to send around the seas. It is why we raid. We would trade if we could but we are seen as pirates. You heard the official."

He was right but I still had my dream of my own land in Neustria. It seemed a long way away but I had come far already. A few years earlier I had been a slave. Now I was a warrior. Soon I would own my own byrnie. I was young and I had time. I would have Siggi teach me to be a better swordsman. I decided to have Erik teach me to speak the language of the Moors. Who knew when that skill might come in handy.

The island was still deserted when we returned. I wondered if people may have visited from the mainland. It was only when we had been there for some time that we discovered the sea frets and fogs which sometimes hid the island from the mainland. It was isolated. That suited us. We did not use the side which the fisherfolk had used; we returned to our beach. Olaf was buried there. This would be the home for our drekar. We would not be close to the haunted farmhouse. We were superstitious. It did not do to anger the spirits.

Our first task was to build a hall for us. We left just Sven and the ship's boys to secure the drekar and we took axes and tools up the slope. Ten men went to cut timber, ten went to dig turf and sods. The rest of us went, with the Jarl, to find a site. The island was not large and we found a dell with a spring. It was sheltered from the east winds and it faced west. There was a ridge that gave some protection and the trees which grew there were small and could be easily felled. I was sent with four others to fetch the large timbers which had been hewn. This was the first hall I had built but I knew how they were made.

Harold Fast Sailing took charge of the construction. We built the frame of what looked like a drekar. It looked flimsy. It was but a skeleton. Siggi and the Jarl had had the men dig eight huge holes in two lines. As soon as the eight trees were trimmed to the same size they were placed in the holes and packed with cobbles from the beach. We then had to summon the whole crew to lift the framework for the roof on top of the timbers. My muscles burned as we stood there. We had to wait until Siggi and Harold had fastened the roof to the timbers before we could relax.

Jarl Gunnar was pleased. "Broach a firkin of ale! You have deserved it!"

The barrel was soon empty but my arms no longer burned. The next part was equally as hard. We took out the turf from inside what would be the hall and began to stack it to make the walls. Then we had to bring over the rest of the turf which had been cut to build up the walls. I was sent with some of the younger warriors to collect thin branches of willow and hawthorn. I saw why when we returned. We had to scramble up the newly built turf walls to begin to fill in the gaps in the roof timbers. Finally, as the sun was setting, the first layer of turf was laid upon the hawthorn and willow to make a watertight roof.

The Jarl nodded his satisfaction. "Tonight, we sleep on the beach but tomorrow we celebrate our hall!"

Sven and the ship's boys had gathered shellfish. Using the bones of two hams we had carved for our food during the day they had made a stew. All of us yearned for bread but the bread oven would be built the next day and it would be some time before we ate bread again. Although I was tired I knew I needed to work on my shield. I used a torch to search for beetles and when I had enough I crushed them to make a paste. I wanted my horse to have red eyes and the beetle juice was perfect for that. I would need to find some cuttlefish for their ink. But, as I went to sleep, I was happy enough with the work I had done so far.

That night I dreamed. I usually dreamed but that night I dreamt of a horse. I rode the horse and I led my own men. The horse seemed to stride across the land eating up the ground. It was so vivid that I swear I could smell horse. I ached when I awoke. It would pass but I did not relish more work. The dream stayed with me. It lurked in the recesses of my mind. I would be a horseman and I would lead men. When?

The Jarl divided us into three groups. Two small ones began to build the bread oven and the smithy while the rest of us fetched stones and sand from the beach. The floor of the hall would be made of sand, topped with stone and finished off with timbers. The large stones would be used for the oven and the smithy. Siggi White Hair and Ulf Big Nose disappeared for they sought clay. Without clay, we could not have an oven.

When the Jarl was satisfied with the floor we cut down more trees to make the timbers and the one doorway. For food, we ate the salted fish which the dead fisherfolk had left. Miraculously we managed to finish by dark and we had a roof under which to sleep. The fire in the middle was lit. We let the smoke filled the hall. It would drive away any unwanted animals and insects whilst drying out and hardening the roof and walls. Siggi told me that we might have to cut a hole in the roof for the smoke but he was confident that Harold's design would mean we did not need to.

That night we finished off two firkins of ale and those with good voices sang songs and told sagas. It made the hall a home. The new crew had songs we had not heard before and they had not heard ours. Before we could raid again we needed more weapons making. We had our smithy ready but no smith. There was plenty of metal and Beorn Beornsson set to work making arrowheads. The new warriors who did not have spears could still make and use a bow. The ship's boys were sent to find the wood and the feathers to manufacture them. When the fire was hot Beorn began to melt the iron. I helped him by using the bellows we had fashioned from leather and a pig's bladder. It was selfish on my part. When he had finished, I intended to make my metal studs. I had already made the mould from sand. We had a plentiful supply. I also wanted to see how Beorn made the iron molten.

I used different muscles when working the bellows but I soon tired. I was grateful when Beorn said it was hot enough and I helped him to pour the molten metal into the moulds. He turned to go as I put the broken pieces of metal into the crucible we used. He stopped, "Do you need help, Hrólfr?"

"I think I can do this."

He nodded, "Let me help you. We are one clan now. What do you make?"

"Studs for my shield."

He nodded approvingly, "That is good. Many warriors do not do that. They should." With Beorn's help, I soon melted the metal. I was about to pour it when he took some burned charcoal. It lay around the fire and it had cooled. He dropped a small handful in. "It makes the metal harder and besides Thor likes it."

We left the metal to harden, "The smithy is free!" He shouted.

No one else had any metal to work and we let the fire die. I went down to the sea. A few warriors were collecting limpets and other shellfish. I saw Sven there. He was using a line to catch fish. "Have you caught any cuttlefish or squid, Sven?"

He shook his head, "No they are further out." He pointed to some rocks which were just visible above the surf. "Try there but you will either need to dive or a net. Unless, of course, you can use a spear."

I shook my head, "I need the squid blood. I wish to paint my shield."

"Ah. Then use a net. Whatever you do not need we will cook! You know you do not need a great deal of it?"

I nodded, "I want my shield to stand out."

"Then you are a brave man for such a shield attracts warriors who will wish to fight you."

"I just want everyone to know who I am."

"You have dreamed."

"How did you know?"

"I recognise the look. Such as you are chosen by the gods or toyed with by the Weird Sisters. You are like the Ulfheonar or Berserkers. You do not tread the same path as us. I will watch your progress with interest."

It took me all afternoon but I caught enough squid for the ink I needed and crabs besides. It was a good stew we ate that night. Arne had promised us that the bread oven would be ready the next day. I finished off my shield after we had eaten, for the days were still long. My fingers were stained and remained so for days but I had the effect I desired and the shield would have days to dry and to harden. I would apply a coat of resin the next day for I knew where the pines were. It would stop the inks from fading.

As I lay down my shield Siggi came over. "I have been speaking with Sven the Helmsman. He says you wish to be known on the battlefield. That is either very brave or very foolish. You can use a sword but you have little skill. You were lucky fighting those Moors. Had they had swords then I would now be talking to a ghost."

I nodded, "Would you teach me?"

He grinned and nodded, "I will. I know you have the strength and you have the wit to fight for you are able to think. I need to help you harness the two, that is all. We will train tomorrow when the work is done."

I was up before dawn. I could not sleep. I collected the resin first. Then I took my studs from their moulds. Only one was faulty. I put that in my pouch to use as a slingshot. I went to the beach where I hammered my studs in to the shield. I was pleased with the effect. Then I returned to the hall and coated my painted horse with the resin. The shield was finished. All I needed was to add a long leather strap to hold it against my back and it would be ready.

Siggi White Hair was waiting for me after I ate the last of the dried salted cod. The spring water tasted good. We had been lucky with our choice of sanctuary although I suspect the Norns had directed us here. I knew not why. If I expected to be using 'Heart of Ice' I was wrong. Siggi waited with two old swords. He had rescued them from the supply Beorn was going to melt.

"Why not use our swords?"

He smiled, "I thought that you felt affection for that sword. It is special is it not?"

I nodded, "The Dragonheart had it made for me. It is the most valuable thing I own."

"And that is why we use these old things. They have neither edge nor point. I do not wish to be harmed by a lucky blow from you! They will suffice for what I intend." He threw one to me. It was heavier than mine and not as well balanced. Siggi smiled, "See already you realise that your sword is much better. If you can fight with this then what can you do with your own, eh?"

I could see his reasoning. I stooped to pick up my helmet.

"No, we use neither helmet nor shield. I want you to fight unprotected."

"But you have a mail byrnie!"

He laughed, "Which I have earned and when time allows I shall buy a full byrnie as I do not have the death wish upon me. I went berserk once. That is enough for any man. Now, what do you try to do to an enemy when you fight him?"

"I do not understand. Kill him?"

"Good answer. Too many men try to show their opponent that they have more skill than they do. They play with their enemy. Such men are fools. You kill and you kill as quickly as you can. Where will you strike me to kill me? I wear no helmet and I have no shield."

"Then your head."

He shook his head, "Try it!"

I swung my sword at his head. As he blocked it he hit me hard in the stomach with his fist. I doubled up, winded. The rusty blade was placed next to my throat. "You are dead and I have your fine sword."

He helped me up and when I had regained my breath I asked, "Then what should I do? Should I have punched you when I struck?"

"I was only able to punch you because I had blocked the blow. You had all of your weight behind the blow. You would not have been able to do so. I will show you. I will attack you!"

I was ready with my left fist. I would show this old man that I, too, could punch. I was ready for a swing at my head. Instead, the rusty sword darted out and struck the top of my leg. "I thought you would attack my head as I did with you!"

He laughed, "Use your eyes and your wit. You are clever, Hrólfr the Horseman. Watch your enemy, look at his eyes. Try to hit me again."

I was tired of being made to look like a fool. My stomach hurt and my leg throbbed. I feinted at his leg for he would expect me to copy him but instead, I swung sideways at his arm. He blocked it easily but he smiled. "Much better. I watched your eyes and looked at your body. I knew what you intended. Again."

We spent the rest of the morning thrusting and parrying. He still made me look foolish but his praise kept me going. We stopped after I had made my most successful move. Instead of swinging at him, I feinted and then turned away to bring my sword around his back. It was the first time I had surprised him. He was delighted and picked me up in a bear hug. "That is how you use your head! Had you struck me I would have been dead. We will stop now for we have done enough for the day. Come and sit by me. Fetch your sword."

I sat next to him and offered him my sword.

"No, I want you to look at it. How can you kill with this?"

I stabbed forward and then swung it sideways. "A thrust or a slash."

He nodded. "Choose wisely. If your enemy wears armour, then it is hard to cut them. You must weaken the armour first or weaken the man. If you strike with the flat of the sword it will still hurt and not take off your edge." He pointed to his knuckles. "If you hit here then my hand becomes numb. I might even drop my weapon. Now if you have quick hands, and I think you do for you have a quick mind, then you use your tip." He took my helmet and placed it on the stump of a tree. "Stab the tree in the eye."

My hand darted forward and my sword went next to the nasal and under the bronze metal band.

"Good. Now if he moves then you will hit metal but it will make him move his head. When he does that, you use your shield or your seax for he will be distracted. Never make the same blow twice unless you wish to make him think he knows what you do. Vary your strokes and your blows and remember that no matter how good your sword is each time you hit with it the blade and the tip became less sharp. The sooner you end the combat the better. Now come. I am hungry and I smell bread! Someone must have managed to light the bread oven!"

Even though the first batch of bread was slightly burned it did not matter it was worth it. The Jarl opened another barrel of ale. "Before we run out of ale and as we have the hall and oven finished we will raid!"

We all cheered.

He turned to Erik One Hand. "You have proved yourself to be one of the crew I would have you stay here and watch the hall. Will you do that?"

I saw the disappointment on his face but he nodded, "It would be an honour, Jarl." He smiled. "I will see if I can manage some one-handed bread!" We laughed and he added, "And I can tend the nets. There will be dried fish too when you return laden with treasure!"

Arne Four Toes shouted, "Where do we sail, Jarl? Frankia?"

"Not this time. I had thought that Sussex is ripe for the plucking. The Danes have made the land of the East Angles theirs. Perhaps King Egbert still looks to the north and his enemy, Jarl Dragonheart. It is a rich land. I fear the eye of the Empire will be seeking us out."

Alf the Silent said, "There is a place called Haesta or something like that. The tribe are the Haestingas. They have iron workings there and a bay where we can land."

Arne laughed, "You do not say much but when you do it is worth hearing Alf the Silent!"

He smiled. He had said enough and he was a wise man who knew when to stop.

Einar Einarsson nodded, "I have heard of the place but I did not know about the iron. That would be good, Jarl. We could do as Hrólfr has done. Melt iron and add studs to our leather. Until we get mail it will be better than nothing."

"I have seen armour which is like the scales on a fish. Pieces of metal are sewn onto the leather. They overlap." I remembered the men I had seen on the galley.

Einar nodded enthusiastically, "Even better. Then we steal iron and make ourselves stronger."

We spent some time questioning the two of them about the best approach and when he had done so the Jarl said, "Now that you all have a helmet I have a mind to put on a Herkumbl on your helmets. We are one clan and our foes should know it." Sven brought out a carved wooden stamp. On it was a raven's wing. For our first raid, it will just be painted with squid blood but when we return with iron we will make a metal one." A Herkumbl was a clan marking. It helped when you fought other Vikings. Hermund the Bent was an enemy and one day we would have to fight him.

The idea appealed to all of them. Even as we discussed it I was deciding that I would have a horse for my sign when I led a warband. Then I laughed. I had a piece of mail hanging from my helmet, a sword, a second-hand shield and already I was leading warriors. How the Norns must have laughed at my youthful arrogance.

Sven estimated that it would take us almost two days to reach the Sussex coast. It had taken that long to reach Frisia. We left in the afternoon so that we could arrive in the middle of the night. Erik One Hand waved us off. He looked like a forlorn figure on the clifftop. I did not envy him being alone on an island with just the spirits of the dead there. The winds were with us until we rounded the Breton coast. They still helped but we were not as swift through the water. By then it was nightfall. During the day, we used the wooden compass which Sven kept. It meant we could sail confidently. At night, it was not as easy to keep a straight course. As luck would have it we only had the stars briefly but it helped Sven and Harald Fast Sailing to correct our course. When dawn broke, they checked their compass and found that we were still on course.

To the east of us lay Frankia and we avoided that. Our run in with the Count's men in Dorestad meant that there might be Imperial ships watching for us. We could outrun any of them but it was better to be hidden if possible. The sea is a vast place and we saw no sign of sails as we used the gentle winds from the south to head steadily and, we hoped, stealthily towards the coast of the land of the Angles. We slept watch on watch. It was never a deep sleep. The anticipation of action was too great for that but we rested and we ate. We were all happier when darkness fell. We felt that luck was with us when the clouds disappeared and the stars helped us to steer a more accurate course.

Alf and Einar were at the bows. They had both been here before. They were looking for landmarks. They knew that to the east of the small port were high cliffs. If we could find them then they were both certain that they knew of a small beach some mile and a half from the settlement where we could land. We knew that we were approaching land when the swells lessened and we could hear, in the distance, the sound of waves breaking on a shore. Sven shortened sail. It slowed us down and made us harder to see.

A whistle from the bows took the Jarl racing down the centre of the drekar. He came back and pointed west. We were a couple of points too far to the east. We sailed a parallel course to the coast and we all saw the cliffs. When the ship's boy on the masthead spied the beach, he whistled and pointed. The sail was quickly furled and we took to the oars so that we could land as gently as possible.

Ulf Big Nose leapt into the surf before we had even grounded and he raced up the path which was clearly visible to the west. We would not be beaching the drekar. Sven and the ship's boys would let her drift out to sea away from the rocks and use a sea anchor. During the voyage, I had found time to attach a longer strap to enable me to carry the shield upon my back and I put it on over my wolf cloak. As we were at the stern Siggi, Arne and I were amongst the last ones off. We helped to push the drekar back into the deeper water and the ship's boys used oars to scull away from the beach.

Ulf Big Nose appeared and he pointed west. He had found the settlement. I was in the middle of the warband as we headed up the path which twisted and turned its way to the headland. We were partially in the dark as we had no idea if there was a wall of armed men waiting for us. Neither Alf nor Einar remembered one but it had been some years since they had visited. Who knew what might have been built since then? Confidence was high but even I knew the risk the Jarl was taking.

We reached the headland and Ulf pointed across the shallow valley. There was a burgh. It was small but they had fortified the top of the other headland which stood above the small port. There were four or five fishing boats bobbing around but the place was silent. Between the burgh and the water were scattered houses. Alf pointed to the northeast. He had said that was where the mine workings were. Arne nodded and led off the twelve warriors who would accompany him. It was to be hoped that there would just be the miners there and Arne and his men could overpower them. If they could secure the iron, then it would be as valuable an asset as gold.

The rest of us followed Ulf as he led us down the valley. I wondered what strategy the Jarl would employ. The burgh looked to be small. I wondered if it was a refuge in case of an attack. If I had been the Jarl I would have searched the houses first. If they were empty, then it would mean the people were in the burgh. We halted fifty paces below the houses. I glanced behind me and saw the faintest of glows. Dawn would be an hour or so away. The Jarl waved to Ulf Big Nose who slipped up the hillside towards the nearest hut. Our scout was like a ghost. Jarl Gunnar then turned and waved Siggi White Hair to the left and Beorn Beornsson to the right. I drew my sword and followed Siggi. I saw him swing his shield around and I followed suit. I was no longer the new warrior. I had to earn my oar.

We were approaching the huts which were closest to the port. Perhaps the fishermen were early risers or perhaps we were unlucky but a man stepped from his hut as Siggi approached. I understood enough Saxon to know what he shouted, "Vikings!"

That was as far as he got for Siggi hacked across his chest and the man fell writhing to the ground. Pandemonium ensued. The huts emptied as men and women alike raced out. The men held weapons and some of the women had armed themselves with knives. A man launched himself at me with a woodcutting axe. I barely had time to hold up my shield. He was no warrior. As the axe caught on one of my new studs it stuck. I darted forward and my sword slid between his ribs. As he fell Siggi shouted, "Quickly! Kill the men! Forget about the women!" I saw some of the newer men trying to restrain the women. Ketil Eriksson had his face raked for his troubles. The women fled away from us.

With the women gone we soon disposed of the men who remained. They were brave but facing a Viking was a daunting task. Siggi pointed to the Eriksson brothers. "Go around the huts and collect anything that is valuable. If there is loose soil in the centre, then dig it up. There may be treasure. Take all that you can back to the ship."

"What if there is too much?"

"Then, Knut Eriksson, you use a cart like that one there!" The scorn in his voice as he pointed to the four-wheeled crudely made cart caused Ketil to laugh at his brother's embarrassment. "The rest of you follow me to the burgh. The Jarl may need help."

We turned right and headed towards the burgh. The Jarl was closer to the fort. If the Saxons stayed within we were safe enough but if they sallied forth then the Jarl only had eight warriors with him. The sun had begun to spread its thin light from the east. It shone on mail. There were warriors within the burgh. I ran as fast as I could. I was younger than the rest and I only had leather armour. I began to outstrip the rest of the clan. The huts hid my view of the Jarl but I heard the clash of metal on metal. He was being attacked.

As I burst through a gap in the huts I saw that Eystein Svensson was dead and even as I watched a mailed thegn hacked through the arm and chest of Finni Sorenson. The Jarl had five warriors with him and there were ten men with the thegn. As the thegn swung his axe at the Jarl I ran at the two men behind him. Neither wore mail but they both had helmets and swords. I was running at them from their right and that gave me the slightest of advantages. I could use my shield but the first warrior could not. I punched with my shield at the Saxon's head. He reacted by bringing up his sword. I ripped my blade across his middle and pulled back. He looked like a gutted fish as he tried to hold in his insides.

The warrior next to him was able to turn so that he faced me with his shield. He lifted his sword to smash it down and make a killing blow. I blocked with my own sword and then used the Siggi punch into his face with the boss of my new shield. He tumbled backwards, throwing his arms up to regain his balance. As I plunged my sword into his throat I heard a roar from behind as Siggi led the rest of our men to attack the Saxons. The odds were now in our favour. I glanced to my right. The Jarl was still fighting with the thegn. My job was not to interfere but to protect him. I saw a mailed Saxon at the rear turn and run back up to the burgh. I raced after him. The gates were still open. I saw that the Saxon had a short mail shirt on. Even as I ran I wondered why a man who could afford such armour would leave his thegn.

I was gaining on him. The sun was now shining in the eastern sky. As my sealskin boot sent a stone skittering down the hill he turned and saw me. I was alone and he must have felt brave enough to take me on. He had a full-face helmet such as the one worn by the Jarl Dragonheart. His shield, however, had no leather covering. Mine was better. I did not pause as I ran up to him. I swung my sword from on high as I hurried towards him. He brought up his shield to block the blow. I did not aim at his body but his leg. He had no mail there and my sword bit deeply into his leg. He flailed at me with his sword but it was a weak blow and my shield barely moved. I swung my sword again and this time the flat of it smacked into the side of his head. He tried to scramble back but his left leg would not support him. As he dropped his right knee I ended his misery. I plunged my sword into his neck and gave him a warrior's death.

I saw fingers as they began to close the gates. I ran up and smashed them with my shield. There was a scream and the gates sprang open. Two priests lay there floundering like fish. They clutched at their crosses and began to chant to the White Christ. I shouted, in Saxon, "Go!" and pointed towards the open gate. The Jarl had determined that we had no market for slaves. Our orders had been clear. Kill the men and scatter the rest. Priests did not count as men! They did not fight. The two men fled out of the gate. I stepped inside ready to fight any who remained within.

There appeared to be no one and then I heard whimpering from behind the door of the hall. I strode swiftly and silently towards it. I stepped inside and there, cowering under a table were two women and three young children. I opened the door wide and said, "Go!"

The two women looked at each other nodded and, grabbing their children and, bizarrely, a large pot; they ran. It was not a large hall just as the burgh was not a large one. It was, however, new. I searched, not for treasure, but for enemies. There were none. I went back to the gate and shouted, "The burgh is taken!"

I saw that there were one or two Saxons who still fought but most were slain. Siggi shouted, "Hold it, Hrólfr, until we reach you."

I waved my sword in acknowledgement. As much as I wanted to search the hall for treasures I obeyed Siggi and stood my ground. The warrior I had slain was just ten paces from the gate and I went to him. Sheathing my sword, I took off his helmet and his mail shirt. I had earned both. I saw that he was a warrior but a little older than me. After taking off my cloak I slipped the shirt over my head. It only covered my front and back but it was better than just leather. I replaced my cloak and my shield. It felt tight but I would get used to it. The helmet had been dented in the fight but when it was knocked back into shape it would be better than mine. I also took his sword and seax. I had better but it was always useful to have spares. He had a pouch and in it, I found some coins. Finally, around his neck, he wore a cross of the White Christ. It looked to be silver. The young man had been someone who was important. I took his baldric so that I could carry both his sword and his seax. I would have to carry the helmet.

I heard a whinny from behind me. I went back inside the walls. I walked around the hall and there was a stable. Inside was a horse; it was young but it looked to be powerfully built. I guessed it belonged to either the thegn or the young warrior I had slain. I walked up to it and stroked it. I had spent many years growing up in Neustria and I loved horses. I spoke to him. He was tethered. I found a pail and went to the well. I filled it with water and returned to the horse. He drank greedily.

"They left you without water eh? While you drink, what say I get you some grain?" I went into the hall and found the kitchen. There were sacks of grain, food and at least three barrels. Hopefully, they would be filled with ale. This was a rich haul. I found a clay pot and filled it with grain. Other Vikings might not be happy about my wasting grain on a horse but I could not help it. That was part of my nature. I returned to the horse. The pail was empty. I put the pot before him. "You were thirsty. I shall get you some more."

"Who in the name of the Allfather are you talking to?"

I turned and saw Siggi standing there. I felt foolish but I stood my ground. "A horse. He was thirsty."

Siggi grinned, "You are a strange one." He pointed to my mail shirt and the helmet which was laid next to the pot. "You have done well. The warrior you slew must have been rich. Perhaps he was the son of the thegn the Jarl killed."

"Is the thegn dead?"

"He is but he wounded the Jarl in the leg. Harald Fast Sailing is stitching it. I have taken command until then. We need the drekar here. Go and fetch it."

"Can I take the horse? It will be quicker."

"It is yours for you captured the burgh."

The horse had finished the grain and I untied his halter and led him from the stable. I did not bother with a saddle. I knew how to ride. Once outside the stable I pulled myself on his back and kicked him in the ribs. As I burst from the gates Ulf Big Nose stepped back in surprise. He saw it was me and he laughed, "You are truly Hrólfr the Horseman now."

"I go to fetch the drekar!"

"Good for I have run far enough this day!"

I kicked the horse on. I had forgotten the joy of riding. He was not large, my feet almost touched the ground, but he was strong and he galloped happily across the valley. As I climbed the other side I passed the Eriksson brothers and Gunnar Stone Face. They were pushing a cart and carrying things taken from the village. Their journey was for nothing.

I reined in next to them. "Siggi has sent for the drekar. We sail back to the port."

They nodded. Ketil smiled, "You have landed on your feet Hrólfr the Horseman!"

I laughed, "Aye I have. This is a good day!"

It did not take me long to reach the beach for the horse was eager to run. I slipped from his back and, cupping my hands shouted, "Sven! Siggi White Hair wishes us to take the drekar to the port. The Jarl has a wound." I pointed behind me, "We have some things to load first!"

He nodded, "Did it go well?"

"Aye but the Jarl took a hurt."

"We will come closer and make it easy for you."

While I waited, I took off my shield, cloak and new baldric. I could leave those on the drekar. I intended to ride the horse back. By the time the cart appeared the drekar was in the shallows. They threw a rope to me and I tied the drekar to a large rock. We would only have twenty paces of surf through which to wade. It took some time to fetch all that we had collected. The empty cart was carried to the drekar. We wasted nothing and then the Eriksson brothers and Gunnar Stone Face clambered aboard. I handed my treasures to Ketil, "Here take my booty and put it near my chest. I will ride back and tell the others you are following."

Cnut shook his head, "And you do not have to row!"

I smiled and spread my arms, "The gods favoured me, that is all!"

As I rode back, more slowly this time for I wished to enjoy the ride, I spoke to the horse. "I shall call you Dream Strider for I have dreamed of my own horse since I was young." The horse whinnied. "I will see if the Jarl will let me take you back to the island."

By the time I reached the other side of the valley the crew were carrying the contents of the burgh down to the harbour. My joy ended when I saw the four bodies lying there. We had paid a price for our success. I tied Dream Strider to the lintel of a hut by the harbour. I strode towards Siggi whom I saw organising the men.

"The drekar is coming."

He nodded and pointed up the valley. There I could see a line of warriors, "And Arne has finished at the mine. This has been a good day." He pointed to the fishing boats. "Go and fetch two of those. We will tie them to the stern of *'Raven's Wing'*. They will be useful on the island. We can catch bigger fish."

"Aye!"

The two nearest boats were anchored just twenty paces from the shore. I took off my helmet and mail shirt and laid my sword and seax on top of them. I took off my sealskin boots and I waded out to the nearest one. The water came to my chest. I pulled myself aboard and pulled up the stone anchor. There were a pair of oars and I sculled it back to the shore. I repeated with the second boat by which time I saw the drekar as she nosed into the harbour. I put my shirt and boots back on.

The Jarl was carried down to the water's edge on a shield. His leg was heavily bandaged. Harald Fast Sailing said, "Watch him, Hrólfr. We have much to carry from the burgh."

"How is the wound, Jarl?"

"He was a good warrior and he fought well for his people. I was lucky that I just took the blow to my leg." He pointed to the horse. "Siggi told me you had your own success."

I nodded, "Could we take the horse back to the island? He will be useful."

The Jarl considered, "I do not see why not but have you considered what happens when we leave the island?"

I shrugged, "That is in the future. I am young, Jarl. We deal with each moment and then move on."

He nodded, "That is a good attitude."

When the drekar was tied up we took the decking up and began to fill the hold with the barrels, sacks of grain and other booty. Sven reluctantly tied the two fishing boats to our stern. He did not relish the prospect of towing them. Finally, we laid the bodies of our dead by the raven prow. *'Raven'* would watch over them until we could bury them on our island. The ore would be spread out on the deck. We just awaited the last of the ore to be loaded, and then the burgh could be burned and could leave.

Siggi White Hair smiled as I took the horse's halter in my hand, "I look forward to seeing how you get this beast on board. I have tried to take sheep and pigs before now. I always got a soaking."

I confess I had not thought about how I would do it. The deck of the drekar was slightly higher than the quay. It was higher than the horse's legs. I wondered about a plank and then I had a sudden idea. I mounted the horse and rode him a few paces from the drekar. "Stand clear! Clear those chests away from the centre of the drekar." The Eriksson brothers quickly cleared a space and sheltered by the stern. I kicked Dream Strider in the ribs and said, "Come boy! Let us see if you can jump!" I rode him obliquely at the deck so that I could land on the cleared space. I did not ride him hard but I pulled up on the halter when we neared the drekar. He sailed over and I had to jerk the reins to the left to stop us flying off into the sea. I barely kept his back and had to grab a hunk of mane to do so.

To my great surprise, the crew all cheered and began banging their shields. Even Sven was impressed. He laughed, "I thought you were due a ducking there, Hrólfr the Horseman! I can see you are well named!"

The last of the ore was just being manhandled into the drekar when Ulf Big Nose, who was at the burgh firing it shouted, "Riders! They come from the north!"

Siggi was decisive. "Fire the burgh and get back on board." Arne, Ketil, Knut and I were on the quay. He turned to us. "We will wait until they are aboard" He leaned over the drekar to pick something up.

I saw the flames licking the wooden hall and Ulf Big Nose and his three men began to race towards us. He had left it late for I saw the horsemen as they hurtled down the slope after them. We had no bows strung and so Siggi passed us each a long spear.

"Leave them space to get by. Run Ulf!"

I saw him glance over his shoulder. They would make it; just.

"Ready your spears. Spread them out!"

Ulf, Karl and Knut all leapt through the gap and hurled themselves over the side of the drekar. They landed on the deck. The leading horse and rider tried to turn. The horse's hooves found no purchase on the cobbles and it began to slide. Arne's spear took the rider in the side of the head while Ketil and Knut both speared the horse. Its sliding body struck them and knocked them into the side of the drekar.

Sven shouted, "Get them aboard! They are hurt."

The next riders managed to stop and then appeared to be confused as to what to do. Their leader lay impaled upon Arne's spear! Siggi White Hair shouted, "I have had enough of this! He rushed forward jabbing his spear as he went. Arne and I followed. The rider closest to Siggi stabbed at him with his spear and Siggi's mail was struck. The blow, however, knocked the rider from his horse. Siggi lifted his spear and stabbed the horseman through the side. The rest waited.

Sven's voice boomed out. "Back! You have done enough!"

We climbed aboard and the crew cheered. I went to Dream Strider and stroked his mane. The smell of the dead horse's blood could upset an animal. We pulled away from the port as more horsemen appeared. They were too late and our first raid had been a great success.

Chapter 6

The smoke from the bread oven was a welcome sign as was the sight of Erik One Hand as he waved from the cliffs. We had discovered the problem of carrying a horse when Dream Strider decided to make water and then defecate. Luckily, I was the one closest when it happened and I was the one who suffered. Arne Four Toes thought it hilarious. Consequently, I was fairly smelly when we arrived in the bay.

Siggi White Hair said, "I think it would be easier if you took your beast off first, don't you?"

I nodded and began to take off my boots. My mail, helmets and swords were already with my chest.

"Any idea how you are going to get off?"

I pointed to the iron ore which was stacked, in places, as high as the sheer strake. "The same way as I got on."

I swung up onto Dream Strider's back. He had had enough of the drekar and eagerly moved towards the sacks of ore. He was careful with his hooves. When he put his front ones on the sheer strake I slapped his rump and he jumped into the sea. I lost his back and sank beneath the sea but as I had the halter in my hand I popped to the surface like a piece of cork. I rolled onto his back and lying flat encouraged him to swim to the shore. When he stepped ashore I slid down. I let go of his halter. He shook himself and then cantered along the beach just happy to be on dry land.

It took some time to empty the drekar. We had had a rich haul. Our chests were brought ashore. We would not need to raid again for a while. The task of taking our goods to the hall would take longer. First, however, we took the dead to the hill and we buried them close to Olaf. We made a barrow. After the Jarl had sent them on their journey to Valhalla Siggi said, sadly, "They will not be the last."

It was a sobering thought.

The cart and Dream Strider proved to be invaluable. We rigged up a harness and my horse pulled the cart up the path which led to the clifftop.

We did not take the iron ore there. Siggi pointed out that we could use the beach just as easily to roast the ore and then refine it. Most of the iron ore would end up as slag. We would leave that on the beach. The valuable iron we made would be easily carried to the crucible and the forge. That, however, was a job we would leave for a later date. We had a victory to celebrate and treasure to display. We had captured many animals. Dream Strider was not the only passenger. We kept a ram and a ewe from the animals we had captured and slaughtered the other four. We would add to our herd when we raided Frankia and Austrasia. The fowl we kept. They would be good eating but they would not take much keeping and would give us eggs.

That evening as we ate roast mutton and fresh bread we washed it down with Saxon beer. Harald Fast Sailing began a saga about our victory. My horse's activities featured prominently. After everyone had laughed at my embarrassment the Jarl spoke of the dead and of our future.

"It is sad that we lost four men but when I look at what we have gained I am happy. Siggi, I give you the mail I took from the Saxon Thegn. I have a byrnie already and if you continue to charge horsemen then you will need it. We have gained many swords and helmets. It is a start. Tomorrow we begin to make iron and I start to heal. When Harald takes out my stitches then we raid and this time we try Aquitaine again."

Arne Four-Toes said, "Is that wise, Jarl? The last time we barely made it out alive. Remember the Moorish horsemen?"

He nodded. "And that is why we will not raid the southern bank of that mighty river. We will sail along the northern bank. This time we will send scouts out first. It is half the distance we travelled to the land of the South Saxons. If we leave at dawn our scouts have a whole night to find us a target."

"You mean we attack during the day?"

"Aye Beorn. I have not heard of any, save Dragonheart, raiding the river. If our scouts can find somewhere without a stone wall, we will not have a problem."

That caused a debate. I remained silent. I did not know enough yet to contribute. Ulf, our chief scout, also remained silent. Eventually, the Jarl noticed this. "You are quiet, Ulf Big Nose."

He nodded, "I am the scout and I will choose those who go with me. It seems that the gods have given us something we did not have before." He pointed to me, "A horseman. Any man who can make a horse jump onto a drekar and then off has my respect. If we could steal horses, then we could explore further and have the means to escape. If I have Hrólfr the Horseman as a scout, then I think we can do what you wish and that the drekar will be safe. A horse doubles the area we can search."

Every eye was on me. The Jarl said, "Well, Hrólfr, what say you?"

"I serve you, Jarl Gunnar Thorfinnson and I am happy to scout with such an illustrious scout as Ulf Big Nose. I hope I do not let you down."

Siggi White Hair put a huge paw around my shoulder, "You could not. Even if you tried!"

Dream Strider could not escape the island and so he was not tethered. He galloped around the island as though it was his domain. Each day he grew. I suspect he had been stabled too long and it had stunted his growth. When I was not working, I liked to watch him. He did not belong to me. He belonged to himself and permitted me to ride him. He came whenever I whistled. I thought I knew horses but it was not until Dream Strider came into my life that I truly came to understand them. It was funny to see some of the other, younger warriors who tried to entice my horse to them. He would come and eat whatever treat they offered and then gallop off. When he came to me he stayed and nuzzled me. We had a bond from the outset.

Knut and Ketil, in particular, were convinced that I was a galdramenn. "I have heard that the Dragonheart's wizard, Aiden, taught you the horse spell."

"No, Ketil. I swear that I use no magic save the connection between a horseman and a horse."

"I would like you to teach me."

I smiled, "The problem you have is that you try to dominate the horse. A horse is like a good hunting dog; if it likes you then you need to do nothing. If it does not, then you will never control him. Let Dream Strider come to you."

Ketil nodded and Knut asked, "Why did you pick that name?"

"In my dreams, I see horses and there is one, a jet-black stallion, much bigger than Dream Strider and he strides through my dreams. No matter how fast I run I can never catch him. I have often woken murmuring Dream Strider. I did not choose the name, my dream did."

The times when I could ride my horse or even watch him run were few. We had to build a furnace big enough to melt the rock. Then when the rock had cooled down we had to separate the slag from the ore and then re-smelt it. The process took a long time and required much wood. The island soon began to become bare. There would come a time when we would have to spread further afield to get the wood for the fire. Erik Green Eye knew how to make charcoal and Beorn Beornsson said charcoal was better for iron making. We began to make charcoal.

Hrolf the Viking

The Jarl began to heal and the first of the metal was produced. Rolf Arneson had skills with a blade and he carved a raven's wing for our herkumbl. It would not be large but it was detailed. The painted one had disappeared from our helmets. The metal ones, when produced, would be riveted to the front. I liked it for it added metal to the part of the helmet most prone to attack. I had managed to take the aventail from my old helmet and, after I had repaired the dents in my new one, had managed to fix it to the back. Even Arne was impressed by my new helmet. I could see that he was envious. Everyone wanted one of the raven's wings. It was seen as a mark of honour. However, some of us had to go on the next raid without the prestigious adornment. They took time to make. When we left this time, every man had a helmet. Some had managed to sew pieces of metal on their leather armour and everyone now had a good sword. Siggi had sold his mail shirt to Ulf Big Nose. As we two were the only scouts it felt right that we both wore the short mail shirt which covered just the back and the front.

Erik was left again save that this time he had Dream Strider for company. He also had animals to attend. Soon it would be harvest time and then we would need to prepare to overwinter in our new home of Olafstad. As we rowed the first few miles to gain sea room, it was a much more fluid motion. We were now in rhythm. Even when we did not sing we spoke and we spoke in the rhythm of the oars. Hard work and constant exercise meant we found it easy to row and to speak. We only had to row ten miles and then Sven was able to turn and head south by east. The wind from the west now worked for us. We were able to lie on the deck and sun ourselves. Although the land would never get as cold as at home these late days of summer were days to savour. The days ahead would be colder. Winter was coming.

This was not the first time we had approached this mighty river and we were better prepared. We knew just how wide it was; it felt like a sea. We kept to the northern bank. There were settlements there and a couple of towers but fewer of them than on the southern bank. We reached the mouth of the estuary just before dusk. The river appeared empty. Sea birds soared overhead, that was all. Sven had the sail lowered and we took to the oars. I was facing the sunset and the sky seemed to be on fire. The river was flat, especially after the waves we had endured sailing down the coast. We rowed for ten miles up the river. It was then we spied the tower in the distance. The light from the setting sun reflected from its top. We rowed in silence for another five miles and then Sven put us over to land on the northern bank.

Ulf Big Nose and I slipped over the side. The Jarl would not anchor. The crew would row against the gentle current. "Be back before dawn.

Hopefully, we will find somewhere close to this spot on the river where we can shelter and wait for you." The Jarl nodded to Harold Haroldsson and Alf the Silent. They would search nearby for a stand of overhanging trees or a small tributary.

Ulf and I waded through the shallow water to the marshy bank. It was flat land but there appeared to be no roads. I was the novice and I followed Ulf as he loped along. We only had our swords as weapons. It was speed and stealth which would save us. Ulf was not called Big Nose for nothing. He sniffed and pointed left. There was a track of sorts. I guessed it was the path trodden by those fishing at the river. Ulf stopped and sniffed. I did too and I knew then what he had found. It was the smell of horse muck. Where there was muck there were horses. Ulf could move remarkably silently. He was like a ghost or a will o'the wisp. I struggled to keep up with him.

I heard the whinny of the horses. They were not in a stable. Instead, they were penned outside. Their only guard, however, was a formidable one. It was a dog. I heard it growl. Ulf and I dropped to our haunches. He held his hand up to me and then, leaning forward began to whistle. Had I not been as close as I was then I would not have heard it. The growling stopped. While still whistling, Ulf clicked his fingers and the dog began to move towards us. When it reached us it spied me and growled again. Ulf reached into his tunic and pulled out something. He offered it to the dog who ate. He handed me something. It was a piece of dried deer meat. He nodded towards the dog. It was a vicious-looking dog and was the size of a calf. I held my hand out with the food on the palm. The dog ate it and then lay down.

Smiling Ulf stood and we went to the pen. There were four horses. Ulf gestured to me. This was my job. I climbed over and clicking with my tongue approached them. I did so calmly and steadily. As I had expected one of them moved towards me. Knowing we had horses to ride I had brought two of the apples from the island. There was a small orchard and while the apples were not quite ready horses didn't seem to mind the sour taste. Certainly, Dream Strider didn't and ate all that were offered.

I took out an apple and took a bite. I held it in my palm. The horse picked it up, gently and chewed it. Then it licked my hand for more. I offered it the other half while I slipped the halter around his head. He took it. Waving Ulf over I handed him the reins. I mimed for him to walk around with the horse. It needed to get used to his smell. I took out another apple and bit into it. The horses must have smelled the apple once I bit it. That and the fact that the first horse had accepted me made them slightly less nervous. A pair of them walked towards me. I took another bite out of the apple and held out the two pieces. I kept half in my mouth. While they ate, I took out my second halter. I had decided to go for the chestnut. It was larger than the other. I took half of the apple from my mouth and gave it to him as I slipped on the halter.

I led him to the gate. Ulf had already opened it and he mounted his horse as I stepped through. We walked east. When we were a thousand paces from the pen we kicked our horses in the side and they trotted along the path which ran by the river. We made good time. We saw no one and we did not look like raiders. We had neither helmet nor shield and every man carried a weapon.

Within half a mile we had seen one target but Ulf pointed to the stone tower which was nearby and shook his head. We moved on, always keeping to the trees and the undergrowth. When we came to the terraces and the grapevines we lay flat along our horses' backs. The second site we found another three miles upriver was more promising. It was closer to the river and, although it had a wooden wall, it had no stone tower. More importantly, I could see a wooden quay. The place was used to move things down and up the river. We tethered our horses to a tree and then moved towards the quay. There were two barrels. Ulf sniffed and mimed drinking. They were wine barrels. There was loot here already for us. Taking out our swords we moved towards the walls of the town. The path was wide and there was a clearing before the walls of the town. There was a gate. It was as high as a man and there was a ditch. I would have left to return to the drekar but Ulf restrained me and we waited. We seemed to wait an age but we were rewarded by two men's heads appearing above the gate. They had a town watch. We watched the two of them as they walked in opposite directions around the wall. They returned to the gate and their heads disappeared. Satisfied Ulf led me back to the horses.

We walked the horses along the river and when we were far enough away we mounted them. We had seen enough. There was wine and a town. The town watch were not men to fear. We reached the drekar just before dawn. It was closer to our target than it had been for they had found a small tributary upriver. It looked rather shallow to me but Sven knew his ship. There were trees on either side. While not quite high enough to mask the mast two of the ship's boys clambered up and disguised it with branches. We were hidden. We tied the horses up for we could use them when we raided.

Jarl Gunnar was keen to know what we had discovered. "Well!"

"You need to be careful when you sail tonight. There is a tower and a strong settlement. The one we found has a quay and just a wooden wall with a gate. They have two guards."

Jarl Gunnar Thorfinnson seemed relieved, "Good, you two get some rest while Siggi White Hair and I plan."

I was almost too excited to sleep but I knew that I would need to be alert. I curled up beneath my wolf cloak and slept. I was woken by Siggi who held a two-day-old loaf and some cheese before him. I shook my head, "I need ale first. My mouth is as dry as the desert."

He put the loaf down and reached over to take a horn of ale from Ketil. "Here. You will need this. You and Ulf are going out again with the Eriksson brothers."

I swallowed half of the ale and wiped the foam from my face, "We need another target?"

"No, the four of you will use the horses to get to the far side of the settlement and make sure that no one escapes. The Jarl is worried about this tower. If it is only a couple of miles away we cannot risk being disturbed as we were last time. Ulf Big Nose assures us that we cannot miss the quay."

I nodded, "He is right, it is the only one." I saw Knut and Ketil grinning, "We ride double?"

"The Jarl saw that you had picked good horses, strong horses. They can carry two and we will not be taking them back." He saw the look on my face and he laughed, "No more horses in the drekar! The next time one of them may shit on me! And I will not find that funny!"

I took Ketil with me. My horse was bigger and Ketil was the larger of the two brothers. He gripped onto me as we rode through the night. Ulf took Knut and the two of them carried bows. The four of us had left just before dusk. Ulf and I had not scouted the northern wall. This would afford us the time to do so. We rode directly down the river. The drekar followed but we were quicker as the drekar was rowing against the current. We soon lost them. We walked very slowly when we were in the vicinity of the tower and then we headed inland. Animals skittered out of our path but the noises would alarm no-one. They were the noises of the night. The doves which flapped in the trees made more of a noise and we halted until they settled down again. Then we moved on.

I was becoming used to using my ears and my nose. My nose picked up the smell of wood smoke and then my ears heard the voices in the distance. Ulf veered a little to the left and we went slower. The voices were not constant and we had silence and then the sound of conversation. When it became louder Ulf raised his hand and we dismounted. Ketil heaved a sigh of relief as he slid from the chestnut's back. I took the halter and led the horse. If things went awry this was our way out.

What we had not seen the night before was the tilled field. The horses would be seen from the walls. We turned back into the thin scrubby trees.

We tied our horses to them and, after donning my new helmet, crawled across the tilled field. It was covered in crops yet to be harvested. They were some sort of bean and they did afford us cover. A drainage ditch on the far side meant we could shelter and spy the walls. Ulf pointed; it was for my benefit. There was a second gate on the north wall. We waited until we saw the town watch patrol the wall close to us and saw him meet up with the one from the south wall. Then we rose and Ulf led us to the road which ran from the north. He and Knut dived into the ditch on one side and I jumped into the other with Ketil. The gate was just forty paces away. It was closed. We waited.

Time passed and we measured it by the regular patrols of the town watch. After three such circuits, I began to worry. The attack should have started. Had I been alone I would have moved but Ulf remained as stone and I emulated him. I think I learned as much from Ulf as I had from Siggi. Ulf was patient. I had to learn patience. I heard something in the night. I could identify what it was but when I glanced over to Ulf I saw him rising from the ditch and waving me forward. I turned and tapped Ketil. Drawing my sword and hefting my shield around to the front I stepped from the ditch and began to approach the walls. The two men of the town watch ran along the wall, heading for the south gate. A moment later I heard the sound of a church bell sounding the alarm. The attack had begun.

Suddenly the gate opened ahead of us and a rider appeared. Ulf and Knut had their bows in their hands and as the rider was just ten paces from us their arrows plucked him from the animal's back. I put my arms up and began clicking my tongue. The frightened horse reared before me and then stopped. I stroked its nose.

Ketil said, "You could have been killed!"

"And if a riderless horse had ridden to the tower where there are warriors what would they have thought?"

Ulf and Knut had run towards the gate. We had been seen and the gate slammed shut. As we ran to join them I saw a figure on the wall aim something. I took no chances and pulled up my shield. The arrow struck it. When we reached the gate I could hear the sound of battle and confusion within the walls. Although it was slightly higher, if we were to gain entry then we would have to scale the gate for the ditch prevented us from doing so further around.

Ulf said, "Ketil, Knut, hold your shield." He slipped his bow around his back and, stepping onto the shield, said, "Up!" The two brothers hoisted him up and his fingers found the top of the wall.

I sheathed my sword and slipped my shield around to my back. "Now me."

I was lighter and they had now done this once. I managed to get my arms over the wall. To my dismay, I saw Ulf fighting two men and a third ran at me with a sword. As I pulled myself over he slashed at me. Someone was watching over me that night for I managed to get my head over the top as the sword slid along my helmet. My aventail saved my life that night. I had no weapon in my hand. I held the sword hand to the wall and punched with my right. The man had no helmet and my fist connected with the side of his head. He tumbled to the ground and he fell awkwardly.

I drew my sword and my seax. I ran at the back of one of Ulf's attackers. He did not see me coming and Heart of Ice slid through his ribs. His back arched and I used my sword to push him to the ground. I did not pause but pushed next to Ulf and stabbed with my seax. I caught the second man across the arm and as he dropped his sword Ulf took his head.

"Get down to the gate and let in the brothers. I will guard the rampart." He stood and faced the men who were approaching from the west wall. I turned and ran to the tower. I clambered down the ladder. As I reached the bottom and turned a man swung his sword at me. I instinctively flicked up my seax. It took some of the power from the strike but his blade still struck my chest. The new byrnie stopped the blow. I rammed my seax into his eye, twisted and then pushed it into his skull. He slumped to the ground. I had to sheath my weapons to open the gate. I heard cries behind me as men saw me. I could not turn. I had a task to perform. I had just managed to lift it when a spear was rammed at my back. My shield behind me took the force and I swung the bar in an arc. It struck two of the men who had weapons raised to strike me. Ketil and Knut burst in as I hurled the bar at the advancing townsfolk. The two brothers were eager to get into the fray and they threw themselves at the men before us. We had shields, swords and helmets. They had whatever weapon they could find.

I swung my shield around and drew my sword. As I joined the brothers we slew the last of those who were facing us. Three others saw us and ran. I saw a man pitched from the walls and then I watched as Ulf raced down the ladder to join us. He nodded, "You did well. Hrólfr, you and Ketil hold this gate. None must escape. The rich will try to flee with their treasure. Stop them!"

He and Knut raced off. "Ketil, grab this bar with me. We will close the gate again!"

With the gate closed and just the dead before us, we were an island of peace in a sea of war. We could hear the sound of battle as the Jarl and his men fought with the town watch and whatever warriors there were.

While we waited, we searched the bodies of the dead. The baker, I could tell his trade from his flour stained clothes, had six coins on him and a fine dagger. That was all. The spear he had used on my shield was shattered. Altogether we found four metal crosses, twelve coins, two daggers a sword and a couple of poor helmets. Ketil found a leather satchel by the gate and he put our finds within.

He was still doing so when I saw men running to us. "Ketil leave that and stand close!"

A man with a woman and two children had burst from a side alley and ran towards us. I could see by his clothes that this was no baker and the small chest he clutched, rather than his wife or his children told me that it was valuable. His head had been down as he ran to towards us but his wife saw us and she screamed. I suppose my new helmet made me seem inhuman somehow.

The man spoke and I understood most of his words. "Let us go and I will give you money." He tapped the box.

I shook my head. "You will give us your money and you will wait here until my Jarl has finished."

The man clutched the box closer to him. The woman pleaded, "Please do not hurt me or my children! I beg of you!"

I pointed to the wall on my right, "Wait there and you will be safe. You have my word that no one will harm you."

She shook her head, "I cannot see your face! You are a monster from the north!"

I took off my helmet. It was a relief for I was hot and the cool air was refreshing. I smiled, "There. I am no monster!"

The man must have thought he could use the distraction of his wife to escape for he pulled a short sword out and lunged at me. Ketil had understood little of our interchange but his sword was ready. The man ran onto the blade before he had taken a step. Even in death, he clutched the box as tightly as ever. His children started wailing. I shook my head, "Had he obeyed he would have lived. A man can make more money. He cannot remake a life." She pulled her children closer to her. "Ketil, thank you for that. Search him and take the box."

I noticed that there was less clamour but more people were approaching. I turned to the woman. "Tell them that there is no escape this way. If they sit down, they have my word they will not be harmed."

She flashed an angry look at me, "No for we are worth more as slaves are we not?"

I shook my head, "I was a slave once but I promise you that we do not wish to enslave you." I was speaking the truth for we could not afford the time to sail to a slave market. It was treasure and food we sought. We had to supply our little island home for the winter.

She nodded, "I know not why but I believe you." She stood and shouted to the ten or twenty people before us. I think she must have been a woman of some importance for they obeyed and sat down.

As dawn began to break Siggi and Arne approached with Ulf and other warriors. Siggi laughed, "You have done well the pair of you. Come bring these folk back to the hall."

I nodded, "They are afraid we mean them harm. Let me speak with them."

"Aye Hrólfr."

I turned to the people but I spoke with the woman, "You are to go back to the hall."

She looked fearfully at the blood-spattered warriors before her. "You swear we will be safe."

I smiled, "If we had wished you harm then you would not be talking to me now, would you? You have my word. Now come! Soon we will leave you and you can pick up the pieces of your lives."

She nodded and spoke to her people, "Come. We go to the Great Hall."

I picked up the chest and Ketil hefted the satchel and weapons on his back. He said, "What did you say to her?" I told him and he shook his head. "You are young but you have a wise head. I would have laid about me with my sword and they would have obeyed."

I laughed, "And what if they had all rushed us? They outnumbered us. We could have been overpowered and slain. True many of them would be dead but that is what comes of not using your head. Be like ice!"

I saw, when we reached the hall, that we had not escaped unscathed. Three bodies lay beneath their shields. Already I saw men carrying goods to the drekar. The Jarl looked up as I approached. I pointed to the woman. "I think that this is the wife of the headman. I caught them escaping and this feels heavy. The others listened to her. I promised them they would be safe."

Siggi nodded, "They will be, we do not have Hermund the Bent with us now."

"Take the booty to the drekar and then help carry the barrels of wine and the sacks of food. We have come at the right time. They had begun to collect in the harvest."

I saw that animals were being driven to the river. The woman had grown bold and, as I turned, she said, "Will you leave us nothing?"

I pointed to the fields through which we had crawled. "There are crops there as yet unharvested. Your grapes are still on the vines. You will not starve. Your husband thought not of that when he fled with this box of gold did he?"

Tight-lipped she went into the hall.

I had sounded cruel but I had grown up in a settlement just like this one. I knew that somewhere, hidden from us, would be an emergency supply of food. They would not starve. I had no doubt that there would be a lord in the tower and it would be incumbent upon him to feed the people who paid his taxes. I was under no illusions; we were the wolves and they were the sheep. Sheep were there to be shorn. If they wanted protection, then they should employ a good sheepdog. It was how the Dragonheart protected his people.

Siggi and the Jarl were the last two who joined us at the drekar and they did so quickly. "Cast off! Riders are coming!"

We had been lucky. This time we had managed a whole morning without interference but now the local lord had come. We left and were heading downstream when the mailed warriors arrived. They followed us downstream. At first, they kept pace with us but once the river took hold of us we sped down the mighty river. Any joy we had in the great quantities of wine, wheat, gold and food, not to mention animals, was tempered by the bodies of the dead who lay by the prow. For once I was happy to be sent to the oars for it meant I did not have to look at them. Every Viking expected to die with a sword in his hand but I had not yet done enough nor fulfilled my potential. I prayed that the Allfather would keep me alive a little while longer.

Chapter 7

Any morbid thoughts we might have had were driven from us by the late summer storm which tossed the ship up and down as though it was a piece of straw! We lost a sheep and two geese. Siggi was philosophical about their loss. "A small price to pay to Ran. Better a sheep and two geese. It was a good Blót."

It took us longer to reach home and I could see the worry on the face of Erik One Hand. It was like coming home to a fretful mother.

The barrels were easier to land than the ore had been. We just tipped them over the side and let the tide take them to shore. They rolled up onto the beach and we pushed them the last few paces. Rather than take them to the top of the cliffs we put them under the rock overhang. There it would be cool and we could take for trade or take some from the barrels for drinking. Not many of us enjoyed wine but in the absence of beer, it would have to do.

We did not rest for long. The next day half of the men were put to work building an animal shelter and food store while the two boats were sent fishing. Beorn Beornsson had the rest of the men at the forge making nails. The storm had threatened to spring some strakes. We would be prepared. I had few skills in either metalwork or fishing and I was used as raw labour. I did not mind for it meant that Dream Strider would have a roof over his head for the winter.

We began by digging a deep hole. It was as deep as a man's leg. We used the cart to haul up sand and stones. That was my task for Dream Strider seemed to work better for me than any other. The posts were put in the same way as the hall but there would be a second floor. By the end of the first day, we just had a skeletal roof, eight posts and a floor. The work meant we were all ready for the last of the beer, warm wheaten bread and freshly caught fish. The fishermen had caught many and they would dry and salt the surplus the next day. In the long nights of winter, they would be our staple diet. The island boasted neither deer nor boar; it was the only drawback for our island home.

By the end of the second day, we had walls and a roof but the storage area was still unfinished and the first rains of autumn came. The Jarl came from Ljoðhús and the one thing of which we had plenty were seal skins. He had many in the hold. We kept them as a last resort. If we had nothing else to trade, then they would bring some coin and trade. Now, however, they covered the sacks of grain and dried beans. It spurred us on to finish the floor. We managed it by noon of the next day. It meant the food we had taken would now be safe from the elements.

It was only when the storage hall was finished that the Jarl would speak of dividing the treasure. It was not as much as that which we had garnered from Sussex and many of the crew spoke about returning there. Siggi was the voice of reason, "If you want to hunt an animal you stake out a watering hole. We have yet to be hunted because we do not return to the same place. We can enjoy the riches of Sussex, Kent and Wessex but wait until after winter."

Sven nodded, "I would not risk more than one more raid. We will need to look after our ship."

"And I am guessing that you would like a shorter voyage than the others we have undertaken of late?"

"Aye, Jarl. She is a good ship and sound but we treat her hard and these are not the gentle waters of the Middle Sea; this is Ran's Ocean!"

The Jarl pointed north, "We will not antagonise our neighbours, the Bretons, we will go further north to Neustria. There is a mighty river there. It travels deep into the heart of the Empire. Things are easier now than when Charlemagne ruled. We will chance it."

"I have to warn you, Jarl, that we have already lost more men than we can afford."

Beorn Beornsson nodded, "Siggi is right and until we get someone who can make mail and other such objects then we will not become better-armed warriors." He picked up a helmet and tapped the raven wing, "This is piss poor work! I am ashamed of it and yet it is the best I can manage. I am a warrior and I do not work iron. Each to his own trade."

"We cannot just conjure a blacksmith out of fresh air."

I could tell that tempers were becoming fraught. I stood. I did not wish to shout. By standing I grabbed their attention. Ketil chuckled, "Beware! The horseman stands! Watch out he does not emulate his horse!"

I smiled. I did not mind banter and I knew that he meant well. "We have few friends, Jarl but we know that the men of Dyflin, Ljoðhús and those in the land of the Wolf are our friends. They have many there who ply trades we do not yet possess."

The Jarl shook his head, "You are saying that we should sail home. I thought you were the one who said we should winter here closer to our hunting ground."

Siggi came to my defence, "That is not fair Jarl. You are twisting Hrólfr's words. He means well and I know what he means. He is not saying you travel home and winter there; he is saying travel to one of those places and return thence. It would be half a month at most," He suddenly slapped one hand against the other, "And, by Odin's beard, we could get more men to join us! This island is as good a home as I have yet to find. We do not have far to travel to raid and, barring the lack of women, it has all we desire."

Everyone seemed to agree. It became a Thing. Everyone began suggesting ideas. I watched the Jarl. He liked it too but he could not be seen to be swayed so easily. He was not Dragonheart who would happily have changed his mind if he had been persuaded of the merits of an argument. "I will sleep on it and when we have raided Neustria we will hold a Thing again."

As the hall descended into a babble Siggi and Arne turned to me, "You are a thinker, Hrólfr. That is rare." Siggi smacked his own white hair, "As I have proved I do not think I just act. I will stay close to you, young horseman."

Once again Erik was to be left alone but he had formed a bond with Dream Strider. Once I had shown him how to mount the horse one-handed and, while we were away and he could fall unseen, he took to riding the horse. Animals have this uncanny knack of knowing that we are all different as people. He was gentle and patient with Erik where he was impatient with Ketil who also tried to ride him. I was happy for I hated the thought of either the horse or the man we had rescued being lonely. I knew that feeling all too well.

We had a violent storm one night. We lost one of the fishing boats which broke free from its moorings and was firewood by dawn. When the skies cleared and shone blue it decided the Jarl. "We raid this night. The Allfather is telling us that the raiding season is coming to an end. If we are to seek more men and a smith we need to take advantage of this short break in the weather."

We would not be away for long. Neustria was but a few hours away. We knew where the river lay and I had lived there. I knew of at least two monasteries as well as towns that did not have walls. I would be of use once more. As we rowed along the Breton coast I began to look forward to travelling to Dyflin after we had raided the river I knew so well. I hoped it would be the land of the Wolf but that was a longer journey. I would make do with Dyflin. Gunnstein Berserk Killer was a good Jarl. I would be able to spend some of my gold. My aventail and short mail shirt had saved me and I began to dream of a byrnie. My mind drifted as we settled into the sea eating rhythm which only Viking warriors can achieve. I thought of a byrnie I could wear on a horse. The centre would have a split like the ones I had seen worn by the Moors. When fighting horsemen, I had noticed how easy it was to hack at their legs as they passed. I had killed some that way. A split byrnie would still hang down and protect my legs and my horse. I knew that we did not fight on horses but I dreamed of a time when I would. The witch in the cave had prophesied it and I knew, from Kara and Aiden, that my destiny lay with horses. It was why Dream Strider was so important to me.

Once we turned east we were able to stop rowing and prepare for war. I now had a dagger as well as a seax. I had made a sheath for the dagger behind my shield. I was becoming more used to my helmet. The half-mask across my eyes had distracted me the first time I had worn it but I had learned to see beyond the eyeholes. Erik had managed to attach the stone we used to a treadle and our swords were all the sharper for that. When he was alone on the island he would sharpen all the spare weapons. He became highly skilled. Even those warriors who had doubted the Jarl's judgement in taking a one-armed man into the clan now saw the wisdom in that simple act of kindness.

I knew the river we sought, the Issicauna. I had lived there as a slave and been rescued from it by Jarl Dragonheart. The village in which I had lived was long gone for the Jarl's men had destroyed it and killed those who lived there. I think the raid had made men fear Vikings. At its mouth, it was hard to see both banks at once. It was a mighty river that went to the heart of the Empire. Many ships used it. The Jarl was being clever. Even if we could not raid the land we could raid a ship and that was just as good. Some would say better as we could sail the ship home. We would, however, try the land first.

It was dusk by the time we entered the river. The wind was with us. As we did not have to row we were all able to watch. Both sides of the drekar were manned. All around us were enemies. The Empire kept ships that patrolled the river. I suspected that we were too big a mouthful for them but their presence might stop our landing. We looked for lights, we listened for bells and we smelled for smoke. I was at the prow looking to the northern bank. My home had been there. I remember hearing stories of the land further upstream. I had plucked some names from my memory. Now that we were on the river it was as though the memories had resurfaced and were much clearer. I knew that there were monasteries here and I knew there were rich prizes. My pride wanted me to be the one who found it. I wanted to give something back to Jarl Gunnar Thorfinnson.

We had many bends to negotiate but as soon as I heard the bell ahead I knew that I had found the monastery. I pointed ahead to Siggi White Hair. "Up ahead. It is called Jumièges. There is a huge monastery and abbey by the river. It was founded by a king and there are many houses close by."

"Which bank is it on?"

"The north bank."

"I will tell the Jarl!"

Soon we saw the pinpricks of light on the hill which told us that there was something close. There was not just the smell of wood smoke but also incense. It was the monastery. Finally, we heard the sound of cows lowing as they waited to be milked.

The Jarl joined us. "Sven says the current is growing. We will need to row. How far is it?"

I pointed to a darker shadow on the hill just around the next bend. "It is there, Jarl."

"Good. Then we do not have far to row." He turned and said, "Oars!"

We took to our oars eagerly. We did not have far to row. Perhaps our eagerness was our downfall. We were confident, more than that we were overconfident. We had landed successfully and raided almost without hindrance and we thought we would do the same here. At first, all went well. We landed just four hundred paces from the monastery. The tiny lights we saw gave us an idea of its size. It was a huge number of buildings and I saw that they were all made of wood. That was as I had remembered them. We poured over the sides and raced up the hill. We had to get to the monastery before the monks and clerics knew that they were being attacked. We could not afford for them to hide anything. This was our last raid before winter and we needed it to be a good one.

Ketil and Knut raced to the huts nearest the river. When they returned empty-handed we knew that they had been evacuated. The Jarl led us up the hill. We heard the bell sounding and this was not the call to prayers. It was the strident bell of alarm. The Jarl turned, "We are discovered! Run!"

I was young and I was fast. I soon overtook the Jarl and Siggi both of whom wore full mail. I saw the church door. It was ajar and I could see light within. I ran straight in. There were priests and monks inside and they were gathering candlesticks, altar linens and holy books. I charged at them. I bundled two over with my shield. One picked up a candlestick to hit me and I was forced to stab him. The Eriksson brothers followed me in and I left them to contain the monks. I had seen a richly dressed cleric leave by the back door and I followed him. He ran towards another building a hundred paces from the church from which emerged men. Some were armed.

"Raven Wing! Raven Wing!" I shouted the cry which would bring my fellow warriors to my side. Undaunted by the numbers of armed men I ran after the priest. He clutched something. It must have been valuable. I was faster than he was but when he tripped over his robes I was to catch up with him. He had dropped a golden cross. It was large. I knew not what the metal was but it looked like gold. I stamped my sealskin boot on it and braced myself for the armed men who charged at me. The first three were armed with small shields and spears. They wore helmets but had no armour. I knew I had to hold on until help came.

The three spears all jabbed at me at once. That helped me for I just raised my shield and blocked them. Having three men ahead of me the odds that I would strike flesh were high and I jabbed forward somewhat blindly. I felt it slide into flesh and the man I had struck screamed. The priest who lay at my feet tried to grab the book and I stamped hard on his hand. A fourth man joined the others just as I was swinging at the other two and I felt his spear as it stabbed into my leg. I knew that it had grated along bone for the pain was excruciating. The leg they struck was the one standing on the book. Just then Ketil hurled himself at the warrior who had stabbed me. It bought me the time to punch with my shield while slashing a sweep at the two warriors. My sword bit into the thigh of one and Knut came and took the head of the last one.

More men with weapons were racing towards us. I was in the middle and I said, "Lock shields!" I had never done this before but I knew it was the right move for three men faced with greater numbers. Our shields overlapped and we held our swords above them. We kept our heads below the tops of our shields. I shouted again, "Raven Wing! Raven Wing!" We had need of help and we needed it quickly. I could feel the blood running down my leg. I hoped it would hold me long enough for our crew to join us.

The men who charge us hit our shields and ran into our swords. A spear glanced off the side of my helmet and I felt my shield shiver as bodies and spears hit it. The three shields held. I poked forward with my sword and was rewarded by a scream as I hit something soft. I peered over the top and saw that I had skewered a warrior in the eye. As I tore my sword sideways I caught a second warrior on the side of the head. He looked stunned. Had I had strength in my leg I would have pushed against him; he would have fallen. Ketil and Knut were faring better than I was and they had both slain a warrior and were pushing back the ones to their fore.

I was aware that I still had my foot on the book. The priest was crawling away and I was unable to stop him. I heard him as he shouted for help. A warrior must have heard him for I saw a mailed man run towards me with sword drawn. I shouted, "I shall have to turn!"

Ketil said, "Do so we can deal with these!"

I swung my shield around and pivoted on my damaged leg. The blood flowed a little freer but I managed to face the mailed man. I tried to remember all that Siggi had taught me. I was acutely aware that I had not had enough lessons. He did not pause as he ran at me and he brought his sword over high above him. I placed my good leg behind me as I blocked his sword with my own and then punched him in the face with my shield. He was not expecting that and it stunned him. I saw him swing his shield around instinctively to protect his body. His leather armour was inlaid with metal strips but it did not extend below his waist. I swung my sword around in a sweep and hit his thigh. I felt my sword scrape bone and he shouted in rage and pain. We were almost evenly matched now save that I was weakening. I felt light-headed and my boot was filled with sloshing blood.

Sensing victory the Frank pulled back his arm for a sideways sweep. He did not make it as Arne's sword hacked into his neck and he fell dead. Ulf Big Nose was beside me and he put his arm under mine. "You have done well, Hrólfr. Let me take you back to the drekar."

I shook my head, "Beneath my foot is a holy book and yonder crawls away a richly endowed cleric."

Ulf laughed in my ear as he almost picked me up. "Let others gain some glory for the three of you deserve great honour."

As we turned and I limped with Ulf back down the hill I saw that the monastery was on fire. I doubted that we had done it deliberately; there was no gain in that but I remembered the oil and the candles. In a wooden building fire was always a danger. The smoke from the fire was spreading across the hillside. It made it like a fog. I could hear shouts, screams and cries but I saw nothing save shadows. I was desperate to close my eyes and to sleep but I knew that if I did I would awake in Valhalla. I had to stay awake.

Once we had passed the lower huts I saw the river and the drekar. Ulf shouted, "Sven! Hrólfr is hurt." He laid me down on the bank. "Now I will go and get some glory!" He turned and ran back up the hill. I lay back and looked up at the sky.

I must have closed my eyes for the briefest of moments for I felt movement and looked up to see Sven and Cnut, one of the ship's boys as they took me aboard. "Where are you hurt, Hrólfr?"

As they laid me next to my chest I took off my helmet, "My leg. It was a spear thrust."

"Cnut fetch some ale. Hrólfr, lie back and I will stitch this. I am a sailmaker and not a galdramenn but I will do my best. You have a boot full of blood here!"

I heard the sound of the boot being emptied over the side by another of the ship's boys. Cnut raised my head and poured some ale into my mouth. I had forgotten how thirsty I was.

"Cnut take off his mail and put it with his shield and sword. Hrólfr will not be fighting again for some time." Sven was clever. The act of removing my mail made me forget about my leg and so he was able to begin stitching.

My hands grabbed Cnut's shoulders and I squeezed as waves of pain raced up my leg. I saw him wince and I relaxed my grip, "Sorry Cnut."

He smiled and helped me to lie back down, "I have seen the wound. I would have shouted for the Allfather. You bore it well." He reached over to my shield and took the dagger. "Here, bite on this. Rurik One Ear found it comforting when Sven stitched his arm."

I did so and my teeth bit into the wood of the handle. The pain was still excruciating and so I dug the nails of my fingers into my palms. It seemed to help. After what seemed an age Sven finished. "Cnut pour vinegar on the wound. Sorry, Hrólfr this will hurt even more but we must do it."

I nodded, "I know. I need the leg. Whoever heard of a one-legged horseman!"

If the stitching had been bad, then the wound being doused in vinegar was even worse. It burned. Unlike the stitching, the burning continued. I prayed for the oblivion of sleep. None came. I lay there and closed my eyes. I could hear the sounds of men being brought back and, in the distance, the crackle of fire and combat. I had time to reflect on the raid. The monks had been warned by those fleeing from the river. The Jarl should have used scouts as we had further south. He was overconfident and too eager. I realised that the fact that the clan had not returned to the drekar meant that we were still winning and the Jarl thought that we would triumph in the end.

I must have slept, or passed out for a short time. I was awoken by Arne gently moving me so that he could get to his chest. "Did we win?"

He nodded, "Aye but it cost us. Here Siggi. Let us move this hero." The two of them lifted me and placed me before the oars.

I saw that I was next to Rurik One Ear. He was sitting up and grinning. He said, "Best put him on the side with my good ear!"

I saw bodies being brought aboard along with great quantities of treasure. There were sacks of food. Monasteries ate well.

The Jarl was the last one aboard and he shouted, as he stepped over the sheerstrake, "Cast off. We go home! Raven's Wing!"

We all shouted and I banged the deck with my hand. As he came alongside me the Jarl knelt down and said quietly. "I will not forget what you did. You are young but you have heart. The three of you did what the warband should have done! We have all learned a lesson this day."

We began to head downstream and I saw the sun begin to rise in the east. "Siggi, what did the Jarl mean about lessons?"

He and Arne shook their heads, "Some of the new warriors forgot orders and they did not secure the abbey. They saw the chance to slaughter and raid the huts. You and the Eriksson brothers were left isolated. You obeyed orders and it almost cost you your life."

Arne Four Toes added, "At least you have a good byrnie from it."

I shook my head, "That is yours Arne Four Toes. I would be dead had you not slain him. The mail is yours."

"But it is good mail!"

"I know and there will be others. Besides I have a mind to have mail made for me!"

They both laughed. "You have ambition, Hrólfr the Horseman. Most warriors your age would be grateful for whatever they could get."

"I am patient, Siggi. I can wait."

We reached the sea without incident but the Jarl was keen to get back to our island. Each moment spent on the river meant danger for us. I dozed. When I awoke, the sun was setting and the crew were moving. "We are home. Come, Arne, let us rid ourselves of this warrior who has snored all the way from Neustria!"

"I can walk!" I tried to stand and I fell.

Sven shouted, "You burst those stitches and it is the brand for you!"

Siggi shook his head, "You have the head of a pig! Do as you are told!"

They lifted me to the side where they lowered me to Knut and Ketil who stood in the shallows. They grinned at me. As they carried me ashore Ketil said, "You bring us good fortune, Hrólfr. We both won mail shirts from the dead we slew. They are not as good as the warrior you felled but they are better than what we wear! That was a good raid!"

I glanced over and saw the bodies being carried up the path to the graveyard. They would not think so. The two brothers made a chair from their arms and managed to get me to the hall without falling.

"We will bring your chest and your shield. You will be hall bound for a while."

Chapter 8

I hated the inactivity which ensued. Rurik One Ear had only been wounded in the arm and could move around. He could even help the rest of the crew as the bounty from the raid was brought to the hall. I was not allowed to see Dream Strider. I had to lie in the hall and watch the activity around me. Erik One Hand found it quite amusing, "Now you see my frustration! I have to watch while others do what I would. At least your leg will heal and you will walk again. I can never grow another hand!"

I was duly and rightly chastised. He was right. I had much to be grateful for. That evening after we had eaten I had to endure the aftermath of the raid. The Jarl and Siggi singled out many of the newer members of the crew. Thanks to their reckless action we now had but seven of the original crew of the *'Raven's Wing'* left alive and I was injured. The ones who had disobeyed orders squirmed and their fellows, like Rurik, who had done his duty gave them glowering looks. When the bounty was shared that was reflected in the distribution. After the Jarl's share, those who had obeyed orders like myself and the Eriksson brothers received far more than the others. To be fair to them they did not complain.

It took a week to prepare for the voyage to Dyflin. The Jarl and the more senior members of the crew had decided to make the shortest possible journey. Rurik and I would stay with Erik One Hand. Neither of us was happy. The opportunity to go to a busy market like Dyflin with gold to spend was tempting but we both knew that we would be of no use during the voyage and we accepted our fate.

By the time, they came to leave I was using a crutch but, thanks to Dream Strider, I was able to ride around the island. I rode down to the beach to see them off. It was only as she set off and I saw her in the distance that I realised what a small drekar she was. *'Heart of the Dragon'* dwarfed her. I waited until she was a dot on the horizon before I rode back to the hall. It was getting on and off Dream Strider which was hard and so I stayed on his back. I spent that first day exploring, fully, the island. It was not a large island but it had variety. The northern shore had mainly cliffs and just the one bay where the fishermen who had lived here had kept their boats. I shunned the house for I was sure the spirits of the dead Franks haunted it. Even though I had had nothing to do with their deaths I was a Viking and I rode quickly when I neared the house. The south of the island had many shingle beaches and bays. We had, luckily, chosen the best one but there were now more places where we could gather shellfish.

It was strange to be with so few people. This was the first time in my life that I had not been in the middle of a crowd. Both Rurik and Erik were quiet men. As they were both one-handed; at least for the time being, I had to do some things for them. When Erik began to practise with a sword left-handed I joined him.

"Are you able to use it one-handed?"

"A little. I practise when there is no one on the island. You have found me out."

"I think it is good. Have you thought of using a shield on the stump of your right arm?"

He nodded, "It was too heavy."

I had a sudden thought, "Rurik, the bounty we brought from Portucale; where is it?"

"On the top floor of the store."

"See if you can find one of those small shields we captured from the Moors."

Happy to have something to do he wandered off.

"But I can barely use a sword; what use will a shield be?"

"At first it will keep you alive and later you will learn to use a sword left-handed." Rurik brought one back. "Here I will fasten it to your arm." It had two leather rings through which we put his stump. He seemed a little self-conscious at first. "It will not stay on if you lower your arm but that is a good thing. Keep it up."

Rurik suddenly laughed. I gave him an angry look for he was mocking Erik. He realised what I thought and shook his head, "I was just thinking that if Erik ever gets to fight an enemy he will confuse him. He will have to strike sword to sword." He patted Erik's left arm. "Strike quickly and you will confuse your enemy."

Now that we had something to do I was able to sit on a log and practise with Erik. I was happy for it gave me something to do and Erik soon became more confident. Rurik could not wait for his own arm to heal so that he could help too. We developed a routine in those first few days. We tended the animals first. I rode a circuit of the island while the two one-armed men made the dough for the bread and lit the ovens. Then we would all go down to the sea. Beorn had said that seawater would help the healing process. While Erik watched us Rurik and I would strip off and bathe. I soon found that Dream Strider liked the sea and it made it easier for me to get into the water. While I found it hard to walk it was easy to swim and each day my leg became stronger. In the afternoon, we would empty the fish traps and ascend to the hall where we would bake the bread and prepare the fish for our meal. Then we would practise with the swords.

On the third day, I decided that, as I couldn't walk, I would practise combat skills on horseback. While Rurik and Erik sparred, both left-handed, I took a few javelins and, setting up a piece of hewn wood as a target, rode Dream Strider and threw the javelins into it. My first attempt almost unhorsed me and I learned to keep my weight forward and to use less force. I managed to hit the wood five times out of eight which pleased me.

Rurik and Erik watched me for a while as they rested between bouts. Rurik wandered over when I stopped. "Have you not thought of using stiraps? They would keep you on the back of the horse."

"Stirap?"

"Aye, you must have seen them in Neustria. The nobles there use them. They are metal rings into which you put your feet. They are attached to the horse so that you do not fall off." He suddenly grinned. "We can make some tomorrow. The swordplay has made me think that my arm is healing and I have been keen to try my hand at ironwork!"

We were all keen and excited for it was something we had never done before. I was happy to sit and pump the forge so that it became incredibly hot. As Rurik worked the metal Erik and I shouted out suggestions. Rurik was happy to comply for it was all new to him. We suggested he make the bottom flat so that my boot would fit better. Because he was making it for me we used my boot as a template. By the end of the day, we had two stiraps and we spent the time after our meal working out how to attach them. This was where my expertise came in. I had seen saddles in Neustria and they all involved wood which was covered in leather. The wood helped keep the rider on the animal's back.

It took me two days but I eventually made a saddle that fitted Dream Strider perfectly. I was not certain if he had worn one before but, at the end of our first seven days alone on the island, we were ready to try the saddle and the stirap on Dream Strider. My leg had improved so that I no longer needed the crutch. We used a piece of blanket cut from an old one and then I laid the saddle on his back. At first, he was skittish and I sang to him. I had learned he liked soothing singing. He let me tighten the strap under his middle. As an added precaution, we had fitted a second belt that went around his chest. Then we were ready. As Rurik held his head I wondered how he would react. I used a rock to climb upon his back. The saddle meant I could not vault on as I usually did.

The moment I sat on his back he took off; he managed to tear the reins out of Rurik's hands and gallop off. I barely had time to grab mane. There was no way I could put my feet in the stirap and I just clung on with my knees. The pain from my wounded leg was intense. Had I relaxed my grip I might well have fallen from his back and that might have undone all the good work Sven had done on my injured leg. I sang and spoke to Dream Strider as quietly and calmly as I could. At first, I thought it was not working but he gradually slowed down. Eventually, I was able to lean forward and grab the reins. Once I had his reins in my hand I could turn his head. We were approaching the cliffs to the south and I did not relish the thought of plunging off the island to the rocks below. When I turned him, I pulled back until he slowed down. He was lathered. It was a sure sign he was upset. I stroked his head and then risked slipping my feet into the stiraps. Surprisingly it did not seem to bother him. It was the saddle on his back he did not like. I rode back to the others. It was a small victory. He gradually became used to the saddle.

Over the next few days, I learned that throwing the javelins with my feet secured gave me more accuracy. Then we tried a charge with the spear. Rurik and Erik stood bravely and trustingly as I charged at them. I was not thrown from the saddle. Over the coming months, I would learn how to perfect this technique as well as how to vary the length of the stirap. The days passed pleasantly enough. The three of us enjoyed each other's company and we were all learning new skills. Once Rurik's arm healed he was able to spar more aggressively with Erik who had gained confidence. My leg improved each day. The seawater and, surprisingly, the stirap helped.

We attempted to brew some beer. We were not alewives but we had all seen it made. Our first attempt had been little better than slurried water. By the third it was drinkable. We would have ale for the crew when they landed. We had no doubt that they would have bought ale in Dyflin but they would all appreciate the gesture.

We expected the drekar back within twenty days. After seventeen days, we spent more time fishing and hunting. The ironworking was forgotten. I still rode and I still swam but the priority was having food ready for the winter and for the returning crew. We also wandered the island looking for and collecting berries, nuts and wild fruits. Nothing was wasted. It was when I was close to the old deserted farm that our idyll ended. As I rested and allowed Dream Strider to drink from the old rain-filled trough by the haunted building I spied a boat. It was heading from the east. It looked to be a large fishing boat. I did not think it boded well. I did not remount immediately for I would have time aplenty to warn the others. I stared out to sea. I saw that there were six men aboard and, although they were rowing I saw helmets and weapons. They were Franks or Bretons and this was not a peaceful visit.

I led Dream Strider away from the skyline and mounted him. I galloped back to the other two. They were also on their way back. "Franks or Bretons! Six of them!"

Rurik nodded, "They may be friends of those that Hermund the Bent slew. They will find us here and blame us."

The frightened slave within Erik One Hand emerged. He said, "We could take our own fishing boat and head out to sea?"

I shook my head, "And where would we go? Sail to the land of the Angles? No, Erik, we were charged with defending our home and we will do so. There are but three of us and yet I would stop them."

Rurik nodded, "I agree, but how?"

I pointed to the food store. "We use that. We can take up the ladder. You two can stay at the top and use bows and javelins against them."

"And you?"

I patted my horse, "I have Dream Strider. I have javelins, a spear and my sword. I can move faster than they can and while they may expect Vikings they will not expect a Viking who is mounted. I can lead them a chase around the island and tire them out. If I can hurt a couple, then the odds will be evened out."

Erik held up his stump, "Even with a one-armed man?"

I laughed, "Aye Erik, a one-armed man, a man with one ear and a rider who cannot stand on his right leg! We are Viking! We are Raven Wing Clan!"

"It is worth taking the chance." He reached up and clasped my arm, "In case things do not work out well I will see you in Valhalla. It has been a privilege to serve with you."

"And you too, Rurik One Ear! But do not consign us to our graves too soon. So long as we live then there is hope."

I rode to the hall and picked up my shield, helmet, javelins and spear. I had a great deal to carry. I put my shield around my back and held my two javelins and my spear in my right hand. I waved to my comrades and galloped back to the wood which lay between the hall and the home of the dead fishermen.

My time with Ulf Big Nose had been well spent. I had learned to hide in plain sight. I found a place where I was hidden by a large oak. A long branch came from the oak and stuck over the trail. So long as I remained still then they would not see me. I was ten paces from the trail. I had practised with the javelins and knew that I could throw accurately twice as far as this.

I heard them long before they reached me. From their words, I knew that they sought our hall but they did not expect to find any of us. "I do not think that Vikings will leave treasure buried in the ground! They wear it upon them!"

"Fool! The Leudes said that he knew they had left the island and they would not take their gold on a dragon ship. It will be buried beneath the floor of their hall. We will dig it up and be rich men."

"What of the Leudes' share?"

"We will give him enough to satisfy him. These Vikings are rich! The Leudes said that their leader wore mail!"

The sound of their voices gave me an approximation of their position. I knew exactly when they would appear before me. I waited until two men had stepped into view and then I hurled first one and then a second javelin. My first hit one in the neck and he fell, spurting dark blood. The second struck the man in the calf but it came through the other side. Before they could react, I galloped at them. They had no idea I was alone. Their shields were on their backs and, as they struggled to pull them around, I galloped, brazenly through the middle of them. I was on a horse and I had a half-face helmet. I frightened them. As they cowered I jabbed my spear at them and was rewarded with flesh. One of them fell screaming from a wound in his leg. I galloped to the south.

Although only one man was dead two were hurt. I doubted that they were fatal wounds but they were injuries, nonetheless. I did not ride hard; I wanted them to follow. I saw that one remained with the two injured men and the other two followed me. They could now see that I was alone. I glanced over my shoulder. I knew the island well and I guessed that they did not. They ran and began to close with me. I allowed them to get within thirty paces and then I wheeled to the right and led them west. The ground sloped down to our bay and they were encouraged by the fact that the slope was in their favour. As Dream Strider increased speed so they lengthened their stride to try to catch me. It was a mistake. One of them tumbled over and was unable to stop himself. He fell awkwardly.

I wheeled Dream Strider around and holding my spear before I galloped towards the last warrior standing. He tried to stop himself but the slope prevented him. I thrust my spear at him as he cowered beneath his shield. Had he worn mail I would not have been able to hurt him but as it was I stabbed down and my spear pierced his right shoulder. As I turned to finish him off I heard a shout and saw the other three coming towards me. The wounds I had inflicted were not enough to incapacitate them. I turned Dream Strider and headed back to the hall. A plan was forming in my mind.

I rode directly there. I knew that they would be able to follow my tracks but that did not matter. I would still reach there first. As I galloped towards the hall Rurik appeared from the door of the store. I reined in beneath him. "There are six of them. One is dead and four are wounded but they still come. I am leading them here. I will draw their attention to me. Use your bow when their backs are turned. If you can slay one, then we may have a chance."

"Be careful Hrólfr! This is too good a tale to end with your death!"

"I have no intention of dying for men who just come to steal our treasure. Hide yourselves. They will not be far behind me."

I rode to the hall and waited. I stroked Dream Strider's mane. I would give him some of the winter fruits as a treat after his exertions this day. They came. Three walked ahead while two limped behind. The one who was unwounded led with the man I had speared next to him. The one who had fallen was the third and his head bled yet. When they saw I was alone and not moving they gathered into a line of five. They would have to have their backs to the storehouse if they were to face me. I could still escape left or right. They spread into a half circle and advanced. They thought to trap me in a net.

Rurik's first arrow was accurate and it struck the man with the head wound in the back. He pitched forward. They looked at each other in surprise. Before they could react a second arrow hit the man whom I had speared. He too fell. They gathered together and made a wall with their shields. They looked at the two men. They were obviously dead. They looked from me to Rurik. Now that there were just three of them they did not fancy the odds. They turned and ran.

Rurik yelled, "Wait for us!"

I did for I knew that I could catch them as I was mounted. I waited until my companions descended from the store. Rurik rubbed his shoulder. "I am glad that we did not need a third arrow. I fear my arm would not have been able to pull back the bow."

"Come, we can catch them. They are tired and all but one are wounded."

The two of them ran alongside Dream Strider as we galloped towards the north coast. It did not take long to begin to catch up with them. One of them was lagging behind. The unwounded man was stretching his legs. It was not a clan we followed it was a band of bandits who thought to make coin while our ship was away. As I rode alongside the last man I smacked him on the head with the flat of my sword. He fell in a heap. I saw the haunted farm ahead and knew that they would think they had escaped us. That would not happen. I kicked hard and Dream Strider opened his legs. We began to catch the last wounded man. I rode beyond him. Rurik and Erik would catch him. I wanted to catch this man who deserted his comrades. He had fled three men with wounds and he had yet to test himself. He was not a warrior.

He ran towards the sea and their boat which was drawn up on the sand. Had he turned and faced me he might have lived. Had he been a warrior he might have decided that one on one he might win. He did neither and he kept running towards the boat. I rode behind him and swung my sword. I hacked deeply into his neck. I struck hard and his head was almost severed from his body. As he fell and his head hit the water it separated and floated, briefly. The dead eyes stared at me and then it sank beneath the waves. I allowed the tide to take out his body and then I returned to the two survivors.

When I reached Erik and Rurik, Rurik shook his head, "One was dead when we reached him. This one has not long to live. I cannot understand his words."

I stared down at him. His eyes were closed but I saw that he was breathing still. "Who are you?"

He looked up at me with wild eyes, "You are not supposed to be alive! How can a man fight a ghost?"

"What do you mean?"

"I know you! You were a slave and you should be dead yet you ride a horse like a Leudes."

"Speak clearer! I do not understand you! How do you know me?"

"You are a ghost!" His eyes closed and he died.

Rurik, who had not understood a word, said, "What was that about?"

"I know not but he called me a ghost. I have never seen this man before. I do not understand it."

Erik said, "I saw his eyes, Hrólfr. He was terrified of you."

We gathered the bodies. We removed the few valuables from them and burned their remains. Rurik and Erik sailed their boat around to our cove. It would not do to leave a reminder for their friends. If I was a ghost, then better they thought that and stayed away from our island.

We were more watchful from then on. I rode all around the island first thing in the morning and last thing at night. I took to sleeping in the store. If an intruder came at night, then Dream Strider would wake me. The times alone were important to me. Who had the man thought I was? I had never seen him before. My home was far from the land of the Bretons. I now regretted burning his body. I could have looked for signs of his clan and his origins. Perhaps he had travelled here from my former home. Yet even that would not explain anything. I was a slave. What difference would it make if I were dead or alive?

The three of us were all glad when we saw the drekar as it appeared on the horizon. When we saw a second we wondered if this was our Jarl. I recognised **'Raven's Wing'** and breathed a sigh of relief. I counted the oars and saw our drekar had each one manned. The Jarl had found a replacement crew. The second drekar looked to be much smaller. I took her to be a threttanessa. She was lithe enough and she rode high in the water. She was not heavily laden as was **'Raven's Wing'**.

I did not saddle Dream Strider but attached the cart to him and led him down to the beach where we awaited the arrival of our comrades. One of the jobs we had completed was to drive a huge timber into the top end of the beach. We had packed it with rocks and, as the ship's boy jumped ashore with the rope, we tied the drekar to the mooring timber. Had we known there was a second we could have made a second mooring post.

The Jarl jumped off and waded through the water. He looked relieved to see us. "Thank the Allfather you are safe."

Rurik looked at me and then the Jarl, "Are you a galdramenn, Jarl? How did you know we had trouble?"

"Come we will walk to my hall and I will tell you. The others can empty the drekar." We turned and headed up the slope. I handed Dream Strider's halter to the ship's boy. The Jarl asked, "What was this trouble, Rurik?"

He told him of the events of the last week. When he had finished, I said, "One of those who died said he thought that I was a ghost and that I should be dead."

We had reached the hall. Rurik poured the Jarl some ale and he began his story. "Hermund the Bent has caused us great harm. When he landed with the fishing boat he told the Franks that it was you who had slain the fisherman and his family. He said that he had killed you and that was why he had to flee. He named you 'Hrólfr the Horseman'. He said you had the mark of the slave on you. There is now a price on our heads. The Count of Neustria has ordered any who capture us to take us to Tours for judgement."

Rurik said, "But it was Hermund who killed them!"

I shrugged, "He is a liar and without honour."

"I am sorry, Hrólfr. I should have seen Hermund's, black heart. And there is more. The Count of Austrasia had also put a price on our heads for the burning of his abbey at Jumièges. We are wanted, men. King Egbert of Wessex has declared all Vikings to be enemies of God and the south coast of his land is being lined with burghs." He quaffed the ale, "This is not bad. So, it seems we must make our little island a fortress."

The door of the hall opened and Siggi strolled in, "I might have known you would be taking it easy!" He picked me up and hugged me, "How is the leg?"

"The seawater and the swimming helped."

The Jarl said, "And they were raided by men from the mainland. Hrólfr is a ghost, apparently!"

Siggi seemed to approve. "You killed them?"

Rurik said, "Aye. That is their boat in the cove."

"Good, your brother comes!"

I looked at the Jarl, "Your brother lord?"

"Aye, my younger brother became bored at home and he pestered his father to give him a drekar. Poor Gunnstein does not realise that he will have to pay his father back for his boat. It took me a year of serving with the Dragonheart to pay off *'Raven's Wing'*."

Siggi poured himself some ale and after tasting it, smiled, "Aye well *'Sea Serpent'* is little more than a knarr. It should not take him long."

"You forget, Siggi, that there is a price on our heads. Wherever we sail men will hunt us."

Siggi laughed, "We are Vikings! We do not expect to be greeted with smiles and maids who fall on their backs and spread their legs for us. We expect them to run from us and to be terrified. We have the winter to make weapons and to plan our raids. Hrólfr was right to suggest we winter here. We can raid as soon as the weather improves. Why we can raid when the weather is bad." He pointed to the land. "If three men can defend this island then two boat crews of Vikings should fear nothing! We make Olafstad impregnable!"

Winter Interlude

Gunnstein Thorfinnson looked like his brother. He was barely twenty and yet he had scars on his arms. He had been on raids. He had a mail byrnie and a fine helmet. I liked him as soon as I met him. Although his crew only numbered twenty-seven with the new crew brought from Dyflin and the smith and his family we had to build a second warrior hall as well as a hut for the smith. Our little clan was growing.

Rurik, Erik, the Eriksson brothers and I were given the task of building the hut. It had to be close to the smith. Our new smith, Bagsecg Bjornson, was one of Bjorn Bagsecg's children. I had seen him in Cyninges-tūn. He was now married with two children; one a babe in arms. If his wife, Anya, was intimidated at the prospect of being on an island with almost eighty men she did not show it.

The six of us working together soon made a hut which abutted against the smithy. Bagsecg said, "It is a trick of my father's. In the winter, you get the heat from the smith to keep the home warm and in the summer the smoke keeps away the insects."

Anya said, "It is a shame it does not also wash the clothes to get rid of the charcoal and iron too!"

"I am a smith. What else would you expect?" Poor Bagsecg might be a mighty smith but his sharp-tongued wife still ruled the roost.

She had no answer to that and so she rounded on us, "And I wish my feet to be dry!"

Erik One Hand could not rid himself of subservience. He had been a slave for many years. "The sand, the stones and the wood are effective. It is what we have in the hall but we can dig a better ditch around the outside if you wish."

His voice sounded so pleading that she relented and smiled, "No, Erik One Hand. This will be good." She looked at us as we began to take away the wood we had not needed. "The Jarl will need to find some women for you. It is not healthy to have so many men living together!"

Ketil said, "We wanted to bring some back this time but the drekar could carry no more. After the winter, perhaps."

Bagsecg patted his anvil, "And I have the winter to make mail, weapons...."

"And gold," piped in Anya.

"Aye and gold." He looked at me. "It is why I came from Cyningestūn to Dyflin. I was the youngest smith in the land of the wolf. I had the leavings of my father and brothers. We did not like Dyflin."

Anya shook her head, "Jarl Gunnstein is a good man but the men who came there were barbarians! They stink and they have no manners."

"Aye, here we are safe and I can ply my trade."

I grinned at Bagsecg, "And I would be your first customer! I would have a mail byrnie!"

They all looked at me in surprise. Ketil said, "You are younger than us all! Where would you get the coin for a mail byrnie?"

I found myself reddening. Had I not proved that I was a warrior? "Wait here and I will bring gold!" The Eriksson brothers laughed as I left. I went to my chest and took out the gold necklace I had taken from the Moor. I also took two gold coins. When I returned, I dropped the gold necklace onto the anvil. "Would that pay for a byrnie of mail?"

Ketil picked it up and bit it. "This is gold! Where..."

I snatched it back from him and gave it to the smith, "We raided before you joined us, Ketil Eriksson. I am one of the original crew remember. I am Raven Wing clan!"

Ketil looked contrite, "I am sorry, Hrólfr. I forget that you are a warrior. You need a thicker beard!"

I shook my head and handed the gold to Bagsecg. "Well?"

He nodded, "Aye!"

Anya shook her head as she took it from him, "And how will I spend this? We are on an island?"

"Never mind woman, go and see to the bairns. Take your gold with you!" When she had gone, he said, "This would buy a full byrnie."

"I have something different in mind, Bagsecg. I wish one which is split at the front from the waist to the knees."

He nodded, "That would make movement easier but you would not be as well protected."

"I wish it so that I can ride a horse with it. It needs to be the finest of mail links. I need it to be light."

"That is more work and..."

I handed him another coin, "And this will be payment which your wife does not see."

Ketil chuckled, "I can see I will have to play bones with you, Hrólfr. I could become rich!"

"I gamble with my life, not with bones!"

As the nights lengthened and the storms increased our life on the island settled into a comfortable routine. With the halls built we had somewhere sheltered to work when the weather made life hard. Men used animal bones to make combs, needles and other intricate work. I groomed Dream Strider. When the weather allowed, we fished, set traps, made ale and collected wood for arrows and spear shafts. With our own smith, we now had a plentiful supply. Anya proved to be a skilful fletcher and she earned coins by collecting the goose feathers and making arrows. Anya liked gold!

And of course, we kept a good watch. Every seven days a different four men would spend the week in what we termed the haunted house; the old fisher folk's hut. No one enjoyed their duty but we needed a watch to be kept on the mainland. The worse times were when there was a fog. We dreaded them sneaking over under the cover of a sea fret. The Norns did not send any enemies to us or perhaps the Allfather gave us special attention. As Yule approached Siggi, the Jarl and Gunnstein Thorfinnson took to planning raids for the spring. As I had some knowledge of Neustria I was often included. I took it as an honour for I was still young. Siggi White Hair told me, one night, it was because I had an old head for one so young. "Perhaps being a slave has done that for you."

I shook my head, "I visited the witch and went into the bowels of the earth. When you emerge, it is as though you are reborn and you realise that you must value each day. We are given a short time on this earth. If you are to make a difference you take life seriously."

Siggi was older than the two brothers and despite the fact that he was not Jarl he took the lead in all the discussions. "We need slaves and we need women. Forget gold. We have had four fights in the last ten days. Someone will get hurt unless the men can release their seed."

"Hibernia then?"

"Aye or the land of the Cymri. I would have said Wessex but it is too risky now. We need to raid wisely."

I ventured, "What about the land of Corn Walum? King Egbert has fought there but it is not yet his, at least I do not think it is."

Gunnstein said, "I think you might be right. The men of Wessex slew many of the warriors there. It is a poor country but they have women."

Siggi clapped his hands together, "And tin!"

We all looked at Jarl Gunnar. We had discussed it but it was his decision. He nodded, "It is not far to travel and we can be there in two days."

"It will have to be fine weather for *'Sea Serpent'*." Gunnstein ventured his opinion. It was a mistake.

"If it is not then you can stay and guard the island." The younger Thorfinnson looked aggrieved. "We will have to have some warriors guarding the island when we leave to raid."

Gunnstein nodded, "Aye you are right." He looked up. "What about the land of the Bretons? That is close and we can be there and back before anyone knows."

"So far they have left us in peace. They are our nearest neighbours. There will come a time when we may have to fight them but not yet. They are no friends of the Empire. If they do not bother us, then I will leave them alone. We may raid Neustria for it seems they are set on our destruction and I fear they may try to end our threat when summer comes."

"Then you have your plan, Jarl. We get slaves and then we raid Neustria. As I recall there is a port just at the mouth of the Liger, Nantes. The Bretons attack it all the time. It would be an easier target than Tours which has a Roman wall." Siggi White Hair made the final decision but he made it sound as though the Jarl had made it. He was wise.

And thus, we decided what we would do when the year turned. The winter passed quickly. Unlike Ljoðhús there was no snow. There were no wolves and our animals began to give birth. It was as though we had found a piece of Valhalla here on earth. Only the lack of women cast a shadow over our world and when the wind began to blow from the south the Jarl decided that we would raid. Our clan went to war once more.

Chapter 9

My mail was not finished and so we set sail with me wearing my old leather armour. I had sewn in some strips of thin metal which we had made from the poorer quality iron. I sewed them on my shoulders and my arms. My mail vest also gave me some protection. Poor Erik had been desperate to come but the Jarl pointed out that he could not row but now that he could fight left-handed he could help his brother who had been forced to remain and guard the island. Erik just wanted to feel needed and he was happy with the judgement.

It was not a pleasant two-day voyage we endured. We took advantage of a wind from the south which meant it was slightly warmer but, more importantly, it took us to Corn Walum that bit quicker. Some of the new crewmen had raided the coast and told us of a fjord which was deep enough for a drekar and had many villages along its banks. Our plan was simple. We would sail as far up as we could get and find a village to raid. Then we would sail down the fjord, back to the sea using the current to aid us. If we found more villages then we would raid them. We sought no treasure and we sought no weapons. It was women and slaves we needed.

We saw the coast before dusk. Karl the Red was the one who had raided there before and he stood at the prow. He used hand signals to direct us. We sat at our oars. Fully crewed we were very fast when we needed to be. Once we entered the river we would row hard for we would take down our sail. We wished to be invisible. It was just after dark when we passed the river mouth and we began to row. We did so silently. We heard a bell tolling from our steering board side as we headed up the vast patch of open water. Karl the Red had told us that it was seawater until we reached the river the locals called the Fal. He said there was another smaller fjord close to the village with the church. I knew that the Jarl had noted the bell. We were here for slaves but a church would have treasure and that was always useful. The book of the White Christ which had nearly cost me my life had brought twenty gold pieces in Dyflin. I had no doubt that it would fetch much more when it was sold in Lundenwic. That rich port was barred to us.

Where the river began, there was a village on the headland. It was on the north bank and there was a creek next to it. We turned and headed for it. The smell of smoke drifted down the hillside towards us, it was a good sign. Ulf Big Nose leapt ashore and began to head up the slope. We tumbled out into the water. Five of the new men would remain with the drekar. We had that luxury now. Once again, I was one of the first to follow Ulf. I knew how to move in the dark and keep my senses alert. Ketil and Knut were close behind me and, since our fight with the bandits, Rurik One Ear had been a constant at my side. He had learned to run with his good ear next to me.

I almost ran into Ulf Big Nose. His hand came out to stop me and he pointed. I could see that there was no wooden wall. The huts were unprotected. As my eyes adjusted to the dark I saw that animals were moving in the pens where they had been placed. A solitary man stood on guard. Ulf pointed to Ketil and Knut and then the man. He drew his hand across his throat. They nodded and, with swords drawn, headed off. Ulf wasted no time and he led Rurik and me forward. Our task was to get to the far side of the village as quickly as we could.

We were halfway through when the dog barked. A man came out of the hut next to me. He had a sword drawn and he swung it at me. It was a blind reactive strike. I was fortunate in having quick reactions. My blade came up and knocked his poor blade away. I swung my shield so that the edge of it smacked him in the mouth. He tumbled to the ground. A woman screamed within. Rurik and I stepped over the man's unconscious form. I saw, in the corner, a woman and her two children. They were cowering. I knew enough of their language to tell them to move. She shook her head. Rurik just grabbed the woman and hauled her out. The two children clung to her hands. It was an effective way to move them.

As we emerged into the village I said, "I will help Ulf!"

I ran towards the sounds of fighting ahead of me. Four men with farm implements were trying to attack Ulf. The fact that there were four of them made it harder for him to fend them off. They may have only had scythes, billhooks and wood axes but they could all inflict serious wounds. Even as I approached he managed to knock one to the ground with his shield but an axe caught him a blow to the side of his head. As he stumbled the villager with the bill shouted in triumph as he pulled back his billhook to slay our scout. I plunged my sword into his back as I hit the man with the axe on the back of the head. The scythe swung viciously towards me and I barely had time to get out of the way. A stunned Ulf managed to hack his sword down the man's back.

The two whom we had both struck and stunned crawled and rolled into the dark. "Thank you, Hrólfr. Give me a warrior any time. You know what a warrior will do. These farmers do not know how to fight! Let us wait here. There are no more huts beyond us. I need a moment to clear my head."

I gestured to the dead men. "There are at least four dead men in the village. They fought well for their women."

He gave me a shrewd look, "And you think we are wrong."

"It does not seem right."

"It is the Allfather's way. A man should protect his family, his clan and his land. He should also protect himself." He pushed one of the bodies with his boot. "These were brave but they wear no armour and they do not have swords. We will take their women and we will look after them. We will even protect their children and those who are born of these women to us will be Vikings. They will be stronger. You cannot change the world, Hrólfr. There are wolves and there are sheep. We are the wolves."

Ketil ran up to us. I saw that his face was spattered with blood. From his grin, I suspected that it was not his own. "The Jarl says we are done. The men are dead or fled and the women and animals are being herded towards the drekar. He wants to raid the church too."

As we wandered through the body-strewn village I asked Ulf. "Is it wise to raid the church? We have what we came for."

"He is the jarl and we swore an oath. If it is the wrong decision, we will chastise him in the Otherworld."

I was not certain I was happy about that. I had much to do in my life. However, the jarl's decisions whilst sometimes flawed had not yet resulted in disaster. I had to hope that we still amused the Weird Sisters. In the end, we had no problems. We emptied the wooden church and took the few precious objects it contained.

The drekar was not as crowded as I had thought it would be. We had twelve women and eight children. Arne Four Toes told me, as we sailed down the fjord, that some children had run off. Twelve women would do. I noticed that all were young. Some were barely older than I was. The animals were penned with them. There was a ram and two ewes, a goat and a handful of chickens and geese. I knew that the animals would make a noise and awaken the second church. I wondered if that would deter the Jarl from attacking.

When we pulled in to the shore I knew that we would be attacking. "Siggi, take the front four oars. You are the best of my men. Climb the hill and surprise the church. We will anchor below in the small bay and I will bring twelve more to help you." He pointed to the geese which were honking. "They would wake the dead."

Siggi snorted, "Not if their necks are wrung!"

"They will give us food and that we need!"

"Come on you wastrels! Let us be about our business." Siggi wasted no time in getting us ashore.

We slipped over the side and by the time we had reached the land the drekar was slipping down the fjord. As we looked up we could see the outline of the church or the cross atop the wooden tower at least. We drew our swords and made our way up. The sun would soon be up and I guessed that some of those who lived by the church would be up already. Although too early for planting men would work the soil at this time of year. We moved silently. The Jarl had been right, we were the best eight men on the drekar. Seven were from the original crew and Rurik One Ear had more than proved himself a good warrior who could be relied upon. As we paused to get our bearings I heard the sound of the geese in the distance. Would it disturb those on the land? We could do nothing about it.

As we moved on, following Ulf, Siggi and Arne, I heard a dog bark. We stopped and waited for the shout of alarm. There was none. We moved on again and I smelled smoke and I smelled animals. There was a pen of some description ahead. We moved beyond the animals towards the church. Siggi waved to Ulf Squint Eye and Harald Fast Sailing. They would take care of the animals. I saw a chink of light at the door of the wooden church. There was someone in the church. Siggi strode straight towards it. His boot kicked it open and he stepped in. There was a scream as someone's life was ended. All need for secrecy was gone. I followed Arne and Ulf Big Nose who ran beyond the church to the houses.

Once again it was villagers who raced out to meet us. They were half asleep and half-dressed. They had grabbed whatever weapons they had. The difference this time was that when they saw us they turned and grabbed their families to flee. We were the Northmen; we were the wolves of the sea and their lives were more valuable than what they had in their huts.

"Search the huts in case they have left anything."

I took the nearest hut. It appeared to be empty and then I glanced in the corner and saw something move. I approached. It was a pair of pups. I put my hand down and clicked, as I did with Dream Strider. One growled and then ran off between my legs. The other stood its ground. It bared its teeth. I liked that. It was not afraid of me. My hand flicked out and grabbed it by the scruff of the neck. "Come you shall have a home on our island! We need a dog!" As I stuffed it inside my tunic it nipped me. I laughed, "Good! You have spirit."

Once I left the hut I saw Siggi and the others. They had books, linens, candles, candlesticks and metal plates. The others drove the animals. We followed the track down to the sea. To our left the first rays of the new day were visible. We had barely gone ten steps when we met the Jarl and the rest of the men.

"No slaves, lord, but holy books and animals."

"Good. Let us go home!"

By the time we had safely placed the animals on the drekar dawn had truly broken and we could see the huge water before us. I could see that Karl the Red had given us good advice. On the opposite side of the water lay a burgh. We would have faced serious opposition there. We took off our helmets and swords and settled down to row. We had gone barely a mile when the puppy stuck his head out from my tunic and yapped.

Siggi White Hair almost jumped off his chest in surprise, "What in the name of the Allfather...?"

"I have a dog. I thought we needed one on the island. It can warn us of enemies."

Siggi laughed, "Not yet a dog! It is barely whelped. What is his name?"

"I have only just got him. How can I have a name for him? I do not yet know what he is like."

Siggi put his hand out to stroke him and was rewarded with a nip from the puppy's razor-sharp teeth. Siggi laughed, "He nips well enough!"

"Then I have his name. Nipper!" When the puppy gave a high-pitched bark we all laughed. It was *wyrd*.

The women keened and moaned all the way home. Two tried to throw themselves over the side with their children but Knut and Ketil stopped them. We had to use half the men to watch rather than row. It made our journey home longer than it should have. Siggi was not happy and neither was Sven. After the second woman tried to throw herself over Siggi roared, ranted and raved at them. They pushed themselves as far towards the raven prow as they could go. After that one look from Siggi made them quail.

The *'Sea Serpent'* still patrolled the southern harbour and we knew our home was safe. Unloading was not the easiest of tasks. As soon as they were landed the women and children tried to flee. It was an island! They were soon caught. Siggi had had more than enough. He had a halter placed around each of the women's necks and they were led up to the hall. While we had been away Gunnstein Thorfinnson and his men had built a slave hall. It was similar to our hall but smaller and with but one door. The bar was on the outside. Until they learned to be compliant they would be locked away each night. I used some of the rope to make a halter for Nipper. I did not mind him running off but I doubted that he would be able to fend for himself yet. I would feed him awhile and after a few days let him off the rope so that he could wander the island.

Erik had brought Dream Strider down to the beach. He nuzzled my face when I approached him. Nipper barked and Dream Strider looked down on the golden-brown creature. "I hope you two get along!"

It was dusk by the time we had taken everything to the hall. Food was ready and we ate first. When we had eaten, we gave food to the slaves. Language was a problem as they spoke their own dialect which was more like Breton than Saxon. For that reason, I was called upon again. Using a mixture of Saxon and Frank I told them that this would be their new home and that some would be chosen to be the women of warriors while the others and the children would be fed in return for labour. They wailed once more until Siggi growled.

Anya appeared and shook her head, "Siggi White Hair you might be a fine warrior but you have not got the sense of a chicken without a head! These are not warriors. They are women taken from their homes and they are terrified. Hrólfr, speak to them gently and smile when you do so." She gave a broad smile so that I could see what she meant. "You are not as frightening as the rest when you smile."

Ketil could not resist shouting, "Watch out Bagsecg, your wife finds Hrólfr attractive."

She whipped around and retorted, "And I can see by the scratch marks on your face how attractive you are to women. They should call you Ketil Foul Fart!"

He quailed before her. She was the size of a mouse but she roared like a wolf!

I spoke again and I smiled as I did so, "You will not be harmed and any man who takes you will make you his bride." I pointed to the beads and jewels some of the warriors wore. "See they are rich men."

One, bolder than the rest said, "And what of you, young warrior? Are you one who will be choosing a bride?"

I coloured and spluttered, "I am not yet ready to take a bride."

For some reason that put the women at their ease they laughed and then they began to smile and to chatter. They went into their hall without fuss.

Anya turned on Siggi and Ketil, triumphantly, "That is how you deal with women." She pointed at me, "If they had a choice then they would choose Hrólfr! Think on that!"

Arne Four Toes nodded and said, "You have a way with animals, Hrólfr the Horseman: horses, dogs, women!"

Everyone burst out laughing. The Jarl put his arm around my shoulder. "I am happy, Hrólfr. You have skills others do not. I am pleased the Weird Sisters sent you my way."

The spring storms burst upon us the next morning. Rain pelted down and was mixed with hailstones. When it let up at noon everyone left their halls to get some fresh air. The slaves stood looking expectantly at the Jarl. He came over to me, "Tell them that I expect them to prepare the food. Show them where the store is and what we would like to eat."

Already I was sick of this. I had hoped I would be able to ride Dream Strider but that was not meant to be. The sooner they learned to speak our language the better. I decided to employ Erik. Like me he had languages and if he would speak with them then life would be easier for me.

"Erik, come with me. We will start to teach them our language." I walked over to the women and told them what the Jarl has said. I introduced Erik to them and then said, "Both Erik and I have been thralls. We are now free." I pointed to the warriors who were standing around and talking about the raid with the crew of *'Sea Serpent'*. "There lies freedom. They want wives and if you are a wife then you are not a thrall."

The one who had flirted with me the night before smiled and said, "You are no fool, Viking. It is a pity that you do not wish a wife for it would not be unpleasant to be your bride. Very well. We can see that we are on an island and have nowhere to run. You slew my husband at Lannfyek so I am a widow."

"Good, it will be better if you learn our language. Erik and I will try to teach you words. Come we will go to the store hall."

Dream Strider was in his stall and Nipper was tied up next to him. As the women and children began to ascend to the food I fussed both the dog and the horse. An older woman said, "You are not what I expected from a Viking, master. You appear almost kind and yet you slew our men last night."

I shrugged, "It is who we are. We cannot change our destinies, can we?"

I reached the top of the ladder and she said, "Can we worship here?"

"The White Christ?" She nodded. "Aye but do not try to make the men Christian for they will beat you. It would be better if you did so privately but we will not take your crosses from you. So long as you do the work you are required to do worship whomsoever you wish."

I noticed that the more I spoke with them the easier it was to understand their dialect. This would not be as hard as I thought. I went through the food they were to cook and I gave it the Norse name. I also told them how we liked it to be cooked.

"Now, is there an alewife amongst you?"

A short dumpy woman, the oldest of the slaves stepped forward. She said, "Aye. I can brew."

"Good, then you do not need to prepare the food. We have a hut to make ale. Erik, take charge. You, what is your name?"

"Brigid."

"Then, Brigid, I think that you will find many of our men who wish to be your husband. You will have the pick of the pack!"

I think she was secretly pleased. Whilst the plainest of the women she had a skill that would make her as beautiful as a goddess to some men. By the time we had eaten the food that night, all thought of escape and all tears ceased. They were resigned to their fate and I knew that the women would be treated well. At least here they would be protected.

We had a week in which the women settled into their new lives before we set off again. The Jarl's brother was envious of our success and he and his small crew were keen to raid. I think the Jarl worried about his little brother for he said that we would all raid. He chose the small port at the mouth of the Liger. It was close enough for us to be there in hours rather than days and he knew that our neighbours, the Bretons, were at war with them. We would take advantage of their isolation. Unlike Lannfyek in Corn Walum, this one had a citadel. The Romans had left a fort here. It was like the one at St. Cybi. Rising above the port it gave the inhabitants somewhere to which they could run.

Siggi returned from the counsel of war and sat with us. "We sail tonight. The Jarl has decided that we will leave ten men here to guard the women and the island."

Arne Four-Toes said, "I do not think we need leave that many. The women are settled."

I saw Knut and Ketil look at each other. Everyone knew that despite what had been said about Ketil some of the women found him attractive. The two brothers had found many opportunities to be close to the women. They would take wives soon.

Siggi shrugged, "He is Jarl and besides he wants his little brother to be equal. It is Gunnstein who will lead the raid. We take no slaves. The Jarl says we will raid Hibernia for slaves. If we take them from here they are close to home and their men might come for them."

Harald Fast Sailing nodded, "The Jarl is using his head. Besides treasure is easier to manage than slaves and brings greater rewards."

Hrolf the Viking

I did not think that the Eriksson brothers would think so.

I visited with Bagsecg, "Is the mail ready? We raid tomorrow."

Bagsecg pointed to the blank swords next to him. "It will be some months before it is ready, Hrólfr. None of the boy slaves is big enough to help me. The next time you raid see if you can find someone who could learn to use the bellows."

I nodded. I was disappointed but it was not the blacksmith's fault. He had been brought to make weapons not to be my armourer. I would have to wait. I went to the wheel and put an edge on my three weapons. I examined my mail vest. It had not been the best when I had taken it from the Saxon but the blows it had taken had damaged some of the links. I had been fortunate so far. If I fought someone with a good sword, then the vest might not survive. So long as it took one blow that would be enough.

I rode Dream Strider in the afternoon. Nipper was now trained well enough to be allowed to run free. He slept in the stables with Dream Strider and the two of them had become unlikely companions. My dog still lived up to his name. He growled at any who approached. Siggi liked that. He did not want a watchdog to pet. He wanted a watchdog who barked. As we galloped across the island I noticed that Nipper had grown. His frame was filling out. As well as the scraps I fed him from the table, he had proved himself to be a good ratter. That was also good for our store was safer now. I reached the west end of the island and turned around to canter back. This was a good island. We had barely used all the land that was available to us. There were still many trees despite our building and ship repairs. The drawback was the water. There was just one spring. It had sufficed so far but if we had a hot summer then who knew.

We were at our oars before dark. The Jarl wanted us to strike just after the citadel was locked and barred for the night. He was a clever man; he reminded me of Dragonheart. He thought things through. If we always attacked just before dawn, then our enemies would prepare for that. His variety of targets and times kept them guessing.

We rowed southeast. We had three islands to pass before we reached the mouth of the river. Two of the islands were uninhabited and so they were useful as markers for our course. It was another reason the Jarl had chosen the target. His brother would lead the raid and the three islands would help him to find it easily. The weather and the sea were both kind to us and we flew down the coast. The beach we would use was a large one but it was some way from the houses. The port was around the headland in the mouth of the river. We knew from previous raids along the river that the port had a town watch. We would walk.

The moon had yet to rise when we reached the beach and it was dark. The smell of the houses and their fires were inland of us. We gathered on the beach. Despite the fact that Gunnstein and his men would lead the raid Jarl Gunnar was no fool. Ulf Big Nose was designated as scout. I felt a little put out that I was not with him. I had thought I had shown some skills in that area. I obeyed orders. Ulf and Gunnstein's scouts loped off followed by the crew of *'Sea Serpent'*. I swung my shield around as we followed. We had left four men to guard the ships. The Eriksson brothers had been given that task and neither had been happy about it. I ran alongside Siggi and Arne. It had been some time since I had had the chance to do so.

On the boat, Siggi had told me that there was a church in the village that had the bones of some saint. It was called St. Nazarius. For some reason, the followers of the White Christ valued such relics. If we had the chance, we would take them. They would fetch gold in Dyflin. We knew they would fetch even more in the land of the Lombards but we would not risk the Middle Sea just yet.

Gunnstein was young and he was reckless. He and his men just charged into the village rather than sneaking in. We heard the commotion and Siggi snorted, "Young fool! Surprise is gone!" There were two ways of raiding; one involved stealth and the other terror. Gunnstein was going for terror.

"Raven Wing! Run!" The Jarl's voice set us off running. I drew my sword and followed Siggi and Arne. They ran up the hill. The citadel was there but so was the church. Siggi was going for treasure. Gunnstein would find few pickings lower down the hill. The clamour had aroused the inhabitants and five men rushed from the hall which was next to the church. They had had time to grab helmets, shields and weapons. Siggi did not hesitate but threw himself amongst them. I saw a warrior begin to swing his axe at Siggi's unprotected right. I brought my sword over and knocked the axe head down. My sharp sword took a chip from it. The man turned to face me.

I had not fought many axe-men before. I knew that a blow from an axe could be deadlier than a sword but I also knew that he would have to swing. He could not thrust. I could do both. When he did swing at me I was surprised at the speed. I held up my shield and angled it. The blade caught on one of the studs. I heard the clang and saw the spark. More importantly, I felt the blow that shivered my arm. My sword darted forward. He was expecting a swing and the thrust took him by surprise. I got through his guard and my sword scored a deep wound along his cheek. Emboldened and before he could swing again I punched with my shield. It was not my strongest blow for my arm was still numb but it made him step back. I then feinted to stab at his face again and he flicked his shield up. I changed the angle of my strike and stabbed him in the knee. I twisted as I withdrew the blade and he shouted in pain. I had quick hands and, bringing my arm back, I swung at his neck. My sword bit deeply and he fell.

Before I could even think of moving on a sword smashed across my chest. I looked up in horror at the man who had appeared from nowhere. The pain in my chest had taken my breath away but I managed to swing my sword across his face and make him retreat a step. I turned to face him and pulled my shield up. Siggi had told me never to drop my guard and my success with the axeman had blinded me and made me forget my training. If I was to survive this encounter I would need to think.

I saw that this was a young warrior; older than me he was quick and alert. I saw it in his eyes. I had that advantage. He could not see my eyes. They were hidden behind my mask. My other advantage was that I was slightly taller. I had no doubt that he had seen my feint before I had slain the axeman. I would need to be cleverer. I held my sword up above me with the tip pointing down. If he gave me the chance I would stab above his shield. When I saw him pull his sword back I knew that he intended a sweep. As he swung I stepped into the blow with my left leg and my shoulder behind my shield. I stabbed forward as I did so. Our swords struck at the same time. His made my already painful arm numb once more. It also increased the damage to my mail vest. A tear had appeared. My sword, however, had found flesh. I had pierced his shoulder. I brought my sword back and stabbed it upwards. His shield hid the blow from him and I came up under his shield. I felt the tip strike and I pushed hard. It tore through a gap in his leather armour and entered his stomach. I saw the pain in his face and I pushed harder. Suddenly my sword tore through his body and emerged at his right shoulder. Life left his eyes. I pushed his body from my sword.

Siggi and Arne had raced on. Rurik was behind me. He nodded to my mail as he passed, "Your vest!"

I looked down and saw that it was split down the middle. It would offer no protection to my front. I ran with him up towards the church. Siggi kicked in the door to the church. By the time Rurik and I joined him a priest lay in an untidy heap and Arne was already gathering candlesticks and candles. Siggi shouted, "Rurik! Get the plate. Hrólfr, come, we will find the relic! Look for a box!"

I remembered that Aiden had told me how the priests liked to keep their precious relics close to their altar. Arne had taken everything from the top of the wooden altar and I kicked it over. There was a stone beneath it with a clear line around it. "Siggi! I have found it."

"Good lad! Take out your seax. You lift that side while I lift this." The fact that the large stone came up easily showed that this was regularly lifted. We dumped it on the floor rather too heavily and it cracked. There were two boxes within. One was small, about the length of a man's arm, while the other looked like a treasure chest. I picked up the small box and Siggi the other. I saw the look of disappointment on his face. "No coins in this one. Come we will take them back to the drekar." He handed me the large box. "This is not heavy. Take them both. "Rurik, it is time to go! Watch our backs!"

As we made our way back to the drekar we could hear that the raid was over. There were moans from the wounded but little sound of combat. The dead we passed were our foes. When we reached the axeman and the others we stopped. Siggi said, "I will get your rewards for you." He took the sword and axe from the men I had slain and he cut their purses. He placed their valuables on top of the two chests I carried and said, "You go back to the drekar. I will bring your weapons and search these others. Rurik, go with him!"

By the time we reached the drekar others were there already. Sven had put a gangplank so that we could walk aboard. We had more animals. I laughed as I saw Beorn and Harald Fast Sailing trying to get a sow and her young aboard the drekar. Beorn said, "Put those treasures down. This is work for the animal master!"

I handed the boxes to Rurik, "Take care with these. They may be worth more than gold!" I put the purses in my tunic and went over to the pigs. The two men were trying to manhandle the sow. I shook my head. "Leave the sow. Get the young on board. She will go herself if we do so." I picked up a squealing pig and walked up the gangplank and dropped it in the bottom. It continued to squeal for its mother. Beorn and Harald did the same. When I picked up a fourth the sow gave a snort and clambered after me. I dropped the piglet and then got out of the way of the sow's snout. The young huddled around her.

"Stay away from her and the young."

Beorn and Harald brought the last two, "You truly are the animal master."

"It is just common-sense Harald Fast Sailing. You know drekar but not animals. I could not sail this ship. Each to his own."

"Aye but this skill of yours, it is truly *wyrd*."

It took until dawn to load the two drekar. The Jarl shook his head as he boarded, "My foolish little brother. He is brave but he is reckless. He has lost four of his crew. He will be shorthanded."

Siggi nodded as we settled on to our chests, "Aye, Jarl, but he has learned a valuable lesson. His oathsworn have bought him experience."

The Jarl said, "Aye, with their lives."

Chapter 10

I felt honoured that the Jarl asked me to be there when the two chests were opened. Gunnstein, Siggi and Sven were there also. The smaller one contained some bones. Siggi nodded, approvingly, "Gold! As valuable as gold!"

The Jarl smiled, "And the other chest is larger and just as light. It may contain even more." The air of anticipation was almost palpable as he carefully opened it. To our great disappointment, it contained nothing save some parchments with the indecipherable writings of the Franks and the Romans.

Siggi snorted his disgust and pointed to the fire. "What a waste! We might as well use it for the fire!"

The Jarl shook his head, "I do not think so. What say you Hrólfr?"

"My time with the Dragonheart and Aiden told me that while this may not have a value in gold it may have secrets in the scribbles."

"But how do we read them?"

I shook my head, "We do not. We send them to the Dragonheart. If there is value in them then he will share with us."

"Aye, you are right. Dragonheart has honour."

Gunnstein was keen to make amends for the rash actions of his men. "Let me take them, brother! We have gold we took from the village and I know there are more who would go a-Viking with us from Cyninges-tūn. Besides Bjorn Bagsecgson has armour and I would buy a byrnie. His son is still busy with the swords."

"It is good and we will take these relics to Dyflin and then find more slaves. The ones from Corn Walum have settled in well."

"Bagsecg asked if we could get some boys who could work at the forge. The ones from Corn Walum were too small."

Siggi White Hair spat into the fire, "One thing Hibernians have is muscle! The west coast is the place to raid."

Gunnstein said, "I have heard of men sailing west beyond Hibernia. They say there are lands to the west."

Sven said, "I would not risk that. The west coast of Hibernia is enough for me. I would not risk sailing off the edge of the world."

I could see Gunnstein mulling over the idea. He was young and he was curious. He was the kind of captain who might risk his ship and his men on such a venture.

There was little to be gained in waiting and we set sail just three days after our raid. The spring storms were still a threat but we were able to take larger crews. If we had to row, then we could battle the seas and the wind. Knut and Ketil had taken two of the slaves as their wives and others had expressed an interest in the women. The result was that there was a greater demand for female slaves.

We sailed together. Two dragon ships kept any other predators at bay. We were too big a mouthful for any but the largest of drekar. The Saxon ships, even if they hunted in numbers were no match for our ships. We were sleek and we were fast. We remained within a length of each other until we reached the Angle Sea and the holy island of the Welsh. Gunnstein would sail to Úlfarrston while we put in at Dyflin.

Gunnstein Berserk Killer had sailed with our Jarl and the two were good friends. I knew from my time in Cyninges-tūn that the Jarl who had ruled Dyflin before had been a treacherous man. Jarl Dragonheart had defeated him and installed his friend as ruler. Although Gunnstein Berserk Killer had scoured his halls of the confederates of Hakon the Bald we were all wary as we entered his hall. Jarl Gunnstein Berserk Killer had grown a little portly since the last time I had seen him. He did not raid; he had no need to for Dyflin was the crossroads of the Viking world. We could all trade there. He grew rich just by sitting there and collecting taxes. He also took tribute from the Hibernian kings and princes. Few wished to risk the wrath of the Vikings. It was worth it to pay him and avoid a raid by his mailed warriors.

As we had walked from the quay to his hall I had been impressed with the bustling nature of the town. Every race was represented. I saw Saxons and Danes, Celts and Franks. It was the only place save Miklagård where such a variety of people could exist without confrontation and violence. Dorestad had had almost as many but that was a dangerous place. Dyflin was just lively! That was the result of Gunnstein Berserk Killer's hand. His word was law. I was glad that we were his friends and allies.

"Welcome my friends! What tales from the west? We are starved of news here."

The two jarls sat together in the middle of the long table. Siggi and Arne sat close to Jarl Gunnar. I was some way away. "We have brought some relics to sell. They are the relics of a saint called Nazarius."

Gunnstein Berserk Killer nodded, "I have heard of him. A Breton prince tried to steal them away once. The Franks will not be happy." He nodded. "We cannot give you their true worth, we will have to sell them on."

"That is understood." Jarl Gunnar waved his hand towards our clan, "These warriors have coin which is burning to be spent."

"Then you have come to the right place." He laughed deeply, "Taking money from traders is easier than fighting but not as rewarding. I miss those days. Are you not ready to settle down? I have six sons now!"

"We have some women but not enough."

"Ah yes, I have heard that you have made your island a stronghold."

I pricked up my ears. Siggi White Hair asked, "Where did you hear that, my lord?"

"We had some travellers call in not long after your last visit. They said that you had an island close to the land of the Bretons and you had built a hall."

"Were they our people?"

"Aye. They came in a leaky drekar. It took my shipwrights four days to seal the leaks. They were heading for Mann."

"Who led them?"

"Hermund the Bent was the name of the leader."

Siggi's voice became cold, "Hermund the Bent!"

I saw no deception in the eyes of Jarl Gunnstein Berserk Killer as he said, "I know him not but one of your countrymen was with him; Harald Black Teeth. He has been here before with your father. He has men following him now. I did not care for either man. We were glad to see the back of them for they spent little and caused trouble."

That almost settled it but I remembered the fight where I had saved Hermund the Bent's life. "Jarl Gunnstein Berserk Killer did this Hermund have a fresh scar running down his cheek?"

"It is Hrólfr, is it not? Good to see you again. You have grown. Aye, he did."

I said, "Then it was Hermund the Bent."

"And who is Hermund the Bent?"

Siggi said, "A murderer and a foresworn villain." The word 'murderer' was enough to silence the table. "He slew one of our clan and a family of fisherfolk. He spread a rumour that Hrólfr here had done it and that he had slain Hrólfr. He is outlaw."

Jarl Gunnstein Berserk Killer stood, "Then I am sorry we gave him aid. Let it be known now that this Hermund the Bent and those who sail with him are outlawed from Dyflin." Everyone banged the table giving their approval. He sat down and shook his head, "And he has fled to Mann. Each time we scour that island the rats return."

"Just so long as we know where he is we will give thought to his demise."

Gunnstein Berserk Killer nodded, "*Wyrd*. Where is your brother?"

"Gone to Cyninges-tūn for more warriors. We will meet with him here."

"You stay? If so you are more than welcome."

"No, Jarl, we come to ask permission to raid the lands to the west."

"And you have it. They do not pay me tribute but the land is poor. They have little to take."

"Little save slaves."

"Then it is rich in those. We have slaves in our pens you could buy."

The Jarl laughed, "I think it will be cheaper if we just take them. You say they are poor but they have churches and those always have treasures worth taking."

Our departure was delayed for many of the crew enjoyed the pleasures of Dyflin so much that they were in no condition to row. Olvir the Child Sparer had got into a fight with a Frank and now boasted a badly cut arm. He would be of no use on the raid. He received no sympathy from Arne and Siggi. "If you cannot best a Frank then stay aboard next time. Had he been one of Jarl Gunnstein Berserk Killer's men I would have understood but a Frank!"

"It was the ale. It was stronger than I am used to."

"Then that is even worse! Your punishment will be that you do not share in the raid. The drink has cost you much."

Poor Olvir was the subject to much mocking. He had to endure it too. He knew that he had made a mistake. It mattered not that he had broken the Frank's jaw and his arm he had let down the clan.

I had never been to the west coast of Hibernia. Haaken One Eye had told how the Dragonheart had raided the churches and monasteries there and reaped great rewards. We were after easier prey than him. What I had learned was that the coast was made of many fjords and narrow rivers. The people there fished for the land was poor for farming. Those with good land kept cattle and had walls around their homes but there were few of those in the part we would raid. As we did not know the land we would have to raid in daylight. As a result, we left Dyflin at night and sailed around the coast in darkness. On the morning of the second day, we found ourselves in the seas to the west of Hibernia. To the west lay vast seas without any land. As we rowed up the coast it was a worrying thought. What if a storm came up and swept us over the edge of the world? I saw Siggi and Arne clutch their Thor's hammers. I had no such protection. I determined to have one made as soon as I could. I made do with the hilt of my sword and relied on the spells of Kara and Aiden. We passed cliffs, rocks and inaccessible beaches. Perhaps we were not meant to raid this area. I could not see anywhere we could land.

Cnut, the ship's boy, had sharp eyes and he spotted the spiral of smoke. It was to the north and east of us. "Sven, find us a bay. Put us ashore and we will head for the smoke. Where there is smoke, there are people."

"Aye Jarl."

We rounded a headland and Sven spied a patch of yellow sand. The rocks on either side were far enough away to risk a landing. He headed the drekar's prow towards the shore. It was unusual for us to go ashore in daylight. In many ways, it was harder than at night for we felt exposed but as we saw no one we hurried across the beach as soon as we landed. "Arne, Hrólfr, go with Ulf!"

"Aye Jarl."

There was a high ridge to the east and a smaller one to the west. The smoke appeared to be coming from the other side of the narrow pass. We raced up towards it. For once we knew that we would be better armed and protected than any we found here. The Hibernians were wild fighters who often fought naked. If they had a sword, then they were lucky. Many used a vicious-looking club. Whilst handy against one of their fellows it offered little protection against a Viking with a shield, a helmet and a sword. As we crested the col we saw a small crude settlement. There were no more than a dozen huts and they were little more than turf shelters.

A wail from ahead told us that we had been spotted. The women and children ran and the handful of men grabbed their weapons and ran towards us. We knew that the rest of our warband was behind us and so we ran directly at the eight men and youths who stood with spears, a crude sword and a wood axe. Holding our shields before us we ran at them. I held my sword to the side. My shield smashed a fire-hardened spear and then the face of one man while my sword tore through the middle of another. Two men were knocked over by Arne and Ulf and then we were past. I did not turn around but I heard a roar as the rest of the warband crashed over the col.

We were now in a foot race with the women and the children. Had the women abandoned the children then they might have escaped for they were fleet of foot but some of the children were young and two of the women carried babes in arms. I saw that we were crossing a strip of land and there was another bay some two hundred paces ahead. I realised that they were heading for the beach and, just offshore, were three fishing boats. Another eight men were aboard the boats. They were heading for the protection of their men.

As we overtook the women they stopped and gathered their children around them. The last one had no children and she ran into the sea. She intended to swim out to the fishing boats which were sailing back to shore. I ran after her and, using the flat of my sword, smacked her hard on the back of the head. She fell face forward into the water. Sheathing my sword, I picked her up and carried her back to the beach.

The Jarl and the rest of the warband were there and they began to herd the women up the hill. The Jarl said, "Siggi, keep ten men here and discourage the men in the boats from anything heroic."

"Aye Jarl." As much as the men might want to come to the aid of their women the line of armed warriors would deter them.

I carried the unconscious young girl over my shoulder and climbed back up the col. Ketil shouted, "I see you have been fishing, horseman! What bait did you use?"

I laughed and said, "My charm! She only ran because she knew you were coming! You really should bathe!"

We had more than enough men to shepherd the women and children back to the boat. We had eleven women and eight children. There were also two babies. Unfortunately, there were no boys to help Bagsecg but that could not be helped. By the time we had put them on board the drekar, Siggi and the others had returned. Siggi pointed to the high ground. "The fishing boats are coming around the headland."

"Aye well, they will soon give up. I am guessing they will raid the next village along." That was the way. They would take women from the next weakest village and so it would go on. Eventually, there would be a handful of men with no village and no women. They would turn to banditry or serving someone who would pay them to fight. It was a cycle of life.

We began to row as the women wailed and keened. The men in the three fishing boats had to watch, impotently, as we sailed by. They shook their fists and, no doubt, cursed us but they could do nothing. Siggi snorted, "They should be grateful the Jarl allowed them to live."

I had some sympathy with the men. How could they have known that such wolves as we were sailing their waters? The men they had left would have been enough to fend off an attack by a rival clan of Hibernians but not us, not the Raven Wing Clan.

The women refused all food on the way back to Dyflin but they did drink water. For once I had no words I could use. They cursed us no doubt but once one of them, who had tried to jump over the side, had been slapped by Siggi, it ended all such resistance. They sat and awaited their fate.

We had to row and Arne said, "We have enough women. We can go back to proper raiding now."

"We still need slaves for the smith!"

I turned and smiled, "Then we buy them. They will not cost much and I agree with Arne. This is not the work for a Viking."

It was evening when we pulled up next to the quay. There was no sign of *'Sea Serpent'*. Jarl Gunnstein Berserk Killer had given us permission to use his slave pens to hold our captives. It was a favour for an old friend and to make amends for helping Hermund the Bent. As we escorted them to the pens the woman I had hit with my sword kept giving me dark looks. Ketil found it amusing. "I see your charms have worn off, Hrólfr!"

"I am not looking for a woman yet, Ketil. You have settled on the first one you saw. I am choosy."

As the Jarl's brother had not yet returned I took the opportunity of visiting Dyflin's markets with Rurik. Since our time on the island alone we were a little closer. Close by the river there were many kinds of traders. I could have bought mail but it would have been far more expensive than that which Bagsecg was making for me and it might not have been the same quality. Rurik did buy a short byrnie. He seemed satisfied with it but I noticed that the links were not as well made as those I had seen in Bagsecg's workshop. There was a trader from the far north, the land of the Rus. He had some of the Saami bows. These were as expensive as byrnie but they were much more powerful and could send an arrow further. Snorri the Scout had had one and he had sung its praises. A bow chosen by an Ulfheonar was worth consideration. I haggled with the merchant. I paid slightly less than he was asking but I was never very good at bargaining. Rurik thought I could have paid much less. I think I had been a slave for too long.

I bought a second pair of sealskin boots. My first pair had proved to be a good buy. My second pair were just as well made as those I had bought from Einar but they were more expensive. I was not paying a friend this time. I had thought I had finished and we were about to turn for home when we spied the jeweller. He had a small stall. He sold Thor's Hammers. I knew that Rurik had wanted one for some time. We went and Rurik haggled. It was then that I spied, in the corner, a rearing horse attached to a leather thong. I picked it up and turned it over in my hands. It was not made of metal but some black material. It was hard but it was very smooth. Whoever had made it knew horses. The proportions were right and the mane and tail flowed as they did on a real horse. It was beautiful and, to my eye, looked like Dream Strider.

When Rurik had paid for his hammer I asked, "Where did you get this? It is unlike anything I have ever seen."

He nodded, "You have a good eye." I was suspicious for that was a common ploy amongst merchants and traders. He must have seen my look for he smiled, "I will not try to sell you anything but what I say is true. I have been here almost a month now and no one has yet picked this up. To me, it is the most beautiful amulet I have."

"Where is it from?"

He pointed to my bow, "As far north as that bow has travelled this has travelled further from the east. I picked it up in the land of the Rus from a merchant who had been to Miklagård and come up the river. He had it from a captured eastern warrior. It is said his people live on the backs of horses. They can use a bow while riding and they are fierce warriors. He was captured in the Ghassanid wars. They executed him and the trader picked it there. I found it fascinating."

"What is it made of?"

"I thought it was jet but it is not. The merchant I bought it from called it ebony. It is a type of wood."

"But it is hard."

"Aye, I know."

"How much?"

In answer, he reached up and flicked up the forelock of hair which always hung down over my forehead. Before I could knock it away he had seen the mark of the slave. He held his hand up. "I mean no offence, Viking." He lifted his own forelock and there was also the mark of the slave.

Wyrd.

"How did you know?"

He shrugged, "I know not. The thought came to me that we had something in common. I am no warrior... " He looked into my eyes. It was strange but I felt the connection then too. "One silver piece is what I paid for it. You can have it for one silver piece."

I shook my head and handed him two, "No for you must have a profit. I wish this horse to bring me luck. I will not begin its life in debt."

He spat on his hand and held it out to me. I did the same. "You look like a boy but in your eyes, I see wisdom. What is your name Viking?"

"Hrólfr the Horseman."

"I can see that you will do great things. I will keep watch for you. I am Sven the Rus. I travel from town to town. I feel sure our paths will cross again. May the Allfather be with you."

Rurik was fascinated by the whole incident. "That little object has travelled from the far side of the world and you paid him twice what he asked. You are a strange one, Hrólfr."

I put it around my neck and said, "Do you not think I was meant to buy it?"

"Of course, but I would worry for I see the Weird Sisters at work. This is a mighty spell if they can summon an amulet from beyond our world and find another who has escaped slavery. These are threads indeed!"

Siggi was intrigued by both my bow and my amulet. "The horse I can understand. You are a horseman and it is meant for you but a bow. I have rarely seen you use a bow."

"Do you remember that Snorri, Jarl Dragonheart's scout, used one of these? He could loose an arrow further than any other. I am not the greatest archer in the world but with this, I shall be a better one," I turned to Rurik, "Did you hear what Sven the Rus said about this? That it came from a tribe who lived on the other side of the world and could use one of these on horseback! The two are linked. I am sure of it."

Even Siggi was impressed, "Truly?"

Rurik nodded, "That was what he said. I can see how it would be more useful for it is shorter than a war bow. When we return to the island you shall have to try it."

Siggi nodded, "For me, we could go home today! When I was young, I liked places like this. Now I like the quiet of the island."

I found myself agreeing with him. I missed my horse and my dog. I missed the island too.

Gunnstein Thorfinnson arrived back two days later. He brought with him new warriors; more than he had lost and a gift from Aiden, a reward for the parchments. He sent a golden wolf he had made for the Jarl. "This should be yours, Hrólfr. We might have used the parchments to light a fire."

I shook my head, "No lord I am not of the wolf." I held up my new amulet. "I am Hrólfr, of the horse!"

Chapter 11

The fact that two of our enemies now lived on Mann made us more than a little wary as we headed across the sea to the Sea of the Welsh. Snaefell's mountain top now seemed a threat. Were we being watched even as we sailed south? There was an even bigger sense of relief as we passed the island of the Angle Sea. The visit to Dyflin and the arrival of many new men made the crew chatter like magpies but I remained silent. I was thinking of the Norn's threads. I had not set out that morning to buy a bow but having bought one how odd that I should have bought one I could use on horseback. In the same way, I had only accompanied Rurik to the amulet maker because he needed one. I had had no desire or need for one. It was as though my feet were being directed.

Siggi White Hair turned to me, "You are silent. Are you unhappy to be leaving Dyflin?"

"No, I am just deep in thought."

He nodded, "Aye you are a thinker. That will be your downfall I daresay. While you are thinking take the slaves some water."

I was happy to do so. I picked up the pail and the wooden scoop. They had been quiet since they had come aboard. A couple of days in the slave pens had shown them that this was their life. It had also meant that they had learned some of our words. As I waited for the scoop to be returned I pointed to the one whom I had struck and then carried back to the drekar.

"You. Name."

She looked like she was not going to reply and then the older woman next to her, I later learned it was the girl's mother, spoke to her. The young woman nodded, "Nerys."

I nodded and, pointing to the side of her head said, "Sorry." and smiled. There was a hesitation and then she nodded and the scowl left her face. It was a start.

When we passed the land of Wessex we saw Saxon ships patrolling. This was a new development. They did not approach us. We were two of the dreaded dragon ships. Even Saxon warships kept their distance but it became clear that they were making sure that we were kept from their shores. I did not know if that was a result of our raid or others. It mattered not. The world was wide as was the ocean. We would find another sheep to shear.

Each time we reached our island and it was still whole we thanked the Allfather. Rurik and I were particularly fervent in our prayers. We knew we had been lucky to survive. The lambs we saw on the hillside as we headed to the hall were a sign that we had been favoured. Our new sheep had given birth. With just slaves and personal treasure to carry back, we did not need Dream Strider. Erik led him from the stall for me. Nipper bounded up to me, yapping. He leapt into the air to almost knock me over as he eagerly licked my face.

Erik One Hand said, "They have both pined for you. It is good that you have returned."

I took my bow and quiver and handed them to him. "Put these in the hall. I will try them out later. First, I ride Dream Strider. He needs the run."

I did not bother with a saddle. Now that my leg was healed I could mount and ride as easily as before. I set off to the west of the island and Dream Strider raced with a freedom I had not seen before. Nipper bounded along next to him. The dog had filled out. He was spoiled by the children of the slaves who gave him titbits from their table. All three of us needed the ride. We twisted and turned through the woods and then I reined in at the cliffs at the western end of the island. I paused to take in the vista before me. We had a good home. As I turned I spied a cave. I had not seen it before. I would tell the Jarl about it. That might be useful. We could store things there. Then I whipped Dream Strider's head around and galloped along the southern coast. As I passed the two drekar the ship's boys waved as they tied up the ships. We now had more mooring posts and the two vessels would be secure.

The ground to the east of the island was more undulating and had fewer trees. We had to be careful to avoid animal holes. That too was an entertaining challenge. I used my knees and Dream Strider used his horse sense. Nipper just used his lightning quick reactions. At the east end, I dismounted and stroked Dream Strider's head. I found myself looking out beyond the land ahead. A warrior had worn my amulet. He had died far from home and I carried the last piece of him around my neck. Where was my home? I had been taken as a slave so long ago that I had no real recollection of where my real home lay. Was it Cyninges-tūn? Was it Neustria? Was it this island? The Norns determined my course and I wished I could ask them where my destiny truly lay. The witch had said in the land of the Franks. Was this the land of the Franks?

As I headed back to the hall my mind was filled with questions. I knew now, with all certainty, that the Norns wished me to be a horseman. How could I do that while sailing on a drekar? I was still young. My beard had only recently started to fill out. I could only estimate my age by counting back winters. I came to the conclusion that I had seen somewhere between fifteen and eighteen winters. The Jarl had seen twice that many and Siggi almost three times. I still had much time to become that which was prophesied. But I was young and I was impatient.

As I rode through the village Bagsecg waved me over. "I have nearly finished your mail. By next month we can try it. You are still growing and we will need to adjust it."

"Good."

"Did you get me a slave or two?"

"We could not find any in the village we raided." I saw his disappointment. "The Jarl bought two instead."

"That is good. We will build a bigger smithy." Anya came out and I saw the bump which showed she was with child.

I smiled. "I see you are like your father. Sire as many sons as you can and then you have a steady supply of workers."

He laughed but Anya scowled, "It may be a girl. What say you to that husband?"

"I say it would be a good thing for the Allfather puts women on this earth to keep men like me in our place."

She shook her head and rolled her eyes, "Hrólfr, did any of the slaves catch your eye?"

"I keep answering that question. When I spy the right one then I will take her."

She pointed to Ketil and Knut who were heading with their two women to the huts they had constructed. "If those two empty-headed lumps can get women then you should too. We need children with brains! Theirs will just have brawn!"

I laughed and led Dream Strider back to the stall. Anya's words did not worry me. There was still time. I dried, watered and fed Dream Strider before heading to the hall. Nipper followed me to the door and then bounded off. He would go hunting. We all had our own space in the hall. As I had been one of the first I had had the first choice and my space was by the eastern corner. In light of my purchase, I saw now that was *wyrd*. Rurik and Erik were close by. Siggi and Arne were towards the middle. They were closer to the fire and the table. That reflected their position in the clan. They were, along with Ulf Big Nose, the senior warriors in the clan. As I passed they were still talking of Dyflin.

"Beorn will have to tell that alewife of his that she needs to make some of that black beer we had in Dyflin. That wakes a man up in the morning."

"Aye, but has she the recipe? The old crone in Dyflin pretended she could not understand us when we asked."

"She can try. It will give us different tastes anyway."

They paused as I passed. Siggi asked, "When can we see you try that new bow, Hrólfr?"

"The morrow will be soon enough for me to make a fool of myself before the whole clan."

Siggi said, "They are the only people who should see a man be a fool for we are family. We may mock each other but we are like a mail shirt against all others. Each metal ring links to the next!"

Rurik was seated on his mattress threading a new leather thong through his hammer. "I saw you speaking with Bagsecg. Is your mail ready?"

"Soon. If we raid again in the next month, however, I will have no mail."

"You are young and you are quick." He pointed to his missing ear. "When I lost this, I thought that I would not be a warrior and yet even though I do not hear on that side I know when an enemy comes. I have watched you fight; you know how to defend. When you wear mail then remember how much it weighs! It can be a burden as well as a blessing. I would build up your body and become used to carrying weight."

It was good advice and I would heed it.

The Jarl decided to wait for half a month before raiding once more. We had more slaves and they needed assimilating into our settlement. As I had found when I was taken, it does not take long. It is especially true if you are taken a long way from your home. The Hibernians were three oceans away.

Gunnstein was keen to raid for he felt he had let himself down on the previous raid. He was contrite about his losses. I think the Jarl had let him lead so that he could learn from his mistakes. He had learned by sailing with the Dragonheart. I was in the hall carving two adornments for Dream Strider's reins and bridle when the two brothers and Siggi entered. They acknowledged my presence and then discussed the raid.

"The Liger is our best target. It is long and we can sail many miles along it. Only the Dragonheart has ventured inland and we can sail even further for we are closer to our home."

Siggi, as ever, was the voice of reason. "And there are many places where we can be stopped. If the Franks wish to stop us they just need to put a chain across the river."

"And we can break the chains. I do not think that we will be able to repeat this raid too often but while we have the men and the drekar let us take advantage of fine weather. The Franks have internal division. I heard that from Gunnstein Berserk Killer. The Bretons are encroaching on the land of the Empire as are the Burgundians. We take advantage of their weakness. I want to make our island home a fortress for the winter. What we have we hold."

Siggi nodded, "So we go for food. That is good. We have enough iron for the winter. We can always return to Sussex next year but for the while, we have enough."

I could hear the disappointment in Gunnstein Thorfinnson voice, "What of treasure? I heard when in Cyninges-tūn, that Jarl Dragonheart seeks a great treasure. He was assembling his men to take it."

I heard the barb in the Jarl's voice, "Then perhaps you should have sailed with him as I did! Jarl Dragonheart has many drekar at his command. He has a land ringed with burghs and can leave it unattended. We are growing, little brother and we are learning."

I glanced up and saw that Gunnstein was reddening.

Siggi softened the harshness of the Jarl's words. "There will be treasure, Gunnstein Thorfinnson, but we do not know in advance what they are. Jarl Dragonheart has a wizard who can read. I have no doubt that the words we sent to him have given him information which is hidden from us. We take our opportunities where we can."

I finished carving one of the adornments, a horse's head, and I rose to attach it to Dream Strider's bridle. As I passed them, nodding my acknowledgement of them, the Jarl said, "We row as far up the river as we can and then turn to use the river. That way we can raid more than one place."

"So, brother, we hide up during the day?"

"Exactly." Their voices faded as I stepped outside.

Once I was in the fresh air I headed for the paddock and pen. We had built it to house all the animals save the sheep. Dream Strider did not seem to mind and as Nipper slept close by the dog chased away any of the piglets which came too close. I saw two of the new slaves feeding the pigs. There were a boy and a girl aged about six summers. Had the boy been a Viking he would soon be readied to train as a warrior. He would learn the sling and begin to fight with wooden sticks. The slaves would do this for the rest of their lives.

I stroked Dream Strider and spoke to him as I attached the horse amulet. I would carve another before I left for the raid. The boy slave stood and watched me. I pointed to Dream Strider and said, "Horse." The boy nodded and tried to repeat it. He got it wrong. I repeated it until he understood. I then did the same with Nipper. The sooner they could speak our language the better. It would make their lives and ours much easier. They finished feeding the animals and I heard them being called. They hesitated and I smiled and said, "Go to your mother!"

I was not certain if they understood but they ran anyway. When I returned to the hall it was filling up with warriors. Our hall was Raven Wing and it was obvious that they all knew of the raid. Sea Serpent Clan had their own, smaller, hall. Men were checking armour. Erik sat wistfully on his mattress, "Do you think the Jarl will let me come with you this time?"

I shook my head, "If I said yes then it would just give you false hope. There may come a time when you come with us but I fear you have made yourself too valuable here."

"We have slaves now to make the bread and brew the ale. The children watch over the animals. What do I do?"

"You guard our home. When we sail, we all feel safer knowing that you are here."

I took my armour down from the nail I had hammered into the wooden roof support. If my mail was not ready, then I would need to make my leather armour stronger. I had metal strips sewn onto my shoulders and arms. I took out the torn mail vest. It could not be used as a vest for it was in four pieces. I attached two to the front and back using the metal I had sewn there already. Then I put the last two pieces, which were both smaller on the lower part of the leather so that they protected my thighs. It did not look pretty but it would be effective.

"You have been to this river with the Dragonheart have you not, Hrólfr?" Rurik turned his good ear to me.

"I have. It is more like the land of the Arabs than the land of the Frank. The last time we raided there before you joined us, we lost many men there. They have Moors who have long curved swords." I opened my chest and took out the one I had captured.

"That is a vicious looking weapon but it only has one edge."

I turned it over, "And that gives it strength and yet keeps it light. When Bagsecg makes a sword, he puts the steel between the two pieces of iron and he beats them together. It is heavy but there are two edges. Now I know not how they make this but I am guessing that they do not need to use as much iron. It becomes lighter and the back of the sword has the weight." I handed it to him. "Here, swing it and see."

He did so and I saw the look of surprise upon his face, "It is light and the action is smooth. It has a sharp point too."

I took the sword back and wrapped it up again in its sheepskin. I returned it to the chest. "But it is a land with many riches. There is wine, they have spices, wheat is plentiful and they have both oranges and lemons."

"What of the churches?"

"They are richly endowed but I should warn you, Rurik, because they fear attacks from the south they have well-defended burghs. These are not poor barbarians such as those we met in Hibernia and Corn Walum. They wear mail and protect what they have. The Jarl is gambling that few Vikings have visited us and they may be taken by surprise. I hope he is right."

"What do you mean?"

"They have horses. They are not small like Dream Strider. They are large and they use the stirap. We can outrun Saxons for they fight on foot. You do not outrun a horse. And remember it is hot there in summer. Your new mail will protect you but it will feel like Thor's anvil!"

We left in the middle of the afternoon so that we could sail down the river during the hours of darkness. The first part was wide and there would be no navigational obstacles. There were two known towns that we could attack. Tours and Andecavis. I was worried about attacking Tours. A Frank had defeated the Arabs there and I felt certain that this would be heavily defended. Siggi told me that he had heard a rumour that outside the city of Tours was a monastery, Marmoutier Abbey. He had been told that there were well over a hundred monks there. That number of monks meant it would be rich. The other town which we thought was worth raiding was Orléans but, once again, I feared it was too big a nut to crack.

We did not have to row for the wind was with us and we would need our strength when we had tonight the current of the mighty river. As we sailed towards the mouth of the river I wondered if they had rebuilt St. Nazarius after our raid. Would they be watching for us? I remembered that the river was wide there. We would be sailing under the dark of moon.

Siggi sensed my disquiet. "Like you I am worried but I think the Jarl is right. We are doing something no Viking has done before. We can lie up during the day and sail further inland than any before us. Those who travel from the far north do not have the luxury of a secure island like ours. Your suggestion was a good one, Hrólfr. We must trust the Jarl to make another good decision."

I was silent for a while and then I risked telling him my other idea, "The island is good but we need to have a home on the mainland. Then we could use horses."

He laughed, "You have a bright mind but I think you must have eaten of the magic mushrooms. Do you think that either the Bretons or the Franks would let us settle there?"

"Gunnstein Berserk Killer lives in Hibernia amongst the Hibernian kings and princes. He has no country, just a city. Could we not do that? We could then use horses to range further afield to raid. If we built strong walls around our hall and used somewhere close to the coast what could we not achieve?"

Arne shook his head, "Where do you dream up such fantasies? The way you describe it sounds possible but the reality is that we could not."

"Dragonheart did."

That silenced them both for a moment and then Arne said, "He has a sword touched by the gods. What have you got?"

"A dream."

Siggi said, "Then do not listen to us and hold on to that."

We began to row once we turned east and headed up the river. This time we led and *'Sea Serpent'* followed. We heard a bell tolling from the church we had sacked. Was it warning those upriver or calling people to prayers? We rowed not hard but silently. We had our sail furled to make us less easy to see and we had to reach a point beyond Nantes before we stopped. Nantes had a castle on the north bank. There was an island in the middle of the river. We knew from our time with Dragonheart that the southern channel was shallower but we would risk it. There were pinpricks of light on the hillside. We could hear the sound of the town watch and those signs told us that we were close to Nantes.

We slowed down our oars as Sven took us close to the south bank. We kept as close as we could to the middle of the channel. Suddenly we all felt our keel as it touched the bottom and then, just as quickly, we were off and free. We were larger than *'Sea Serpent'* and I was confident that she would not be grounded. We rowed a little faster as the river took us north and east. A short while after we had passed Nantes we passed another island in the middle of the river. It looked inviting but we sailed on. When we passed a second a few miles later Siggi and I were convinced that we should stop but we did not. And then there were no islands for many miles. I sensed that dawn was coming and it was just then that we saw a third island. In fact, it was a third and a fourth with a narrow channel between them. It was a perfect place to hide for we would be hidden from both banks. Sven and the Jarl had been guided by the Allfather. It was a good sign. He approved of our action.

We stopped rowing and Sven brought us to a halt close by some overhanging willows. The ship's boys jumped ashore and tied us to the trees. Even though we believed the island to be uninhabited Ulf Big Nose still loped off to investigate the island. *'Sea Serpent'* tied up behind us. The dragon prow peered over our steering board. When Ulf Big Nose returned, we disembarked. He had seen nothing on the island. We were safe. While we began to make a camp so Sven and the boys began to dismantle the mast and lay it on the mast fish. We needed to keep a low profile. I joined the others and headed towards the trees and bushes. We would sleep more comfortably beneath the trees. Six men were assigned the first watch. Jarl Gunnar came to Ulf and me. "You two will not have to watch but after you have slept I want you to scout the north shore. If you can find horses, then so much the better. We need to know what lies ahead. We are in unknown territory now."

We went to find a sheltered spot. It had been cloudy. If it rained, then we wanted to be out of the worst of it. Ulf tapped my leather armour as we lay down. No armour, shield or helmet when we scout. Use a cloak. I will be relying on your language to get us out of trouble."

"But with your nose, we will not get into any eh, Ulf?"

He laughed as he slapped the back of my head. "Cheeky for an apprentice!"

Before I went to sleep I took some leather halters from my chest. We would need them if we found horses.

We slept until dawn and then we were woken by Siggi who was in charge of the watch. As we went to the other side of the island I said, "How do we get across the river?"

"Another reason we do not use mail. We float on a log." He pointed. "I saw the driftwood from the winter storms last night when I scouted the island. We take a big log and float downstream." He saw me readying to ask a second question. He held up a finger. "We will work out how to get back when the time comes. If we have to then we swim! Now come."

I took off my sealskin boots and wrapped them in my cloak. Ulf led us to the jumble of logs and branches. He found one large enough for the two of us and, stepping into the water, pushed it off. The water was colder than I had expected. The branches hid us. Ulf hissed, "Now kick for the shore or we shall end up in Nantes."

I was glad that I carried my boots. It made the kicking easier. The other bank looked deserted. There were willows overhanging the river and some reeds. We made for them. The current was surprisingly swift but we saw the other bank looming up. As the logs caught we clambered up onto the bank. I put on my boots and I looked around for anything untoward. There was nothing. Wrapping the cloak around me I followed

Ulf as he hurried down the path which followed the river. We had only travelled a mile and a half when we saw a hill before us and a village. It was a substantial one. To our left lay a road and we saw traffic moving along it. Ulf said, "Now we become ordinary travellers. We head for the village. Try to blend in with the other travellers. I leave it to you to speak if anyone asks any questions. If they ask about me say I am a Saxon from Lundewic. I can speak Saxon and our clothes can pass for Saxon."

"And me?"

He laughed, "You are a bright young warrior! Make something up yourself."

We moved off the trail and through the trees. Ulf waited until a cart pulled by a man and with a woman following had passed. There was nothing else coming and we stepped onto the road to follow them. If anyone saw us they might take us for the same party. Over the next hundred or so paces we caught up with them. The woman saw us and said something to the man. He shook his head. I could see the village ahead. It looked to be busy. To the south, I saw masts of vessels. They did not look to be large but they would be a danger to **_'Raven's Wing'_**. I smiled and nodded as we passed the couple. They nodded back but looked apprehensively at Ulf. He looked intimidating. When we were halfway to the village he stopped, and took off his boot, as though he had a stone in it. He was buying time.

The couple came abreast of us. For some reason, the fact that Ulf was seated made him less threatening and the man spoke to me. "Where are you bound?"

I had not thought of an answer and so I said the first thing that came to my mind. "Angers. We are looking for work."

He was shrewd and he took in our swords and Ulf's chiselled features. "Soldiers?"

I nodded, "We have been and we have been bodyguards for a Jew. He returned east. We turn our hands to most things."

The woman crossed herself, "A Jew? The killers of Christ?"

I shrugged, getting into my story now, "He paid well and he was harmless."

Ulf had refitted his boot and he stood. We walked with the couple. The man nodded, "Aye well a man has to earn a loaf of bread where he can. We do not have as far to go as you. Angers is a good thirty-odd miles from here. There is little between Ancenis and Angers save trees and vineyards."

"We are fit and we don't mind walking. We prefer riding but walking is fine."

"Your friend does not say much."

"He is a Saxon from the land of the Angles."

The woman clutched at her cross again. "We have heard from our priest that they are beset by the men from the north! Norsemen! Why they even raided St Nazarius. I pray they never come here."

The man laughed, "My wife worries about everything. We are far from the sea here and we are quite safe besides I heard that the Count is preparing men to protect the mouth of the river. We will be safe." He suddenly stopped, "There might be work for you." He pointed towards Nantes. "You could go back to Nantes. They are looking for handy men like you."

I shook my head, "Thank you but no, we have heard of a merchant in Angers who wants two men to protect him when he travels. We will try there."

"You may be right. That will be safer than facing bloodthirsty Norsemen."

We had reached the village and people seemed to know the couple. The fact that we were with them gained us acceptance. No one said anything to us. We had arrived on market day. We walked towards the marketplace. There were other stalls. It was not a large market but there were a dozen people there already. The man lifted the hessian sack from the cart. Inside were more sacks of what looked like beans.

"Good luck. Go with God."

"And with you."

We kept going through the village although we both glanced to the river where we saw the five small boats. They looked to be fishing boats or perhaps traders. If they went downstream then they might spot the drekar. When we were far enough out of the village to speak, Ulf asked me what I had learned. He nodded, "You have done well. I think we had discovered enough. If it is thirty miles to Angers, we cannot reach there."

I said, "We cannot go back through the village. The man will be suspicious."

"Then we will cross the river and go back along the southern bank."

"How?"

"We find a boat or a log. We saw nothing near to the village so we will walk a little way further."

Fortune smiled on us. Half a mile along the bank we spied a small punt. It was the type used by those who fished in the reeds. There was a large patch of reeds bordering the river. We jumped in and began poling down the river. We had spied another island and we let the current take us to it. Soon we were hidden from the north bank by the island. We had seen one more island after we had left the village of Ancenis. The problem would come when we passed the village. We might be seen. The current was strong and we did not need to pole. Ulf used the pole as a steering board. As we neared the island close to the village he said, "Lie down and I will put my cloak over my head. They might not notice us."

It was nerve-wracking but I lay in the bottom and stared up at the sky. After what seemed an age Ulf said. "We have passed it. You can rise" He grinned, "This is easier than walking. You did well today, Hrólfr the Horseman. You did not panic and although I did not understand your words they sounded confident. We might make a scout of you yet."

The news we brought disturbed the Jarl. He sought conference with his brother and Siggi. When they had finished, he said, "Break camp. Put your belongings back on the drekar. We need to move silently and not disturb those in the village. I think we will just sail to the monastery. We can then turn and attack Angers. We sail as far down the river tonight as we can. We have to leave the Liger to attack Angers. I believe that if we can pass this village unseen then we can strike in the heartland of this rich place."

I could see that he was trying to appear more confident than he was. I was noticing many differences between Jarl Gunnar and Jarl Dragonheart. The Dragonheart was more likely to speak from the heart. I would be that kind of leader. If a man had doubts he should express them.

Ulf and I grabbed some food and ale before we found a corner for another hour or so of sleep. That was something we had all learned to do. When you had the chance then you slept.

Rurik woke me, "Come Hrólfr, we are leaving." I saw that dusk was almost over and the sky was darkening.

We could not use a chant to keep the rhythm of the beat and so the Jarl used his arm. I hoped that his brother was equally skilled. I could not help glancing to the right and village of Ancenis. Although shrouded in darkness the smells of the people and fires drifted over. Occasional voices seemed inordinately loud. It seemed impossible that they would neither see nor hear us but who had ever heard of Vikings this far up the river? When we were had passed rowing seemed easier. We had many hours of steady rowing ahead of us. This was what made us different from other warriors. We had trained to do this.

It was not just the physical strain we had to prepare for it was the strain of the mind. If you did not let your mind wander, then the rowing became harder. I had learned to dream of a future not in a drekar but on the back of a horse. I pictured my own clan and my own oathsworn. We would not turn our backs on the sea but we would turn our face to the land and we would range far afield. Working with Ulf Big Nose had shown me that we could use mounted scouts to find our foes and then bring the weight of our band to bear. We would be the first Vikings to fight on horseback. I knew that would surprise our enemies. Most importantly though we would build a hall and walls of stone. The raid by the bandits had set me to thinking. When Rurik and Erik had been in the store they had been protected by height but a fire could have destroyed them. We would build a wall of stone surrounded by a ditch and we would build high walls. I had seen such walls at the Roman Wall. If the ancients could build them then so could we. We would put our roots into the earth and be stronger because of that.

Time passed quickly when I dreamed, even with my eyes wide open, and it seemed no time until we halted by one of the many deserted islands on the river to rest. The ship's boys brought ale and dried fish. Siggi stretched. When he spoke, I knew that there were no Franks close by. "You and Ulf will be scouting again tomorrow. Do not use all of your strength in rowing."

"I am fine. I enjoy scouting. It is a challenge to the mind."

He nodded, "Ulf told me of your quick thinking. Just be careful. Watch men's eyes. They tell you their thoughts if you know how to read them." Enigmatically he finished. For the last few hours of rowing, I gave thought to them.

When we reached the island where we would rest during the day we were exhausted. It had been a journey fraught with dangers; all of them natural. The river twisted and turned, narrowed and broadened. We grounded once and we broke an oar on a submerged rock. Luckily the river seemed devoid of large settlements and towns. We had passed but one large group of houses with a church and that had been on the south bank. I saw the Jarl take interest in it. As I lay down to sleep I thought that if we had a small boat we could row it would be useful! When dawn arrived, I would be getting wet again.

My head barely touched the ground before Siggi White Hair woke me. I took off my boots but Siggi shook his head. "When you came back the last time the Jarl decided to keep the punt. We have been towing it. You get to land with dry feet."

Such small things bring joy.

Rather than using the pole, for the river was too deep where we had tied up, we paddled using the broken oar. Landing on the north bank we hid the punt under an overhanging bush. We had no idea how far it was to either Tours or the abbey. We did know that the abbey was a mile or so north of the town and we knew that the town had a wall. It was a cold morning and the sun had yet to warm the air. Later it would be hot. It always was in this part of the world. There was no riverside trail and we had to use Ulf's famous nose. The ground rose to the north and he led us thence. As we did I saw that another river joined the Liger from the south. It explained why it was so deep so close to the island. We were rewarded by a road just half a mile from the river. We hid close by to watch for travellers. I saw that it was cobbled which made it Roman.

We were about to begin to walk when I heard a whinny. Ulf looked at me and nodded. He pointed to our left. We crossed the empty road, for it was early, and headed over the scrubby land. After a steep climb, I saw a fenced field and there were six horses within it. Beyond the field, there was a hall and it was surrounded by a wall. This was a risk but the benefits outweighed the dangers. While Ulf watched, I crept into the field. I picked up some tufts of long grass and dandelions from a patch close to the fence and ditch. When the horses were between me and the wall I walked towards them. I clicked my tongue and spoke softly as I did so. I kept my gait measured and my head down. Two of them obligingly wandered over to us. I held out my two handfuls of grass and dandelions. They ate them for they were fresh, lush and green. The field in which they grazed had been eaten to the ground. I slipped a halter around the head of one as he nuzzled me and then the second. So far it had been easy but we had to get out of the field.

I led them back to Ulf. He pointed to the east. There was a gate. We kept the horses between us and the hall as we headed towards it. I was surprised that they did not have a guard upon the field although it was early yet. The six horses were valuable. When the Norns gave you a gift it was always as well to be wary. We opened the gate and led the horses to the lane which abutted the field. As we mounted I heard a shout. Looking to my left I saw two men gallop from the hall towards us. Ulf led us down the steep and narrow lane. I guessed that it would emerge at the road and I was right.

Instead of continuing to ride Ulf turned his horse and drew his sword. "Get on the other side. We take them when they come through!"

I drew my sword. I was acutely aware that we had no saddles and the two men who were approaching did. This would be harder for us. We heard their hooves as they clattered down the stone-lined lane. As the horse came out I swung at head height. Although the man leaned back to get out of the way of my sword it struck his chest and then hacked into his neck. His body rolled off the back. Ulf was having trouble controlling his horse and he missed with his strike. The man was a good horseman and he raised his sword to strike Ulf's bare head. I kicked my horse in the ribs. He leapt forward and I stabbed forward with my sword. My blade struck the man in his lower back. The sharpened steel scraped along his spine as he tumbled from his horse.

I grabbed the reins of his horse. "Here Ulf, ride this. It will be easier." I handed him the reins and then rode down the road to where the other horse grazed at the verges. I mounted that one. It was easier riding a saddled horse. The two spare horses followed us. While Ulf hid the bodies in the ditch I slapped the rumps of the two horses and sent them back up the lane. Hopefully, they would think the two horses had just got out by themselves. What they would make of the two missing men I did not know.

As we rode down the road I realised that although more visible now we would attract less attention. We rode side by side and we rode saddled horses. Viking raiders would never do what we were doing. It was easier that way and if we encountered anyone then I could speak. I was keen to ride quickly away from the house where we had stolen the horses but Ulf said, "No, keep this gait for galloping horsemen would be remembered. Two who are riding at a leisurely pace are not."

I noticed that there were many roads joining us from the north. The travellers were all heading towards Tours. While each traveller was wary of others, the fact that we all travelled the same road made us seem closer and less threatening. Ulf was right, we did not stand out. Glancing down I saw that Ulf did not have his feet in the stiraps. I said quietly, "Put your feet in the metal hoops. It is how they ride here."

Ulf nodded. I could see that he was uncomfortable like that. It had taken me some time to get used to it.

We saw Tours in the distance; that is to say, we saw a wall in the distance. It was on the south bank and there was a bridge. The drekar could not pass this place. We looked north and saw, on a hill, a monastery. Ulf shaded his eyes against the sun which had come out from behind the clouds sometime during the morning. He turned and said quietly, "If we ride quickly we can scout out the monastery and get back to the drekar before dark."

I pointed to the river. "That looks shallow but there is a beach here. We could land."

"Aye, but how would we turn around? The river has narrowed. This may be a church too far."

The bridge was a mile or so up the river and the sunlight glinted off the helmets of the guards on the bridge. There was a narrow road that climbed up the side of the slope to the monastery. I kicked my horse in the side and urged him up. Ulf tried to copy me but his horse was not responsive. I said, quietly, "Kick him in the ribs and slap his rump!"

As soon as he did that the horse followed mine up the gentle slope to the bank which lined the river. Now that it was moving we had to keep him going. We cantered along the tree-lined lane. The road was parallel to the river which we could see below us. More importantly, we could see the walls of Tours. There were guards there. I reined in when I saw the monastery before us. It was huge. The Jarl was right this was a plum worth picking. We approached no closer to the buildings as the road we were on went nowhere else. We did not want the monks suspicious. Ulf's sharp eyes took in everything. We turned and rode back to the main road. It was not long after noon and the traffic on the road had become a trickle. Those who were going there had reached it and the ones leaving were still enjoying the town. We trotted down the road. I was eager to be back on the drekar.

We saw no one for a couple of hours. We were approaching the fork in the river where the smaller one joined it when disaster struck. There were four armed and mailed men waiting on the road. We were trapped!

Chapter 12

They were a hundred paces from us. Ulf was the master of decisive action. "Ride towards them and smile. Speak to them. You have a silver tongue and your face looks innocent. When you think it right gallop through them. Use your sword to take one out if you can. I will follow. The first chance we get we go into the river!"

The prospect of jumping into a river with boots and sword on me did not appeal but he was the master. I nodded and urged my mount on. I smiled and turned to talk with Ulf. "They may recognise the horses, Ulf, but if we laugh as though something amuses us it may confuse them."

In answer, Ulf roared with laughter. It was such a loud laugh that our horses were a little startled. We drew nearer to the four and I saw that their hands were on their reins and not on their weapons. They had puzzled rather than angry looks on their faces.

Ulf shook his head as though he was still enjoying the joke and he said quietly, "That worked!"

It was my turn to laugh by which time we were almost upon them. I gambled and stopped my horse. A frown creased Ulf's face. One of the men said, "Where did you get the horses from?"

"Tours! The Constable there found two bandits riding them. Before they were taken off they said that they had taken them from down the river. The Constable asked us to return them. Are they yours?"

I kept my face and my voice as innocent as I could. The leader of the four was not certain whether to believe me or not. "Aye, they are."

"Then we return them."

"Where are you bound?"

"The Constable gave us a silver piece to return them. If your master gives us another then we will both be rewarded. We will find somewhere to stay. We are soldiers of fortune."

He turned to one of the men, "Gilles, tell our lord we have the horses. We shall bring them to him with the riders."

Gilles rode off and the man said, "Something about this does not smell right. Your story sounds reasonable but we are short of two men."

"Perhaps it was they who took the horses to Tours."

"No, I think not. Ride. The hall is not far away and if our lord believes you then he will feed you and you can be on your way."

I could tell from his voice and demeanour that he did not believe me but I smiled and turning to Ulf said, "We are to be fed! Perhaps some wine too eh, Captain?" I smiled so that Ulf would not be worried. He would have no idea what I said.

"Perhaps!"

Every step we took downstream took us closer to our drekar. We knew that the lane from the hall led to the river and our punt was nearby. We just had three men to deal with. All of them were warriors but I hoped that our behaviour had fooled them. One rode next to Ulf and the other behind. I rode next to the leader. The odds were still in their favour but only just.

The leader turned when we were, by my reckoning, half a mile from the punt. "You are a strange pair. You are a happy and cheerful youth and yet your friend there is taciturn not to say unpleasant. Does he not speak?"

"He is Saxon. We hire our swords out." I turned to Ulf and said, in Saxon, "I said you are Saxon."

He nodded and said, "Aye I am Saxon."

I doubted that they would understand but the interplay seemed to work for we were now less than four hundred paces from the punt and the lane. Ulf said, in Saxon, "Be ready. You take the leader and I will deal with the other two."

He was taking a chance but as they had not reacted to his earlier words it was unlikely that they knew Saxon.

"What did he say?"

"He wonders if we might have a bed for the night too." My hand crossed to my sword although it rested on the reins.

The leader laughed, "You have cheek, I will say that."

I turned to Ulf who nodded. I drew my sword and swung it at the leader. He was taken by surprise but his hand came up to fend off the blow. It was a mistake. His leather gauntlets just took the edge of the strike. The blade bit into his palm but, more importantly, he fell from the horse. I slapped his horse on the rump. It galloped off. I turned to see that Ulf had been more accurate. His sword had sliced into the guard's neck and the last one had taken off to race towards the lane.

"Quickly Hrólfr, get to the punt before they are on to us. I want to disappear!"

I galloped the last few paces to the hidden punt. I dismounted and tying the reins to the saddle smacked the horse's rump. It galloped off. I tore the bushes from the punt as Ulf did the same to his horse. We pushed the boat into the river and jumped aboard. The current took us where we did not want to go, downstream. If we went below the island we would struggle to get back. We both paddled as though our lives depended upon it and began to cross the river. The island had a narrow channel on the southern side and we aimed for that. The fact that we could not see the drekar was good. It meant it was hidden from our enemies. We heard a shout behind us but we did not turn. The boat was low and with luck, they would not see us. It was getting on to dusk. The night was our friend.

As soon as we entered the channel I breathed a sigh of relief. I saw the familiar shape of the Raven at the prow of our drekar. We had succeeded. Ulf steered us to the bank where we were hauled ashore. We could hear the cries from the northern bank. The Jarl looked quizzically at us.

"We had a little trouble, Jarl, but Hrólfr was quick-thinking enough to get us out of it. We have news! First though, food and ale. We have both deserved it."

They were eager to know our news and we were waited on hand and foot. Between mouthfuls, Ulf told them what we had found. After he had finished he said, "It will not be easy, Jarl. We will have to walk almost a mile from the drekar and there is a garrison at the castle."

"Is the prize worth it?"

Ulf grinned, "I have never seen such a big monastery." Sven joined us. "I know not how you will turn the drekar, Sven. The river is narrow. The *'Sea Serpent'* could turn, perhaps, but we are too long."

I wiped the foam from my mouth and said, "Remember the river which joined it."

"Hrólfr is right. But it is some miles downstream."

Sven rubbed his beard, "It is not easy but we can, if we have the current with us, take the steering board off and use an oar to steer. We could turn into the other channel and turn around there."

"Have you done it before, Sven?"

"No Jarl but I have heard of others doing it on the rivers of the Rus. There is no reason why it should not work."

Siggi slapped his thigh, "By the Allfather this will be something to tell our grandchildren about!"

Arne shook his head, "The likelihood of us ever having grandchildren is slim so it matters not."

Hrolf the Viking

We prepared for war on the island. We had no wheel but I used a whetstone to put an edge back on my sword. I donned my leather armour and my wolf cloak. I put the head over my helmet. I knew that it would frighten the monks and as the scout, it would be Ulf and me that they would see first. Fear was a weapon and we used it well.

As the crew rowed up the river Ulf and I stood at the bow to signal to Sven. The most dangerous part was as soon as we left the shelter of the island for I was sure that they would be seeking us. We had killed three of their men.

Once we passed the tributary the river became easier and it was slower. The last three miles were the swiftest we had rowed. I pointed ahead, "There is the beach Ulf."

He signalled for Sven to turn to the shore. While we were away Sven would untie the withy from the steering board and then it could be swung out of the water. It would not take long to re-attach. The two men who would guard the drekar leapt off first and secured us to the shore. Ulf was next off followed by me. We were less than forty paces from the lane which led to the monastery. I could see the lights at the end of the bridge but they would help us for the guards who were there would not see as far. Ulf and I ran. It was up to the rest to stay in touch with us.

When we reached the edge of the trees we stopped. The door of the first building was closed. It was not the church. That was further to the south. We waited for the rest to find us. I could hear the murmur of conversation. It suggested a large number of monks. Siggi joined us and nodded. Along with Arne Four Toes, the four of us ran towards the door. This time Gunnstein Thorfinnson and his men would seal the escape route of the monks. They ran alongside us in two lines.

When we reached the door Arne and I took hold of the two handles and pulled at the same time. Siggi and Ulf ran into the hall as the lights from inside flooded out. Even as we followed we heard the wail as they realised they were being attacked. Ketil and Knut followed us and the six of us ran through the huge hall. There had to be a hundred monks. They were eating and they were eating well. I had never seen a table laden with so much food.

Siggi White Hair might have been the oldest but he hurtled down the centre of the room. One priest stood to stop him and when Siggi ran him through it caused panic amongst the rest. They fled. The candlesticks they were using were all made of metal. Siggi shouted, "Knut! Collect treasure. The rest of you come with me." I sensed a movement next to me and a priest swung a long metal pole with a ball attached to it. I think it was used for incense. Had it struck me it could have injured me. I swung my sword sideways and hacked into his chest. I followed the others. We killed none save those who tried to stop us. Killing took time and we had no time. We had to gather all the treasures as quickly as we could. An older monk with rings on his fingers and a gold necklace around his neck tried to stop Ulf from taking them. One blow from his shield rendered him unconscious and Ulf took them anyway.

When we found the kitchens, it was a treasure trove in itself. There were sacks and sacks of wheat. There was enough to last us the winter. I went out of the side door and found a large handcart, "Ketil, help me load the cart with the grain!" We piled it higher than was safe but time was wasting. We could barely move it at first. We pushed it towards the lane. When we reached the top, it took all of our strength to stop it careering down the slope. We began to unload it. We had almost finished when Cnut the ship's boy shouted, "Warriors! Look!"

I saw armed men streaming over the bridge. "Ketil, get to the Jarl and warn him."As he ran off I said, "Beorn Fast Feet, Gunnar Stone Face, come with me we must stop them."

As we ran along the road I regretted not bringing my new bow. I could have slain some before they closed with us. We would have to slow them down. There were three of us and I counted at least fifteen men who were already over the bridge. Others were following. The shouts and cries had alerted the garrison. Gunnar stopped us just thirty paces from the drekar. "We wait here. Let us lock shields." As we did so he said, "I don't know what your wolf cloak will do to the Franks but it frightens me."

I almost burst out laughing for Gunnar's face and voice never changed. "Well, let us hope it does for we have fifteen men to slay. So long as a few are afeard it will be enough."

We held our swords above our shields and, with left legs braced, waited for the Franks. They came at us not as a wedge or even as a body but individually. Perhaps they saw three men standing before them and thought we would run. We were Vikings and we did not run. The leading warrior shattered his spear on my shield and ran into Gunnar's sword. Beorn took a blow from a spear and hacked at the warrior. He hit his arm. I was on the right and had no one to defend my side. Two men ran at me. I deflected a spear and twisted my sword up to score a deep wound on his arm. The other fell back with an arrow sticking from him.

I heard someone shout for them to stop and form up. I said, "They are going to attack together, let us fall back. Sven has the boys using their bows."

"On three. One, two, three."

Although we had not practised this we were used to working in rhythm and we stepped back as one. We took three steps and then the

Franks ran at us. They came together but they fought as individuals. As they came the three of us punched with our shields. At the same time, we stabbed over the top. I found flesh but I felt a spear strike and tear my leather mail. As I pulled my sword back I saw that I had penetrated a Frank's eye and my sword had entered his skull. I swept my sword to the side and the dead body fell from my blade and into the path of two men trying to get around my side.

Although three Franks lay dead before us I saw that both Gunnar and Beorn had been wounded.

"Back again!"

We stepped back but this time the Franks were pressed against us as we did so. Their spears could not find flesh. They clanged against our helmets and shields. Then I heard a roar and saw Siggi, Arne and Rurik hurl themselves bodily from the bank and into the Franks. Now we had a chance for the enemy were assailed from the side. I brought my sword over and struck a warrior on his shoulder. His mail held but his bones did not and he crumpled to the ground clutching his left arm. As I stabbed at the next man I brought my knee into his face and stepped over him. I could see more men racing from the town. Siggi, Arne and Rurik were whirling like madmen. Although the six of us faced a horde of Franks they were afraid to step close to our whirling blades.

Then from behind me, I heard, "Fall back! Wedge!"

I glanced over my shoulder and saw that the Jarl had formed a wedge. He was leading. The six of us knew what was coming but the Franks did not. As we stepped to the side the wedge ran at the disorganized Franks. They ploughed into them. With swords held above their shields and an impenetrable wall of wood and iron before them, they swept through the shocked soldiers. We joined in at the back and despatched any wounded we saw below our feet. The Jarl stopped the wedge thirty paces short of the bridge. The Franks had retreated as far back as they could get.

The Jarl raised his sword and shouted, "Raven Wing Clan!!"

We began banging our shields and chanting, "Raven Wing Clan!!" "Raven Wing Clan!!" "Raven Wing Clan!!"

When the Jarl lowered his sword, we stopped.

"Let us go back to the drekar!"

We walked backwards. It was less ordered than our attack for men stooped to pick up weapons and treasures from our dead enemies. The Franks did not try to attack. We had stunned them. To our right, I heard the crackle of flames as the monastery burned. The Franks had met the Vikings and they would remember the visit. I picked up the two swords from the first men I had killed. We kept glancing up in case the Franks followed, but they did not. I saw that dawn was breaking in the east but it would soon be obscured by a pall of smoke from the burning monastery.

The Jarl was the last one on the drekar and we all stamped our feet as he climbed on board. Sven then shouted. "You are facing the wrong way! Face the prow!"

Siggi started laughing as we all turned around and soon it spread to all of us. Once we began to row we found the current made it easier but the stern did not cut the water as well. Sven shouted, "You have a couple of miles and then we can turn around."

I turned to Siggi, "Thank you. If you and the others had not returned, we were done for!"

"If the three of you had not held them off then we would have had no drekar to sail."

Arne said, "And we will get those wounds seen to when we turn."

I had forgotten that I had been wounded and now that it had been mentioned I felt blood trickling down my side. It was not a deep wound but I had been lucky. I saw that Gunnar Stone Face would need stitches as would Beorn Fast Feet. They would be scars borne with pride. We had saved the clan.

It was daylight by the time Sven shouted, "Stop rowing! Turn around!"

While we did the drekar shifted alarmingly but he and his ship's boys soon replaced the steering board and we headed downstream again. We had the current with us and did not need to row. Siggi saw to our wounds and, as the ship's boys came around with ale I asked, "Who killed the warrior with the bow?"

Karl Blue Hand said, "It was I, Hrólfr the Horseman."

I reached down and brought out one of the swords I had taken. "Then this is yours. It belonged to the man you hit!"

Karl was popular and the crew cheered and applauded him. The Jarl's voice brought us back to reality. "Celebrate when we are beyond Angers and have anchored for the night. The Norns are watching. We all know how they like to tease men with hope and then snatch it away."

We knew he was right and we prepared ourselves. If we had to fight or row we would be ready. The Weird Sisters had decided to throw an obstacle in our way. Although we had been the one who had taken the withy from the rudder it was *'Sea Serpent'* which suffered the mishap. The steering board sheared. Sven thought that it had happened when they had grounded close to Tours. It mattered not. We had to hove to and repair it. We had just passed a small village on the north bank and so we used the south bank for shelter.

As I was wounded Ulf took the Eriksson brothers to scout the land ahead. If we rested, then we would be able to raid again before we reached the mouth of the river. I waited until Gunnar and Beorn had been stitched. If we did raid, then they would not take part. Rurik helped me take off my leather armour. I could see that the spear had struck between two of the metal plates.

Rurik said, "You have been hit here before."

I struggled to remember when and then recalled the fight with the three horsemen. I must have been struck a glancing blow. The armour was not new and my right side was always going to take more damage than my left. It was a lesson learned. The spear had torn through my tunic and kyrtle. The cut was not deep but it was long.

Rurik said, "I can heal this one, Beorn Beornsson. It is not deep."

Beorn Beornsson was stitching Gunnar and he shouted, "Make sure the wound is clean. If a scratch goes bad, then a man can die. Young Hrólfr still has his uses."

I swelled with pride at the praise. Using a mixture of vinegar, herbs and wild garlic Rurik cleaned my side. It stung but I was a warrior. We did not cry out. We kept a collection of linen that had been damaged. It was clean and Rurik made a dressing for the wound and then wrapped a piece of hessian tightly around it.

Rurik had just finished when Karl the ship's boy appeared, "This is a great gift, Hrólfr, I cannot accept it. I just loosed an arrow."

I sat up gingerly and, with my left hand, took out the second sword I had taken. "I took two and I have another at Olafstad. Why would I need a fourth? Keep it Karl and remember the first man you killed and the life of the shipmate you saved."

"Thank you, I will."

Rurik said, "Make a scabbard! It will rust else." Nodding he wandered off. "That was kindly done. Karl has no father."

"Aye, I know. I remember warriors showing me kindness when I joined *'Heart of the Dragon'*. I am just doing the same.

Ulf and the Erikssons came back. Ulf was scowling which I took to be bad news but his words belied his face, "I found the houses, Jarl. There is no wall on the riverside. It is on the land side away from the road and the hall looks to be partly made of stone. There is a church."

"Is it worth raiding?"

He smiled, "Oh aye, it is. We can attack at dusk. Even if the other drekar is not repaired it is only a couple of miles down the river."

"Are there warriors?"

"We saw none."

"Have you finished, Siggi?"

"Aye, Jarl."

"Then we go and speak with my brother."

When he had gone, Ulf turned and scowled at the Eriksson brothers who had gone back to their benches to rest. "What is wrong Ulf? You look as though you have eaten a bad egg."

"I have grown used to scouting with you, Hrólfr." He tapped my head, "You use this. Those two just look for what they can get."

Rurik nodded, "Their father was like that. I served with Erik the Wild for many years. We thought, when he brought his sons aboard, that we could change them. We thought we had but we were wrong. I think it is in the blood."

"Aye well, I take them scouting no more. They are both brave, I have seen that, but a good warrior uses his head. The sooner you are ready to scout again, the better."

"Do you think we will need to scout again this voyage? We have much treasure from the monastery." I pointed to the boxes and chests we had filled. We had not had time to take up the decking and store them yet.

"Probably not. We would need a knarr to take all that we could from this place. It is almost a town. I saw a hill which would be easy to defend if that had a hall or a tower."

"Perhaps they are not raided by Vikings. The Arabs attack with horses and not along the rivers. A wall on the landward side with a ditch before would be enough to deter horsemen."

Ulf nodded and raised his voice so that the Eriksson brothers could hear, "That is how a warrior uses his mind, Hrólfr. It is a pity others who are older do not!"

The brothers reddened and sank into their cloaks as the rest of the crew laughed.

Siggi and the Jarl stood with Sven at the steering board and we could hear their words. "My brother's drekar will not be ready until after dark. I have decided that we take the chance and raid at dusk. Ulf is right they will not expect it. We saw no other places on this southern bank save Tours and they will think we have fled. It is better than risking Angers and a river we do not know."

Sven rubbed his beard. "It is still a risk, Jarl."

"You fear they might come upon the drekar and take it while we are away?" Sven nodded, "I have thought of that. You will have the eight men who are wounded. They cannot fight but they can row. Use but one rope to hold you and if they come then cut the rope and sail down to the town."

"And your brother?"

"He is leaving half of his crew to repair and guard the ship. He is not happy with his ship's master for allowing the steering board to break. They had no spare."

Sven smiled, "Oleg is like all of the crew. He is young. He will learn."

"Siggi, tell the crew we raid. We leave before dusk." As Siggi passed down the drekar the Jarl came to me, "Are you up to a raid, Hrólfr? You were wounded."

"It is a scratch. I will go with you Jarl."

"You do not have to earn your place on my drekar Hrólfr. Do not try to be two warriors."

I shook my head, "I am not. This is who I am, Jarl. I cannot sit and watch others fight for me. It is not in me. I knew not my father. Perhaps I got it from him."

"Perhaps."

After the Jarl had gone, Rurik said, "I think it is the Norns, Hrólfr. They are moulding you. When we were alone on the island, with Erik One Hand I saw you change. Since you have gone ashore you have changed again." He pointed to Ketil and Knut. "They went ashore and came back exactly the same: wild and reckless! One day you will be a Jarl."

As we prepared for war I thought about his words. Rurik One Ear was a thinker. Living in a half silent world he would need to be. Since that day, I had been taken from Austrasia and that tiny village on the Issicauna by Jarl Dragonheart, I knew that I had grown both in size and as a man. Was that down to the Norns or did the Allfather have great things planned for me?

Chapter 13

Even though he allowed me to go with the rest of the clan the Jarl refused to have me in the fore with Ulf, Arne and Siggi. I was at the back with Gunnar Thorfinnson and his men. My side ached and burned. I took the burning to be a good sign. The dressing was working. I also wore my wolf skin. This time it was to give added protection to my damaged armour. It was a warm afternoon as we headed down the river bank. There was no wall but as soon as we were seen there would be resistance. We had to be ready to move quickly once the alarm was raised. Until then we were stealthy.

I hated being at the back. I could see nothing. When I saw the smoke rising from the roof of the hall on the hill I drew my sword. It meant we were drawing closer. Some of Gunnar Thorfinnson's men gave me strange looks but I saw that the Jarl's brother emulated me. At that moment, I saw the inexperience of the young leader. A rich father had meant he had a drekar but that could not buy the experience he needed to lead. There was a sudden shout from ahead and then the men before us ran. The alarm had been given. When we heard the clash of arms we knew that men were fighting us. These were not monks. These were men with weapons.

I pulled my shield around tighter and as I ran I was aware of the ache in my side. My wound would trouble me. I had to put the discomfort from my mind. There were spears ahead of me and, rising above the others, I saw that there were two horsemen ahead. They were in mail and they were shouting at more men behind them. That told me that this was a large number of men we fought. They had nobles ordering the fight. It would not be easy.

I stepped over Audun the Red; he was dead. His throat had been hacked by a weapon. There were others from our crew and they were lying on the ground amongst Frankish warriors. We kept moving to join the fray. The huts on both sides made the ground on which we fought narrow. Ulf, the Jarl, Siggi and Arne would be at the fore leading the fight. It was my duty to fight at their side. Only my wound had stopped me from scouting with Ulf.

I saw Knut Eriksson assailed by two men. He was in a gap between huts, to the side. Although neither of the Franks had mail they both had a helmet and a small shield. I put my shoulder behind my shield and ran at the one to his right. My sudden strike took him by surprise. He fell backwards allowing Knut to turn his attention to the other. The man on the ground was not about to go quietly to the Otherworld. He flailed his sword at my shins. I jumped to avoid it. That was a mistake as I felt my wound ache when I did so. When I landed, I crashed upon his knee. He screamed in pain. His arm flew up involuntarily and I silenced him with my sword.

I rejoined the press of warriors hurrying to help the Jarl. Siggi, Arne and Rurik were with the Jarl and heading purposefully towards the two horsemen. The gap between the huts had widened. Franks lay dead before the Jarl. The rest of our men were spread around in individual combats. The narrow passages on either side were filled with fighting warriors. I ran towards the Jarl shouting, "Knut, the Jarl needs our help!"

Knut slew his enemy and followed me.

I saw one of the horsemen make his horse rear. It was deliberate. He was using his horse as a weapon. A hoof caught Arne on the head and he fell. Enraged Siggi ran forward, recklessly, and plunged his sword into the belly of the horse. As he did so he pushed up with his shield. It protected his head and forced the wounded horse backwards. The dying horse toppled over and Siggi and Rurik leapt at the horseman on the ground. They hacked and slashed at him until he was dead.

The second horseman had a long spear and he was keeping the Jarl at bay while shouting for men to support him. I could see them running from a small burgh on the hill. I ran towards the horseman's right side. He was jabbing the spear at the Jarl who was trying to avoid it and the horse's hooves. The warrior wore mail to his knee and so I swung my sword hard at his hand. He had leather gauntlets but my blow was so hard that he dropped the spear. I suspect I broke some of the bones in his hand. With his left hand, he whipped his horse's head around to make it snap and bite at me. I did the unexpected. I stepped closer in and, as I did so, smashed the boss of my shield against the horseman's knee. The mail gave him protection from cuts but not blows. At the same time, Knut hacked at the horse's head. It reared as its throat was cut and then fell on the horseman. The Jarl stepped on top of the dying horse and slew the warrior.

In our moment of triumph, Loki played a trick. A second wall of warriors burst out of the town to join the ones descending from the burgh. I think that most men facing such odds would have fled for there were many of them and we were surrounded by the wounded and dying of the clan. The difference was we were Vikings and we fought for each other. Siggi was bloodied but unbowed. He stepped between the Jarl and me and shouted, "Shield Wall!"

Knut stood next to me and we locked shields. Ketil ran to the other side of the Jarl along with Beorn Beornsson. Rurik locked shields with Ketil. Behind us, the rest of those who had survived the first attack placed their shields over our heads. Our swords emerged like teeth from the front. The ones from behind added their blades. The Franks hurled themselves at us. There were now three ranks of us jammed between two huts with a dead horse and rider before us. One Frank used the horse to throw himself high into the air. He intended to smash a hole in our wall. It was brave. As he fell Siggi rammed his sword into his middle shouting, "Flying Franks die as easily as horses." Olaf punched his shield at the dead man and his body slid to the ground.

I could tell that Siggi had the smell of battle in his nostrils. I said, "I pray you do not go berserk, my friend!"

He laughed, "Not this day. This day I hew heads!"

I jabbed forward at the Frank whose spear tried to find a gap in the shields. I moved my head slightly and felt the spearhead scrape and grind along my helmet. As my sword found flesh Ketil and I moved our shields up. It trapped the spear. I twisted the sword and heard a scream. The Frank should have let go of the spear but something made him hang on to it. I pushed harder with my sword and he fell to the ground. We had another obstacle before us. Swords and axes crashed onto the shields held above our heads. Had we had spears we might have pushed them back but we did not and we had to endure the assault until the fourth rank arrived.

When we heard Gunnar Thorfinnson shout, "Rear rank! Push!" we knew that they had reached us.

I felt a shield pushed in my back and Siggi shouted, "One, two, three, push!" It was our turn to move but we had to move as one. There was an art to pushing in a shield wall. Everyone stepped forward with the left leg as they punched with their shields. The Franks were taken by surprise. They were fighting as individuals. Two fell but the whole line was forced back. The second action followed; we all stabbed and slashed with our swords. As they were still reeling from our push some found flesh. Their shields were not locked.

I saw the Jarl's sword cleave a head from a Frank's shoulders. He shouted, "Raven Wing and Sea Serpent, we push as one! One, two, three!"

This time the push from the last three ranks and our step forward happened at the same time. It was a much more powerful move. I had switched my sword from above to below. Alf the Silent had put his sword next to my head. As he jabbed forward I brought my sword up. The Frank was watching Alf's blade and he had a shocked look on his face as my blade entered his groin and then tore up through his middle. He gurgled blood and then dropped. I stepped carefully onto his body as we moved forward. The shield wall now had a life of its own. I could not stop even if I had wanted to. We were now walking steadily forward. Our feet were in time, as our arms were when we rowed. Blades hacked and stabbed from behind the impenetrable wall of shields. It was almost as though we were not individuals but one enormous killing machine.

Suddenly we broke the back of their defence. The wall of warriors had thinned and stretched around our flanks but the centre was now weak and one last push saw us trample over those who, moments earlier, had been trying to kill us. Those in the third rank killed them as we burst into the town. Before us we saw no more warriors; they were behind us and they were dead or dying. The people of the town had been encouraging their warriors and their menfolk and now they fled screaming.

The Jarl turned and saw the bodies of his crew and his face darkened, "Kill every man! No quarter! Any women and children will be enslaved!"

Men had blood that was boiling. They were in a killing frenzy. As eager warriors raced forward the women and children who had yet to flee did so. Some ran down to the river taking a chance on survival there.

Not all of the warriors were dead and as our shields were unlocked a Frank wielding an axe charged at me from the side. I held up my shield as he brought his axe from a long way behind his head. I was ready to strike with my sword. Siggi's lesson had been well learned. As he struck I stepped to the side and angled the shield. The head caught between a metal stud and the boss. My left arm was numb with the strike. I thrust forward with my sword for he was busy trying to extricate his axe. He wore a leather cuirass. Boiled and then moulded it was tough but I had a point on Heart of Ice and my sword was well made. It pierced the leather and I brought my left knee into his thigh as I stepped forward. My right side was still weak for such a blow. Even so, the effect was to overbalance him. He fell backwards and then rolled to the side. Weaponless he rose to his feet and ran towards the river. Before I could follow him, something clanged into the side of my helmet and made my head ring. Turning I saw a boy with a slingshot. Before he could throw another stone, a spear was hurled at him by one of Gunnar Thorfinnson's men and the brave boy died. They were narrow margins on the battlefield. Had he escaped he would have been a hero. As it was none would ever remember the boy who had hit a Viking and saved a warrior's life.

The battle was not over for there were still Franks who fought to save their homes and to buy their families the chance to escape but it was not combat. It was a slaughter. They were farmers with weapons who faced us; we were warriors. That was the day when the Sea Serpent clan came of age. They learned how to fight in a wedge and they learned how to despatch warriors who fought to the death with no thought of surrender.

As soon as the last man was killed we stopped to look to our comrades who had fallen. I ran back to Arne Four Toes. He had been felled by a blow to the head. When I found him, to my amazement, he was alive. He was seated with his helmet in his hands. The side of his head and face was a bloody mess and he seemed almost drunk but he was alive. "Siggi! Arne lives!"

Siggi raced over for, like me, he was certain that his friend had perished in the battle. "You should be dead! That blow would have felled an ox."

"Perhaps I have a hard head. Did we win?"

"Aye, we did." He pointed to the bodies of Audun the Red, Karl Karlsson, Sven Three Fingers and others. "They died well but I can hear Loki laughing at us. Did we think it would be easy?"

The Jarl's voice rang out, "Gunnar, fetch your drekar and mine. We will feast here tonight. We have fought enough today!"

"Aye brother! A great victory! Men will talk of this for years to come!"

Siggi White Hair frowned, "What if other Franks come? Should we not risk the river?"

As Gunnar and his men hurried upstream the Jarl took off his helmet and joined us. We were a dwindling band, "Look at the men, Siggi. Can they row? We have fought two battles in one day. The men are heroes. We eat and we feast. If enemies come, then we will fight them but the only men who could come to attack us are north of the river in Angers. It is why I bring the drekar. If they come and try to cross the river we let the current take us to the sea and to home."

Arne did not nod but he smiled, "It makes sense, Siggi. Besides I am weary and I need to rest. I will row in the morning."

"And I am starving!" Siggi nodded and shouted, "Ketil, do something useful. Butcher the dead horses. I made a start on one of them for you!"

We found no beer but there was wine aplenty. It was a little tart for my taste but it numbed the pain of my wound. Although the stitches had held blood seeped out. With the drekar tied up to the river bank, we all felt safer. While the food was being cooked, we ransacked the town. The church was emptied. We had a fine bronze bell which Bagsecg could melt down as well as linens from the altar and many candles and candlesticks. The more metal we could find the less iron ore we would have to steal. There were also great quantities of spices that could be sold for more than their weight in gold. There were many barrels of wine and there were bolts of cloth. They were probably the most welcome of our booty. Now that we had slaves we could have finer clothes made for us.

The hams, cheese and grains were also welcome. We had learned our lesson with the pigs and the boar was killed and cooked while the sow and the four piglets were led aboard the drekar with the fowl we had found. This time we caged the fowl. The warriors who had not fought kept a watch that night and we slept well. Before we left, at dawn the next day, the Jarl had every building fired. He wanted to leave the Franks a message. We had empty oars but we did not have to row too hard as we headed downstream. When we came to the junction of the Maine, which led to Angers we saw horsemen on the bank, many of them, and two boats waited close by.

Siggi White Hair had not had enough killing and he shouted, "Come! Take us on if you dare!"

They did not but they watched. Sven said, "We had best prepare for an attack at Nantes. Staying overnight was necessary but it has allowed the Franks to prepare a welcome for us."

The Jarl nodded, "Then we will meet whatever they have blade to blade. We have lost warriors but we are stronger because of it."

I shook my head and said to Rurik, "I am not so sure. It is not just the warriors who have been lost but the ones who are wounded."

Rurik said, "We must trust the Jarl. No ship has ever brought back such riches. We have enough to buy golden armour."

Siggi snorted, "Stick with iron and steel! Golden armour would make an attractive target for all your enemies!"

Sven's words created a certain amount of unease as we headed down the ever-broadening Liger. He was a measured, thoughtful man and if he feared a trap then we should be prepared. I sharpened my sword and then took out my bow. I had brought it with us but not used it. Something told me that I would soon.

Karl, who now sported the sword I had given him, shouted, "Ships ahead, Captain. A line of them across the river."

Siggi White Hair snapped "Count them, boy! Do they fill the river or are there gaps? How big are they?"

There was a pause and then he shouted, "There are ten of them and there are gaps between. Two are as big as *'Sea Serpent'*."

"That is better." He turned to the Jarl, "What do we do, lord?"

One thing I admired in the Jarl was his ability to make decisions and make them quickly. Sometimes they were not the right decision but you knew where you were.

"Signal my brother to follow us in line astern. Those with bows get to the prow. The rest on the oars. Siggi, I want to break through their line."

He stood and faced the crew, "Right you motherless dogs, today we shall row so fast that the drekar will rise out of the water and we shall fly over the Franks! We are Raven Wing and today we shall be as the raven!"

The men banged and cheered. I took off my helmet and went to the prow. As I passed him the Jarl said, "I want you to target those on their rudders. Let us see how good this Saami bow is eh Hrólfr?" He glanced up at the raven standard flying from his masthead. "Make the raven proud!"

There were eight of us. Apart from Erik Green Eye, the rest were young warriors. I chose my best arrow and knocked it. I knew that my side would hurt when I released it but I would have to bear the pain for the sake of the drekar. If they managed to stop us, no matter how good we were, they would overwhelm us with sheer numbers. We would not be able to use a shield wall on water. As Siggi set the men to rowing we were almost knocked over with the power they created. I knew they could not keep it up for long; they did not need to. We had to break through the line. Even as we approached I saw the middle two ships converge to trap us. They were the point of an arrow and the other boats fanned out behind them.

I had seen Snorri send an arrow over four hundred paces but that was from a wall and with the wind behind. I had to estimate and aim at a moving target. I aimed at the steering board of the ship to the right of me. There was a crowd of men there. I released it when it was three hundred and odd paces away. I guessed we would be closer when it hit. I did not hit the steersman; the Allfather himself would have had to guide my hand for that but it did hit the warrior next to him and the warrior pitched overboard.

The other seven all released their arrows but they barely made the bows of the ship. What they did do was strike two of the rowers. I saw men hurry with shields. I knocked another arrow and adjusted the flight. This time I hit no one but the arrow plummeted into the deck a hand span from the steersman. I quickly sent a third for we were just a hundred and fifty paces apart. The other archers were raining arrows on the rowers and as luck would have it they hit a number and oars were sent into confusion. Despite the steersman's best efforts, he could no longer hold a straight course and I finally managed to hit him. My arrow struck his leg and as he fell the steering board went overtaking the ship away from us.

Rather than heading for the gap Sven and the Jarl took the bold step of aiming directly at the second boat which was coming for us. The gap was now down to less than a hundred paces and I aimed at the warrior who was urging on his rowers. He wore mail and had a fine helmet. At a hundred paces, there was no more powerful bow than the one I held. The arrow went through his mail and pitched him amongst the rowers. The other archers showered arrows on the stern. The steersman fell with three arrows in him and the ship swung around, directly in our path. We were going to strike.

Sven the Helmsman was a skilful captain. "Steerboard side back water! Fend off their bow!"

There was no one in command and the ship came towards us as though the Norns were directing it. The ship's boys used the spare oars to keep the Frank from striking us. We would strike him! The Raven on the dragon prow had a long beak and it tore through the stays on the Frankish ship. Our bows collided. *'Raven Wing'* was better built. The Frankish ship sprang some seams and strakes. As our hull ground down the bow, the planks were torn from her and she began to sink by the bow.

The Jarl shouted, "Archers to the stern!"

I saw what the problem was. The first ship had regained control and was now heading directly for *'Sea Serpent'* with the smaller boats in attendance. I think we could have escaped but we could not leave our comrades to die. As we reached the stern I knocked an arrow. The ship was less than fifty paces from us but heading for the bows of the Jarl's brother's ship. My arrow hit the man next to the steersman. Erik Green Eye was a fine archer and his arrow struck the helmsman in the middle of the back. As another raced to take over the rudder two arrows hit him. The ship began to drift away from the threttanessa. Our last flight of arrows cleared the stern. Any of the officers who were still alive were hiding from our arrows. We were through the trap. Nantes receded in the distance and ahead of us lay the sea. We had escaped.

We were, however, sailing a damaged ship. We went back to our oars while the wounded and the boys bailed all the way along the Breton coast. The Jarl took an oar. We had a saga to sing and stories to tell. We had to reach our island home. The archery, the combat and the rowing were taking their toll on me. My side ached and burned so much that I dreaded passing out. There would be much shame if I did so. I forced myself to concentrate on watching *'Sea Serpent'*. I wondered about the wisdom of bringing such a small drekar with such an inexperienced crew. It had almost cost us.

As we headed up the coast I found my eyes drawn, not to the drekar, but to the land. Would my dream of a home in the land of the Franks ever be realised? The ones we had met had been defeated but there were so many of them. The horsemen near Angers were a warning of the numbers they could bring to bear to hunt us down. We needed more men but we needed experienced men.

"You did well today, Hrólfr." Siggi's voice was quiet and measured. He was a different man when we fought but now he was reflective. With his white hair, he could have been a grandfather.

"No, I was lucky. The bow deserves a better bowman than I."

"You need to practise. You are better with a sword and shield now. In fact, you are becoming one of the best. You just need to take the time to practise with the bow. It is a wondrous weapon."

I nodded, "It was expensive but worth it."

"You cannot put a price on a good weapon. That sword of yours; I would love to have had a weapon such as that. Mine is an iron bar by comparison."

"You should have had Bagsecg's father make you one."

He gave me a rueful smile, "When we were in Cyninges-tūn I was poor. It is only since you raided with us that I became rich enough. If we return, then I shall have one made."

Chapter 14

The poor drekar barely made it to the island afloat. Water surged and sloshed around our feet. We emptied the drekar as soon as we could. Gunnar Thorfinnson's men and the slaves all helped. We then hauled the drekar out of the water and as close to the high-water line as we could manage. It was only then that we could relax. I went with Siggi, Sven and the Jarl to look at the bow. It could have been worse. The strakes had not broken but the force of the blow had sprung them. Sven would need to hammer them back with fresh nails and then caulk the whole of the bow.

I rubbed the keelson into which the prow was fixed. "I am no shipbuilder but if Bagsecg could fashion a strip of metal thin enough it would help seal the front and give us added strength."

Sven rubbed his beard. "It would need to be both thin and narrow for we could not afford too much weight at the bow."

Siggi smiled, "We can ask him. A good thought, Hrólfr. You should know though that Sven is very protective about the drekar. It is like his bairn!"

Laughing Sven said, "Then you should be thankful that my child has brought you safely home."

Jarl Gunnar said, "And we are. I will make a Blót on the morrow. Ran and *'Raven Wing'* deserve it."

Erik had brought down Dream Strider. Nipper inevitably followed. When I fussed and stroked my horse's mane, Nipper jumped up also demanding attention. Siggi laughed, "And Hrólfr's children welcome him too!"

I knew I was being mocked but I did not care. The two creatures gave me unconditional love and loyalty. I thought back to the two horses which had been slain and I shuddered. I would hate for my mount to suffer such a fate.

We had so much booty that it took a whole afternoon to take it to the halls. The animal pen we had built was almost overflowing and we would have to build a second. The storehouse groaned under the weight of barrels and sacks. We had much work to do but it was work we relished for it was a measure of our success. As we ate, that night Erik told me that they had seen ships come close to the island and then sail away when they saw the smoke and people. That worried me. I preferred to be invisible and not to attract attention.

"Did you tell the Jarl?"

"Aye as soon as he landed. He too was worried."

"And you Erik, were you bored?"

He gave me a shy look, "I have taken a woman." He nodded to Brigid the alewife. She was bringing a fresh pail of ale for us. She smiled as she approached. They spoke not with their voices but with their eyes.

When she had gone, I said, "I am happy for you."

"I tell you this for I sleep in the alehouse now. I know she is plain but I have but one hand... Besides she has a good heart. Looks may fade but a good heart can keep you warm in the coldest winters."

Shaking my head I said, "You cannot know what the Norns plan for us. You are happy and she looks happy. It is *wyrd*."

He beamed, "Aye I know. My life changed the day **'Raven Wing'** sailed into the harbour that day. I did not know it then but I have made a sacrifice to the Allfather to thank him. I did not expect to be happy after I lost my hand but now it does not seem important. My left is as useful as a right and I have a place here. I have a mind to ask the Jarl if he will allow us to sell our ale."

"He might but you would need to buy your grain from him."

He nodded, "I have coin. I did not spend my share of the treasures we have taken thus far. And I have some seed. I thought to sow some barley. When you were raiding, I had the young boys help me to begin a malting floor for Brigid. It will help us malt the barley."

I nodded, "You sound like you have learned much already. I am impressed."

"You have many skills, Hrólfr: you are a warrior and a horseman. I am limited. This is something I can do. We will make the best ale we can."

I toasted him and quaffed the horn of ale I held, "And this is good ale! I shall miss your company in the warrior hall but I am happy for your new position."

As I looked around the hall I saw that many of the returning warriors were now looking at the slave women. Even Arne and Rurik were casting their eyes over some of the females. From the looks in the women's eyes, the feelings were reciprocated. The slaves had been here long enough to forget their past. That was oceans away. When the treasure and booty

Hrolf the Viking

was shared out then the warriors would be rich. The slaves were only slaves until a man chose them. That was the Jarl's decision. He had taken the idea from Jarl Dragonheart where slaves enjoyed great freedoms. Jarl Gunnstein Berserk Killer still used slave pens. I did not think it was such a good idea.

That night many liaisons began. There were huddles of cuddling couples in the warrior hall. I sat with Siggi, Sven, Gunnar Thorfinnson and the Jarl. I was not sleepy.

"Is there no woman for you, Hrólfr? Even Rurik One Ear is enjoying the company of a woman."

Siggi laughed, "Rurik has the advantage, Sven, that he can pretend he does not hear her! Hrólfr here has sharp ears. Besides he has greater plans."

I did not like to talk about the future. The Norns might hear and so I changed the subject. "Erik One hand now lives with the alewife. He wishes permission to begin selling ale."

The Jarl nodded, "Why did he not ask me?"

"He was a slave, Jarl. I have been one too. It is a great leap. He is a little afraid of broaching the subject."

"We will have to sell him grain."

"Aye, he knows. He has coin," I laughed, "seed money! He is also planning on growing grain."

Siggi frowned, "That is a big step. We came here to stay for the winter. Is this now our home?"

"It seems that it already is. I like it."

"Then we must protect it, Jarl." The Jarl and his brother looked at Siggi as though he had spoken a foreign language. "Sven here will need time to repair the drekar. Erik told Hrólfr that there were small ships sniffing around the island. What if enemies come? We need to hold what we have. When we raid how will our home be protected? If this is a temporary base, then it needs no ditch and no wall but if it is our home then we must protect it. We should know that!"

Gunnar Thorfinnson looked disappointed, "I had thought we would repair the *'Wing'* and then raid again. We have great riches already!"

Sven shook his head, "Your steering board broke; were I you, I would have my crew make sure my drekar is seaworthy. Ours was damaged in action!"

There was an edge to Sven's voice. He was criticising the young warrior and the Jarl sensed it. He spoke quietly. Tempers were becoming frayed and that was largely due to the drink. Brigid had brewed a strong ale and most had drunk deeply. "Sven is right, little brother, as is Siggi. I know you are keen to continue to raid but we are only as strong as the drekar we sail."

His brother nodded, "Sorry Sven, you are right."

"Tomorrow we divide the booty. That should make everyone happier. I will make the Blót and then we shall see about our defences. What do you suggest, Siggi?"

There was a puddle of foam on the table and Siggi used it to draw out his idea. "Had we known we were going to make our home here permanently then we might have thought about our halls a little better. We have made them low down to make them harder to find. We will have to use that." He drew a circle in the foam. "We dig a ditch just below the high part of the ridge and pile the soil on top. If we build a wooden rampart all the way around it will slow up an enemy."

Sven said, "We have little enough wood on the island."

Siggi pointed beyond the wall. "We use the captured fishing boats and hew them from the mainland. Wood floats; we tow them back."

"That would take a long time." Gunnstein Thorfinnson preferred action to labour.

"Aiden, Dragonheart's galdramenn, told me that the Roman warriors would erect a small fort each day when they marched and then take it down at night. We could do that. Make each oar responsible for one section. We could not do it in one day but the sooner we start the sooner we finish."

"Hrólfr is right. The Romans could build a mile of road a day."

I had a sudden thought. "If we brought some of the stones and cobbles from the beach then we could make a strong gate. We would only need one."

"Do you know how to make such a gate from stone?"

I shrugged, "Grind up stone and mix with sand. If we use water, then it might make a paste to hold the rocks together." I could see they were not convinced. "In the bay, there is a rock which when worn away mixes with the sand. I have seen some above the waterline and it was set like stone."

"Then we leave the gate to you. We will make a wall."

Sven said, "And another storeroom. The one we have has too much in. Food will waste and rot."

And so, we spent some time being not warriors but men. We wore no armour and carried no swords. We repaired the ship and we dug ditches. Siggi chose four of us to go with him to the mainland for the trees. He asked me to take my bow as it had proved so useful in the sea battle. He still worried about Arne Four Toes' head and so he took the Eriksson brothers and Rurik. The Eriksson brothers might not be the cleverest of men but they were strong and could wield an axe.

We sailed to a quiet spot well away from any houses. There was a stand of thin trees that would be perfect for ramparts. I was sent as a scout and as a sentry while the four of them hewed trees. The hewing was not difficult. The ones we wanted were as thick as a man's leg. The hard part was trimming them so that they were manageable. I went through the wood to watch from the far side of the trees. There was farmland to the east but I saw no one. A few sheep grazed on scrubland. It looked as though the wood had been more extensive at one time and had been cleared.

My time with Ulf Big Nose had not been wasted and I found that I could use my ears and nose far better than I used to. When I was satisfied that there was little danger of someone stumbling upon us I headed back. My nose caught the scent of an animal on the breeze. I knocked an arrow and I waited. Ulf had taught me patience. It paid off. A small herd of deer came through the woods, grazing as they came. I was still learning how to use the bow and I wanted them as close as possible. There was a large stag. I would leave him. Ullr would wish it so. Instead, I chose a large female. She looked older than the hinds she was with. I pulled back and aimed at the chest of the beast which came towards me. As soon as the stag's head came up I released. He had scented me and he took off. I was so close to the female that I could not miss and my arrow plunged deep into her chest. She tumbled for a few paces as the herd fled and then she fell, almost at my feet. Slinging her across my shoulders I headed back to the others.

Ketil was standing with his hands on his hips. They had chopped down twenty trees and stripped all the small branches from them. "How do we get them back? The boat is too small to carry them."

Siggi shook his head, "It is a good job you have a broad back, Ketil for you have nought between your ears. Haul them to the beach and I will show you." He saw what I had over my shoulders and said, "Put that in the boat and then help us."

I hurried down and threw the carcass in the bottom of the boat. I passed them each hauling a log. The longer poles had been cut into two. I grabbed one and headed back. I estimated that if we split them we could manage half of the ramparts we needed. Siggi had not returned for more. He was tying the logs together into a raft. I saw the wisdom of the plan. They would be buoyant and easier to tow. As I dropped my log he said, "We will have the Erikssons paddling this across."

When the logs had been brought Siggi said, "Now fetch the branches too. The smaller ones can be used to make charcoal. Bagsecg needs those and the rest can make supports."

It was late afternoon by the time we headed back to our island. Arne Four Toes watched from the haunted farmhouse and he gathered some men to carry our precious cargo to the ditch. It did not take us long and I was impressed with the size of the ditch and the mound. By using an existing dip and a small ridge we had a formidable barrier. Ulf Big Nose was in the bottom of the ditch and only his head was showing. When he saw me, he pointed to the gap where the gate would be. "And tomorrow I will enjoy watching you conjure stone pillars from the beach."

As I headed for the store I wondered if my hands could deliver what my mouth had promised. Siggi gave me Erik, Rurik and Ulf Long Nose to help me. We used Dream Strider and the cart to haul up the stones and the sand. I found the white stone which seemed to act with the sand to make something harder and we took that up later. The three of them looked at me expectantly. How I needed Aiden and his books. I was certain there was some way of finding out how to make it as the Romans did.

Erik said, helpfully, "We could use animal dung and hay such as they use on huts."

"Aye, and it might come to that. Let us spend the rest of the day seeing if this works." I tipped out the stone which I wanted ground down. It was a type of limestone. "Grind this down. I have another idea." While they pounded the stone into dust with hammers I groomed Dream Strider. The horsehair would make the set stone stronger.

When we had a large pile, I went to the gate posts. We had dug holes and there were two large trees from the island. They were the same girth and height. We had packed stones around them already. There was no getting away from this. I had to try something. I had my ingredients: stone powder, sand, pebbles and horsehair. We had less of the stone than anything else and that decided the proportions. We added water to make a very thick paste and then I added the horsehair. It felt too thick to use and I added a little more water.

Ulf shook his head, "What will this do?"

"When I saw it on the beach it had set. I hope this will. Shovel it over the stones in the holes."

The mixture did not go as far as I would have wished and the very top of the stones we had used for packing showed. I was disappointed. As we headed back to the hall for our meal Erik tried to cheer me up. "It might work."

Ulf snorted, "Not in this lifetime it won't."

I was restless during the meal and drank little. Had I allowed my mouth to make a fool of me? It would not be the first time. I wandered out of the hall while the rest were enjoying some of Brigid's fine ale. I went to the gate posts. The slurry we had poured in still looked wet. It had not worked. I went to Dream Strider and, without putting a saddle on him, rode him. I was no Aiden but I could ride and I could ride like the wind. I rode my mount as fast as I dared and when we returned to the stalls he was leathered and it was dark but I knew that I would be able to sleep. In the morning, I would face the derision and mocking of my crewmates and I would deserve it.

I woke before dawn and went to the gate. To my surprise and delight where it had been a wet sludge was now solid rock. It had worked. As no one else was up I fetched Dream Strider and groomed him. I would need more horsehair. When they woke, the others were as pleased as I was. The problem I had was to remember the proportions. We spent the morning gathering the materials and then we began the construction.

"We will make a layer of this sludge and place stones in it. We must choose the largest stones and the flattest stones. The bottom has to be stable. Now that we knew how it worked we were able to use that knowledge. It would take all night to set and so we had plenty of time to arrange the stones. The stones made the slurry rise and we had to put wood around the sides as we worked. We were learning as we did it. We only managed to build up to my knee. It would take many more days to build a gate post high enough to carry the weight of the wooden gates.

Erik had become more confident. He had built a malt house for his wife and he knew about construction. "If you put metal pins in the stones as we build then we can use them to hang the gates."

The four of us became a team. It was new to us all and there was no master, no expert. We all had something to contribute. Siggi and the others had finished the ramparts days before we had the gatehouse ready but there was no mockery. They stood and watched as we laboured. We had learned to do things quicker and the last half of the building process was the fastest. We built a wooden frame that held in the slurry and the stones. We had discovered that the wood peeled away from the stone.

The Jarl came as we were putting the last stones in place. We had to use ladders for that. "If we built four of these with a wall between then we would have a tower."

I shook my head. "We have almost used the last of the limestone, lord. We would have to get more."

He grinned, "Then perhaps we shall; master builder!"

It took another ten days to complete the construction and begin to tidy up the settlement. Once the walls were finished and while we completed the gates the rest of the two crews set to building a second storehouse and animal shelter. We had many more animals and with two young boars amongst the piglets, we were hopeful of increasing our herd. The shelter would make all the difference when the winter winds blew in from the west. It took us as long to hang the gates successfully as it did to build the animal store. However, as Siggi pointed out, the gates were far more important for they might be the difference between our survival and a bloody grave. As an added precaution Siggi insisted on a bridge that we could raise up and place inside the walls. We were so pleased when all the work was done that we had a feast and ate some of the older fowl which would no longer lay eggs.

Ketil and Knut proved to be good singers and they sang some bawdy songs. When they became more serious they sang of our deeds. That was a little presumptuous. That night a sudden late summer storm blew up. It sounded to me as though the air was filled with howling ghosts and spirits. Ketil and Knut certainly felt responsible for they walked around with heads hung the next day.

Sven had repaired the drekar but he worried that the storm might have undone his good work. He and his ship's boys swarmed over her the next day and it was they who raised the alarm. "Sail to the west!"

The message was passed to the settlement. It caused consternation for it was rare to see a sail of any description and we had never seen one from the west. Ships stood well out to sea or headed for the Breton port to the north of us.

The Jarl shouted, "Arm yourselves. Man the walls."

This was the first time we had had the opportunity to see our defences at work. On the inside, we had built up the soil by laying turf so that we could fight over the top. An attacker would need a ladder to do so. We left the gate open for we did not even know if the sail would approach. Sven and his boys raced in. "It is Raibeart and his knarr. He is sailing around to the old fishing place."

We relaxed and yet no one chided Sven for the false alarm. It could have been danger. Most of the crew of **'Raven Wing'** accompanied the Jarl down to the quay to meet with Raibeart. This could be just an accident but it was more likely that he came for a reason. We reached the quay before he did. The knarr was a tidy little ship. Jarl Dragonheart used it to trade. Often it was protected by some of his drekar while at other times it was used to spy. Dragonheart had many enemies and this was a way to keep an eye on them.

When he stepped ashore his face was serious. That was not like Raibeart ap Pasgen. He spoke without preamble, "Jarl Dragonheart has sent me. You are in danger. Hermund the Bent has gathered the sweepings of the sea to come here to raid you. He heard of the raid on the Liger. Every captain from Miklagård to Lundenwic is talking of it. Some say that you took away six ships filled with treasure."

Siggi laughed, "We have but two drekar!"

Raibeart nodded, "Sane men do not believe it. Those who know you do not believe it but Hermund the Bent sailed with you once and his words have credibility among those who have been unsuccessful at raiding. You seem to have the golden touch. The Empire has put a huge price on you and your crew. Hermund the Bent wins whatever happens. Jarl Dragonheart wished that you should know." He hesitated, "He wanted to come but he is assailed on all sides by enemies. He would have sent a drekar with men to aid you for he knows you are his man."

The Jarl waved away his apology, "We fight our own battles. We chose to come here and we will fight for our land." We all murmured our assent. "How many drekar and when can we expect the attack?"

"I left Cyninges-tūn four days since. The winds were in my favour the whole way. The rumour came from Jorvik. It is now more Dane than Saxon. He was recruiting men there. I am sorry. I cannot tell you the numbers nor can I tell you when."

"That was rude of me, Raibeart. Thank you for the information. Where do you go now?"

"Back to Cyninges-tūn. I have some goods to trade at Dorestad and that will be my only stop."

"Then I would beg a favour of you. We did find many treasures on the Liger. We have some Holy Books and treasures. Would you sell them for us in Dorestad? We are hunted there."

Raibeart laughed, "Aye, that you are. You would trust me to get a good price?"

"You are of the land of the wolf. Of course, I trust you. We will come to Cyninges-tūn to collect the payment when this trouble is over. We will pay you a tenth as the broker."

"That is kind. We had better load my knarr. I would not wish to fall foul of the drekar of Hermund the Bent."

"No indeed."

It took some time to load the knarr and it was late afternoon when he set off towards the north. It took courage to do what he did. His ship was unarmed and he had a small crew of just twelve. He had to live on his wits and his skills as a sailor. I wished him good fortune.

As we headed back to the settlement Arne Four Toes rounded on the Eriksson brothers. "Next time stick to the silly songs! You have angered the Norns!"

They nodded their agreement. They knew they had.

Once we had crossed the bridge we had to begin to plan. "Gunnar, I want ten of your men to stay with Sven and the two drekar. If Hermund the Bent has any sense, then he will disable the ships. Without them, we are trapped here." His brother nodded. "Sven, at the first sign of trouble I want you to cut and run. Sail wherever the wind takes you. Hermund the Bent was not the best sailor in the world. You should be able to outrun him."

"And you, Jarl, what will you do?"

"I will stay with my people and we will defend our island. If we are meant to die, then so be it but we will not go quietly!"

Every warrior raised his voice in assent. The fact that we did not know what odds faced us did not worry us. We would fight to the death!

Chapter 15

I was used as a mobile sentry. I rode, the next morning, to the northwest corner of the island where I watched for sails. I was grateful for I knew not if I would have the chance to ride Dream Strider much in the days to come. The rest of the warriors and the people worked tirelessly to prepare for an attack. Bagsecg worked from first light to produce arrowheads and slingshots from the lead candlesticks we had taken. He hammered out as many spearheads as he could. Water was gathered from the spring and the fish that had been drying on the shore were brought to the storeroom. The Jarl was seen as prescient for having the foresight to build a second store. We would need it now. The two crews made our home as impregnable as we could.

I spent all day either on the tip of the island or riding around it. When I returned at night I was greeted with a sea of expectant faces.

"No sign of an enemy."

"Perhaps they will not come."

"They will come, Arne Four Toes. If men are recruited from the cesspit that is Jorvik then it is for a reason. Hermund the Bent knows us and knows this island. He will come. We use this grace to make us a hard nut to crack."

I was more worried about nighttime. What if they came then? Our sentries would only see them when they were close to the walls. Could we afford to keep men on the walls all day and all night? Perhaps it was those worries which gave me my bad dreams. Warriors crept, like the ghosts and spirits of the dead from the very walls behind which we sheltered. I woke up with a start, sweating and fretful.

Rurik was woken by my movements. "What is it? Have you heard something?"

I shook my head. "I dreamed that warriors' spirits materialised from the very walls."

He smiled and shook his head, "We built these walls. None are dead in here. Now in the farmhouse... aye there are spirits there."

That was where my idea was born. I went the next morning to see Siggi. I explained my idea and, rather than pouring scorn upon it he thought there was enough merit in it to take me to the Jarl. He was eating with his brother.

"Hrólfr has an idea, Jarl. I think it deserves a hearing."

"Speak."

"I worried last night that our enemies would come at night." I pointed to the west. "If they come that way then the men on the drekar will see them. They have to come from the north and there, we know, is only one place they can land."

"The fisherman's hut and bay."

"Aye, lord. I think we should have a couple of men placed there. They can act as sentries and give warning."

"That is a good idea..."

"There is more Jarl." Siggi White Hair was one of the few with the temerity to interrupt the Jarl.

"Carry on Hrólfr."

"Hermund the Bent will lead and he knows the island but he also knows of the people he murdered. He will avoid the farmhouse; it is haunted. If the men who watched waited, then they could kill in the night and prey on the men Hermund leads. If they were looking over their shoulder, then they might think that spirits hunted them."

"I am not so sure about that."

Siggi said, "Our men did not murder anyone and yet they fear to be close to the huts at night."

The Jarl viewed me with a critical eye, "This is not you trying to be Ulfheonar is it?"

"No, Jarl, I would not be so foolish. I do not have the skills but nonetheless, I believe that three or four of us could move around this island we know and make them look over their shoulders. That is what we need; fear in their hearts. If we make them think that we are behind these walls they will think that their sheer weight of numbers will gain them entry. Imagine them each night waiting for the knife in the night and the cry of death."

"You have convinced me of the idea but who would do this? Who has the heart to hide by the dead?"

"I would."

"Then you have more courage than I do, Hrólfr the Horseman."

"And I."

I turned to Siggi and, summoning up all the courage I could muster I said, "Not you Siggi White Hair."

His face reddened, "Not me!"

"We need three or four men who are quick, young and can disappear. You will be needed behind the walls to give our people courage. I mean no disrespect, Siggi. I doubt not your courage."

He was silent and then he smiled and nodded, "It takes courage to face an old bear like me and you are right. I would not be happy with slitting a throat and running away. The blood would boil and so would I. Then you need Ulf Big Nose for he is silent and he would be leader."

The Jarl said, "And Alf the Silent."

I nodded. I had been thinking of him.

"And me. I will go."

We all turned as Gunnstein Thorfinnson spoke. "You little brother? Have you the skills to be patient? Can you follow the order of someone like Ulf Big Nose?"

He straightened his back a little and jutting his jaw said, "Brother I have made mistakes. I know that. But I have watched and I have learned. My men and I are part of this clan. We are new and we are raw but we would be part of this. I swear that I will obey orders. Let me do this."

The Jarl looked at Siggi, who nodded. "Then I will send for Ulf and Alf. I will order no man to do this. If they volunteer, then so be it."

When they came, it took a heartbeat for them to agree. Ulf looked not at me but at Gunnstein Thorfinnson. "I give commands!"

Gunnstein Thorfinnson nodded, "You give commands."

Ulf nodded, "We need a fifth."

The Jarl frowned, "A fifth?"

"Someone who can bring the message back to the settlement. He does not need to be silent. He needs to be quick." He rubbed his chin, "Karl Swift Foot. He is young but he can run as quickly as Dream Strider. We will need bows. They can kill silently." He smiled, "We need black feathers. If we give the shafts the feathers of the raven, then it will add further fear to their hearts and minds."

Siggi nodded, "And it sends a message to them that the dead are coming for them."

I left for my patrol while Ulf and Siggi organised our ghosts. I looked out to sea but my mind was on the night and on our task. I had returned to the end of the island and, as it was late in the day mounted Dream Strider. As I peered north and west I saw something against the setting sun. I forced myself to close my eyes and open them again. There was no mistake. There were sails and there was more than one. It had to be Hermund the Bent.

I estimated that they would take some hours to reach the island and so I watched for as long as there was light. I counted three drekar. When

I entered the gate the faces were worried rather than expectant. Siggi said, "We thought something had happened."

"And it has. I saw three drekar heading this way. They will reach the island before morning."

The Jarl nodded, "Send a message to Sven. Ulf, you know what you must do. May the Allfather be with you."

"I will fetch my bow and catch you up."

I dismounted and led Dream Strider to his stall. Erik One Hand hurried over, "Have they come?"

"They are Erik. Tomorrow you get to test your skills with the sword."

"Aye but I have something to fight for. I have a wife and an unborn child."

"You are to be a father?"

He nodded shyly, "I am. Brigid felt it kicking."

"Good I am happy. Will you care for Dream Strider? I know not how long I will be away."

"Of course. I have missed him"

I rubbed his mane. "I will return, Dream Strider."

I went to the hall and grabbed my bow. I emptied the quiver for I would need the black fletched arrows. I donned my helmet and took my wolf cloak. We would not need our shields. Bagsecg had had no time to finish my mail. *Wyrd*. If I survived I would wear it. Ulf and the others waited impatiently. Rurik One Ear handed me my arrows and I put them in my quiver. The five of us left without further ado and we loped off behind Ulf.

When we reached the hut, he said, "You are now under my command. I am Hersir until this is over." He nodded to me, "Hrólfr is the only one who has worked with me as a scout before. The rest of you listen. Use your eyes and your ears. Use your nose but from now on be as Alf the Silent and do not use your voice! We use hand signals. Hrólfr knows them. Hrólfr, go and watch from the headland while I teach them."

I went and looked out on the dark bay. The drekar would be beating down past the Breton coast. They would have to steer clear of the rocks which were there. That would add time to their voyage but once they saw the bay then Hermund would use his knowledge to move quickly inland to the hall. A whistle summoned me back to the hut.

"I want Hermund the Bent to come here. We light a lamp so that he thinks there are people within. Gunnstein Thorfinnson go with Alf the Silent and Karl Swift Foot." He handed him a thin cord. "Cover the path with small stones from the beach. Walk up the side so that you do not disturb them. Lay trips at the head of the path. Half bury stakes so that when they fall they impale themselves. Work backwards so that you do not fall foul of your own traps. When you are done then go to that piece of high ground behind the midden. The stink will hide our smell."

When they had gone, he led me into the hut. He lit the seal oil in the dish. A soft glow filled the hut which seemed stark and empty. "We need to make your ghosts and spirits. Find any clothes you can."

I heard him hammering behind me. I found a chest in the corner. I opened it and found a couple of shifts. They must have belonged to the woman who had been murdered. I returned with them to Ulf who had been fiddling on close to the door.

"Excellent." He dragged the table over so that it was over where the dead fire would have been. "Tie the shift so that it hangs from the roof beams."

It was not easy but I managed it. When I descended, we moved the table to the back wall. He took the mattress which they had used for sleeping and laid it on the top. Then he placed the second shift upon it. He found a half-broken pot and placed it at the top. In the glow of the light, it looked like someone was sleeping.

"Light a fire. I do not care if it smokes just so long as it is alight."

There was kindling and wood chips in the corner. They had been there so long that they were bone dry. Using my flint, I soon had a fire going.

Ulf turned from his work at the door. "Not too big. Go outside and fetch some damp wood which will burn slowly. Slip through the door and go around me."

There was a narrow gap but I made it through. There were plenty of small logs and I chose the eight which were the dampest. I returned and put them on the fire. The room began to fill with smoke. Ulf nodded and pointed to the shift hanging from the roof beams. It was swaying in the air currents. The table and shift now looked, in the smoky interior, more like a body.

"We are done. You go out while I finish this last trap." As I passed him I saw that he had rigged large stones above the door. They were supported by a piece of wood. When the door was opened, the rocks would fall. He pointed to the floor, close to where he stood. There were sharpened stakes in the floor. That was what he had been hammering.

We joined the others at the midden. "Karl go and stand closer to the bay. When you see them return to us. Say nothing. The fact that you are running for the settlement will tell us all we need to know."

"Aye Ulf. May the Allfather be with you."

He ran off and Ulf said, "This is the last time we speak until this is over. When they come, they will investigate the fire and the hut. The traps and the trips will make them wary. The hut and its tricks will also make them both fearful and afraid. They will be in the dark. I want them looking to the ground. I will release the first arrow. You will all release five flights, no more. Choose your targets and do not waste an arrow. Then we run to the west. There are rocks and narrow paths. Hrólfr will lead for he knows them well. We take them away from the settlement. When dawn comes, we go to ground." He looked at me. "You judge."

"Aye Ulf."

"We evade them during the day and then we will strike at night. By then I am guessing that they will be attacking the walls."

And that was it. We waited, each with an arrow ready to knock.

Time passes slowly when you are waiting. Although we could not see the light from the hut we did not look there. We looked out to sea. There were clouds and the drekar would be able to slip in unseen. That was why Karl Swift Foot waited where he did. A sudden movement made my hand tighten on my bow and then Karl ran by. He raised his hand and was gone. Not a word was said. The four of us watched. The midden afforded some protection. It was higher than the hut and as we were kneeling we could not be seen. We listened.

It was the sound of skittering stones that alerted us. They were coming up the path. When Ulf knocked his arrow, we followed suit. The cry, when it came, made me start. They had found the first of the traps. There were no more cries but there were grunts and noises which suggested that they had fallen foul of our tricks. We were thirty paces from the hut. Only our heads were above the midden and we could see the hut clearly. I saw figures approaching and then they stopped.

I heard Erik Karlsson's voice. "They were killed! Who is in the hut?"

"Shut up you fool!" Hermund the Bent's voice brought back many unpleasant memories for me.

"Arne the Unlucky's cry as he died told them we are here. Why do they not come out?"

Harald Black Teeth's voice hissed, "I am not afraid of the dead. I did not murder them. Einar and Erik go inside and see who is there."

There was a pause and then a scream. It was not a scream of pain but of shock, "A ghost! There is a spirit within the hut!"

Hermund the Bent shouted, "Get in there! It is a trick!"

We could only see the warriors who were gathering outside the hut. They were shadows. The whiteness of their faces was just a lighter shadow. They gathered and they watched. The next screams were of pain as the men who ran in set off the traps. There were a few moments of confusion and more shouts before Hermund the Bent restored order.

"See, it is a trick! I told you. Get these wounded men down to the drekar!"

"What of the dead?"

"We can do nothing for them. Leave them here."

Ulf's timing was masterful. He stood and we followed him. He released his arrow high. I knew the power of my bow and I aimed at a warrior forty paces away. We did as he said and released four more arrows in swift succession. As they struck then confusion reigned. Warriors fell to the unseen shower of death. I was almost mesmerized by the effect until Ulf smacked my back and I turned and ran along the narrow path which led west.

"It is an ambush! Shield wall!"

The first part of the plan had worked. I led us along the path until we passed the small stand of trees and then up into the jumble of rocks a hundred and twenty paces from the trees. I halted. Ulf gave me the sign that he approved. He waved his arm and we spread out. He pointed down the trail and held up five fingers. We nodded. We would do the same when they came. I saw the glow in the east which told me that dawn was not far away. We had feared a night attack and that would not happen now.

The jingle of mail warned us of the approach of the warband. They moved slowly through the woods. That would have seemed like a perfect place for an ambush. I saw warriors spread out on both sides as they headed west. Ulf nodded and pulled back on his bow. This time we could aim. The enemy was silhouetted against the faint light of early morning sun. My arrow smacked into the chest of a warrior whose shield came up too late. My powerful bow punched him backwards. My second arrow caught a man to the right of me. He must have thought he was too far away. My arrow pierced his shoulder and he fell. Shields came up and the warband hunkered down. Ulf gave a low whistle and nodded when I turned. I rose and ran down the other side of the rocks. The warband would struggle to find an easy way across and the ground was boggy on both sides of the rocks.

I led the others further west. There was a cave close to the cliffs. I had seen it months earlier. It was a difficult approach to get to it and we could shelter there. I opened my legs as we dropped down to the wider path on the other side. There were bumps and hollows and it twisted and turned. I had ridden it every day with Dream Strider and I knew it as well as my own hand. So long as the others followed my every step we were safe. The lightening sky was alarming but I saw the path drop to the left and knew that the cave was close by. We hurtled inside.

Ulf nodded and made the sign for us to wait. He disappeared. We sat and got back our breath. We each had a water skin and some dried venison. We drank first and then chewed the tough deer meat. It took some time and we had finished it long before Ulf returned.

"They have gone back to the drekar. I think they are licking their wounds. I counted five dead warriors by the woods. Gunnstein Thorfinnson, you take the first watch. When your eyes are heavy wake Hrólfr. Hrólfr wake Alf."

I nodded. I curled up in the shallow cave. I was certain that sleep would not come. I was too full of the joy of battle. When I was shaken by Gunnstein Thorfinnson I was surprised. He smiled, "You snore Hrólfr, like an old man!"

I did not think I would sleep. "Have you heard anything?"

"The sea birds and that is all."

I went to the cave entrance and peered around. It seemed quiet. Climbing to the top of the cliff I kept myself low. I was too far to see the settlement and the drekar but if the wind was in the right direction then I might hear. It was silent. I made water and I watched. Seeing nothing I headed back to the cave. I caught sight of movement in the trees. I dropped to one knee. I spied a branch moving. A leaf could be explained away but not a branch. I crawled back to the cave. Shaking Ulf awake I said, "I see warriors approaching."

"How many?"

"I know not; I just saw movements in the trees."

He smiled, "You did the right thing. Better a disturbed night's sleep than a slit throat." The other two had awoken. "Arm yourselves and follow me!"

I strung my bow. We would need it. Ulf waved me to his right and indicated that I should swing towards the higher ground. I would be alone. I took it to be a compliment that he trusted me but wished to have the other two close by him. Moving as stealthily as I could I moved through the thin bushes and stunted windblown trees. A bird, twenty paces from me, took flight. I knocked an arrow and waited. I was rewarded by a warrior carrying a shield and an axe who slipped towards the others. He was thirty paces from where I hid. I waited until I could see the flesh below his ear and sent an arrow towards him. My new bow was so powerful that the speed of the flight compensated for my lack of accuracy. It tore through his neck and he fell to the ground noisily. The crash of the body and his shield brought a call.

"Ragnar?"

The voice came from directly ahead of me. Without moving my position, I knocked another arrow. This time I saw two warriors. One I could slay with an arrow but not the second. The lack of noise to my left led me to believe that the others had not been discovered. Ulf had given me a task and I had to do it alone.

When they were thirty paces from me I released the arrow. It sped through the leaves which masked my face and struck the warrior on the right in his chest. He wore leather armour studded with metal but the Allfather guided my hand and my black fletched arrow found his chest. Dropping my bow, I drew my sword and my seax. The second warrior knew roughly where I was and moved towards my hiding place. The fact that he had not called out gave me hope. If they were a large number, then he would have shouted for help. They were a scouting party searching for us.

Staying crouched I waited for him to come to me. By remaining still, I made it hard to see me. I knew he would and I had to time my movement perfectly or I would die. He was five paces from me when I made my move. I lunged from the bushes. He reacted quickly but I was attacking from his right. He brought up his sword but he was not able to totally deflect the strike. My blade tore deeply across the back of his hand and into his upper arm. He shouted, not in pain, but in anger. Behind me, I heard more shouts as Ulf and the others began to fight.

The warrior facing me had a shield and he had a leather shirt. He was a broad warrior and would take some stopping. As he twisted to attack me I stepped across his shield and brought my sword around across his back. He had no mail and my blade bit into his ribs. He swung around to try to use his own sword. My left hand darted forward and my seax plunged into his throat.

I ran back towards Ulf and the others. When I reached them, I saw the three dead bodies of our enemies. Ulf looked up as I approached. "Do any remain?"

I shook my head, "There were three; they are dead."

"Good. You did well. Search the bodies and take anything of value then we will send their bodies to Ran. "

The first thing I did was retrieve my bow and the two arrows I had used. Whilst not perfect they could be used again in an emergency. Then I took the weapons, helmets and mail from the dead men. I met the others who had disposed of their own bodies. They carried the ones I had slain. We threw them from the cliff.

Ulf said, "You have grown, Hrólfr the Horsemen. The younger man, who first came to us, would now be lying dead."

The four of us armed ourselves and then headed for the settlement. We moved cautiously; we moved slowly. The fact that we had been hunted by the enemy showed that Hermund the Bent had not left, he had not gone home. He would be attacking the settlement. We saw our wooden wall before we saw the pirates and bandits Hermund Harald Black Teeth had gathered. I saw the Eriksson brothers on the wall. They were shouting down to someone we couldn't see.

Ulf raised his hand and pointed left and right and then back down. I moved to the right. I made my way towards the settlement's walls. If Knut and Ketil could see and talk to our enemies, then I knew where they would be. I crept over the top of the rise. Before me was the camp of the enemy. It was haphazardly organised. The blackened fires showed that. This was not a clan. This was a collection of warriors who joined together for this one raid. If they succeeded they would dissipate like morning fog. I lay on top of the small bank. My wolf cloak covered my helmet. If they glanced in my direction they would see just a shadow.

Knut and Ketil were shouting to five mailed warriors whose backs were to me. I had to smile when Ketil turned around, dropped his breeks and bared his backside. One of the mailed warriors hurled a spear. It was not well thrown and it thudded into the wooden wall. Knut reached down, grabbed it and threw it back. It smashed into a shield. The warriors turned and ran back from the wall.

As they turned I recognised Harald Black Teeth. His blood-red shield with a white skull painted upon it marked him as my enemy. I was sorely tempted to knock an arrow and end his life there and then. The Heart of Ice filled my mind and calmed me. I might kill my enemy but I would die and worse it would warn the enemy that we were still a threat.

I watched him as he hurried back to his warriors moving beyond bow range. They were less than forty paces from me and I dared not risk moving. They began to prepare for an attack. I saw men donning armour and sharpening blades. Less well-armoured men began to gather in small groups holding ladders.

It was at that moment I realised that the main gate was further around the wall from where we waited. I was on the north wall. I heard a clamour from ahead. The enemy were attacking the gate. My heart began to sink down to my sealskin boots. They were doing just what Siggi feared, attacking two places at once! I laid down my bow and drew my sword and seax. I saw that the enemy had moved closer to the walls. Shields protected them from the defenders. It looked to me as though Ketil and Knut had been left in charge of this wall. I was alone. There was no one to give me advice or instructions. Did the Weird Sisters plan for my dream to end here? I had to put that dream to one side. The clan was in danger. There were fifty or more warriors before me. I knew that Ketil and Knut could have no more than twenty men to man the walls.

Harald Black Teeth began shouting to his men, "Today we scale these puny walls! We slaughter these pink arsed boys and give them the blood eagle. The treasure will be ours!" They all cheered. "Remember that they have riches beyond measure! We take their heads to Frankia and their King will give us a thousand gold pieces!"

There was greater cheering. They began to bang their shields. In that moment, I knew that Harald Black Teeth lied. We had a great treasure but not worth a thousand gold pieces. I had no doubt we had a price on our heads but it was not a thousand gold pieces. With a roar, they ran at the wall. Stones clattered off helmets, shields and mail then arrows followed. Only two men fell and neither looked badly wounded. I saw that Harald Black Teeth and his oathsworn hung back while there were four warriors left guarding the camp. As I watched Roald Iverson pitched from the walls I took action. I moved swiftly and silently towards the nearest warrior. He was watching the walls. I dragged my seax across his throat and lowered his body to the ground. The other three continued to watch the walls. There were two standing together. Neither wore mail and their hands rested on their spears. I took three fast steps and stabbed one in the side. Heart of Ice crunched through his ribs. As the other turned I lunged with my seax and plunged it into his throat. The last warrior saw me.

"Jarl! We have enemies! "

He raced at me holding his shield up before him. Although I desperately wished to run, for Harald Black Teeth's oathsworn were running towards me, I had to finish this warrior first. He had a spear so I ran at him. I punched away the spearhead with my seax and, lowering my shoulders, ran at him. My helmet crashed into his head, jerking it back. He spread his arms wide to regain his balance and I stabbed him in the stomach with Heart of Ice. I did not wait to see the results. I turned and ran, sheathing my weapon as I did so, I headed for my bow. I had hung it from a branch and I grabbed it as I ran. I could hear Black Teeth's oathsworn behind me but I resisted the urge to turn.

I twisted and turned down the trail. I was young and I was quick. I heard the warriors following behind me. My consolation was that were four dead men and eight warriors chasing me. Those twelve could not fight on the walls. Each man we killed prolonged the lives of those within. It was up to Ketil and Knut to fend off our foes. The Weird Sisters have a subtle way of teasing men. The steps behind me seemed further away. I began to relax then I stepped into an animal hole. I pitched forward. My bow was thrown clear as I hit the ground.

"Got the bastard!"

I turned in time to see a sword sweep down to sever my head from my body. Unencumbered by weapons I rolled to the side. The sword hit the ground where my head had been a moment earlier. I struck a thin tree and I used it to pull myself up. The sword swept towards me again. Still holding onto the tree, I stepped out of the way, releasing the sapling. It struck the warrior squarely in the face and as I stepped back I drew my weapon. The tree had given the warrior a bloody nose; he wiped the blood away with the back of his hand.

"You worthless little whey-faced runt! I will gut you and let the animals of the forest feast on your flesh!"

Over his shoulder, I saw his companions labouring down the trail. I did not have long. I feinted with my seax. His eyes were still streaming. He brought his sword up involuntarily. His eyes were on my seax and when my sword darted in he did not react in time. My blade pierced his cheek, grinding on bone. He stepped back and spat out a tooth. Two of his companions were closer so I turned and ran. I could not see my bow. I would return for it later.

The enraged warrior shouted, "After him!"

The Norns had taught me the dangers of complacency and I watched my footing as I ran. I headed back towards the cave. Suddenly something flashed through the leaves and I heard a cry. I turned and saw a warrior with an arrow in his chest. The one behind looked around for the danger and he was rewarded with an arrow that struck him in his neck. The other two turned and ran.

Ulf appeared, his bow in hand. We walked back to the two he had hit with his arrows. The two were dying; their eyes were glazing over. Both had their hands on their swords. Ulf would see them in Valhalla.

Gunnstein Thorfinnson and Alf appeared with bloodied swords. The Jarl's brother looked happy. "That is ten more who will not bother my brother."

Ulf spat, "Aye and they will hunt us again. Strip these bodies. I have plans for them. Wait here. "

The two oathsworn of Harald Black Teeth had warrior rings as well as mail; we took them from their bodies. This was a rich haul. The one who had died first had a fine sword. I jammed it in my belt. Ulf appeared with swords from the ones killed by Gunnstein and Alf.

Ulf pointed to the saplings." Tie their bodies between them. I wish to send a message to Harald Black Teeth."

While Gunnstein and Alf took one of the bodies Ulf and I took the other.

Gunnstein pointed to the settlements. We could still hear fighting, "We should go back and help!"

Ulf shook his head, "We go back we die. They will be ready for us. Your brother has let you come with us so that you may learn. Hrólfr learns. How many men has he killed? And yet he has just duck down on his face." I reddened in embarrassment. I was desperate for a beard; a real beard. "We will go to their drekar. There we can help our comrades."

Chapter 16

He led us along the coast so that we avoided any possibility of encountering the enemy. I knew, I know not how, that Harald Black Teeth would have men searching for us. We had killed many of his men. That would take warriors from the walls. I smiled for I knew Hermund the Bent and he would not be happy about that. He would want to concentrate on destroying the walls. If the two disagreed and fought that could only help the Jarl.

It was early afternoon when we reached the farmhouse. The three dragon ships were moored in the bay. They looked to have forty or fifty oars each. They had the prows still attached. One had a serpent's head while the other two had dragons. They were formidable-looking ships. Between the farmhouse and the settlement lay the sprawl of their camp. We saw the blackened remains of a fire and the piles of clothes and spare weapons they had left. They had used the dell which was protected from the winds. The smell of dung told us that it was a poor and ill-maintained camp. They had not designated a latrine. Siggi would not have allowed that to happen. It showed that there was little order to our foes. The camp was spread out over a thousand paces. It looked just like the one we had seen on the north side of the walls. It seemed to be little camps. It was a sign that there was little harmony in our foes. Having spied out their camp we moved towards the farmhouse some three hundred paces away. We hid in the bushes which topped the higher ground overlooking the water.

Ulf took off his helmet and slid forward to peer through the bushes. I copied him. Eventually, Gunnstein did the same and Ulf nodded. The Jarl's brother had taken the criticism of the scout to heart. There were four men seated around the fire before the farmhouse. Perhaps they knew it to be haunted and were frightened of it. Beyond that there looked to be four guards on each dragon ship although it is hard to tell, some could have been sleeping; hidden below the sheerstrakes.

We heard them talk. "I thought that the Jarl would have defeated them by now! We have more men than they do."

"You know that he does not waste men in pointless attacks. He wishes to wear them down. It is their treasure he wants. I have heard that they have so many chests of gold that their drekar almost sank while coming here."

"Then we should just burn it to the ground!"

"But then we would not know where it was buried! Fool! Do you think that they will leave so much gold and jewels just lying around?"

"Harald Black Teeth is not a patient man! He came here to kill Jarl Gunnar Thorfinnson and that runt who rides horses."

Another voice said, "Enough talk, it is your bet!"

When Ulf was satisfied, he slid back down the bank. "We will take the four by the fire. You three use your bows. I will get below the farm and take any you miss." He glared at us, "Do not miss! When they are dead we will go down to the shore."

"What then?"

"Then Gunnstein Thorfinnson, you and Alf the Silent will prop the bodies by the fire and then join Hrólfr and me. We will try to take a dragon ship. If they lose a drekar, it might weaken their resolve."

I frowned, "Or it might make them try to take our ships!"

He grinned, "You are learning, Hrólfr. If they try that then we are not alone. Sven has warriors, and if we know they are coming, then we can be prepared!"

The three of us crept closer to the four men. Their backs were towards us. I managed to get a good view of the warrior on the far side. He had no warrior bands which showed he was not experienced and he just had a leather byrnie. I had a clear target. I knocked an arrow; I had already chosen my best arrow. I glanced at the other two; they were both ready. I pulled back the bow. The Saami bow took some pulling but I was now more familiar with it. I released the arrow. Even while it was heading for the warrior facing me I had knocked another arrow. The three arrows hit almost simultaneously. The warrior who was not hit stood and looked around for the hidden enemies. Two black fletched arrows struck him. He fell backwards onto the fire. His hair flared into flames. I ran to him and pulled him off the fire. I did not want those on the ships to see a burning warrior, it would tell them they were in danger.

I left the other two to arrange the dead bodies around the fire and hurried to the shore. Ulf was hiding by the bushes which grew on the shelf rock above the bay. I lay down next to him. His eyes questioned me and I nodded. He pointed to the nearest ship. There were just four men on board but they did not have a deck watch. From our vantage point by the farmhouse, we had seen that they were playing a game.

"Take off your mail and your boots. We will swim out to the ship. The fools will pay for their laziness. "

Alf and Gunnstein joined us. We had both just removed our leather mail. Ulf just nodded to them and said, "I hope you can swim."

I took out my seax and looked at the sun. It was dipping in the west. It would be some time until dusk. That suited us for it meant we had the darkness to help us to escape.

After checking that no one had moved their position we slipped down to the water. It was cooler than I had expected. I had kept on my breeks and tucked in my belt I had the wickedly sharp dagger. We swam across the still, calm water to the nearest dragon ship. The nearest one was four ships lengths away. The three crews were giving each other enough room in case the sea became more violent. I was a good swimmer. When I had lived in the land of the Wolf I had often swum the waters of Cyningestūn. I closed with the ship quicker than the others.

We had seen the four men seated amidships, by the mast fish. I headed for the steering board. I would be able to climb aboard easier. Grabbing hold of the board I reached up to grip the withy rope. I lifted myself out of the water by placing my feet on the hull just above the waterline. I raised my head to peer over the sheerstrake. The four warriors were on the other side of the mast still playing with dice. I took a chance and rolled over the side of the drekar. The large helmsman's chest which lay close to the stern was big enough to give me cover.

Ulf was the next one over. I drew my seax. Without waiting for the other two the scout waved me forward. They had cleared the deck, I assumed to lift the decking and store the treasure they hope to capture from us. It made our task easier. With bare feet, we moved silently. We were ten paces from them when they saw Gunnstein and Alf as they tumbled over the bow. The Jarl's brother fell awkwardly. Alf stood before him with his short sword ready.

The four deck guards might have been lazy but they were prepared. Grabbing their swords and axes they raced towards our two companions. We ran after them. I was faster than Ulf. I dived when I was close to the rearmost warrior. My shoulder hit him in the back and as he fell forward his sword shot from his grip. Ulf lunged at the second. I lay on the back of the warrior I had hit. He smelled of sweat and fish. I brought my seax up under his right arm. Warm blood flooded down my hand. I pushed harder with my blade and twisted as I did so. The man went limp; he was dead. I pulled out my blade and looked to the bow

Alf had wounded one of his attackers but the other had cut my silent comrade in his side. Alf knew he was dying but refusing to give up hurled himself at the remaining warrior who shouted, "Attack! We are under attack!"

Ulf and I ran towards the two of them who appeared to be embracing. Even as our blades sliced into the back he had used his own dagger to kill Alf the Silent.

Gunnstein rose groggily. His head was badly cut. He had fallen against a sharp piece of iron and he appeared to be limping. Ulf shouted, "Cut the anchor! Hrólfr, find kindling. We shall send Alf to Valhalla in his own drekar."

The crew of the other ship were alerted. I could see them moving around and shouting to the dead guards at the farmhouse. They were too far away at the moment to do any harm to us. I saw them shout again at the four corpses by the fire. I found the kindling. It was by the fire and the firestone. They would have used it to cook while they watched on the ship. I found an empty pot and put kindling in the bottom. I saw a jar of seal oil. I poured some on the wooden deck close to the mast.

Ulf shouted, "Gunnstein, help me raise the sail." With the anchor rope cut, I could feel she was drifting already. The outgoing tide was taking us towards the other ships. I laid more kindling at the side of the pots. I took the flint from the chest by the steering board and then struck it until the kindling and oiled sheep's wool caught fire. I blew on it to make it flame more. I put more kindling on and as the fire caught, poured the last of the seal oil upon it. The flames leapt, almost singeing my eyebrows. "The fire is ready!"

"Then fire the ship! Do not wait for us." The Norns! I tipped the fire onto the oil-soaked deck. I had been expecting flames; I had created an inferno. I had to jump back to avoid being caught by the fire.

Ulf laughed, "It is good you have no beard or you would have lost it already!" He pointed to the shore. "Over the side. The wind and the tide will take it to the other ships." The sail was only halfway up but the tide was driving the dragon ship towards the second one. Its crew was already trying to cut their own anchors. As we jumped over the side I said a silent farewell to Alf. He had said little but he had been a warrior who had always stood by me. He had died well and I would see him in Valhalla.

The water was refreshing and I quickly swam through the water. There was no need for silence now but speed was vital. I clambered ashore and raced for my leather armour. The flames caught the sail. As I began to don my leather I saw that while the third dragon ship had managed to turn to avoid the fireship the second had not. Alf's drekar bumped into it. The second drekar's crew had tried to raise the sail and the flames caught hold of it. The two ships began to drift east. Alf and his funeral pyre were heading for Frankia. Already it was lower in the water. The masts were alight and made the ships alive. I swear I saw Alf's spirit rise through the fire to ascend to Valhalla. I clutched the horse amulet around my neck.

I had dressed by the time the other two reached me. In the distance, the clamour of battle diminished. The day was almost over and with dusk not far away they would see the glow from the burning ships. They would come to investigate. We did not have long.

"Hrólfr, ready an arrow. Gunnstein can you walk?"

"Aye." He looked distraught. "I am sorry I fell."

Ulf shrugged, "It is *wyrd*. The Weird Sisters could not allow us an easy victory. Alf has paid with his life. We will remember him. "

The sun was now setting in the west but there was a glow in the northeast from the sinking dragon ship. We had almost made it back to the cave when we were spotted. It was at the point when we were the closest to the settlement. We could see the walls. I had Heart of Ice drawn and I was leading. Ulf was guarding the rear. Two warriors suddenly stepped out from the trees to our right. They came so quickly that I just reacted. I was quicker than they were. Perhaps they had been fighting all day and were tired, I know not but I lunged with my sword at one of them. It struck his throat and he made a gurgling sound as though he was choking. Then he fell at my feet in a bloody heap.

I pulled the blade out preparing to kill the other. However, he managed to shout before I did so. "Jarl! The enemy!" He got no further for I slashed the edge of my blade against his throat.

I heard Gunnstein slump against the trees. His eyes were glazing over.

Ulf saved our lives that day. "Quickly! Run to the walls! Hrólfr, you must carry Gunnstein. I will watch your back."

I just obeyed our orders and, picking up the Jarl's brother I ran. The day's fighting at the settlement was over and our enemies were limping and trudging back to their camp. The two we had slain were between their camp and our cave. We had just been unlucky. Already warriors were rushing to discover where the danger lay. We were lucky that, in the twilight, we looked much as they did. We burst out into the clearing before the walls. We had just eighty paces to run. As we hurried I took in the dead bodies which lay before the walls. It had been a day for dying. Behind us, I heard our enemies as they realised that we had evaded them.

I heard the shouts from the walls, "More of them! Arrows!"

Ulf shouted, "It is us, you old fool, Beorn Beornsson! Let us in!"

Hrolf the Viking

I took all of Gunnstein's weight. His weakened ankle could not support him. Behind me, I heard a roar as Hermund discovered where we were. Siggi White Hair appeared on the wall as I laboured across the open ground. "Archers now you can release! Get the gates open and have the bridge ready."

Ulf stopped to turn and release an arrow. Gunnstein was now almost a dead weight; the blow to his head must have been worse than we had thought. I knew that the gates would be well barred and there was a danger that our enemies could follow us in. I resolved to carry Gunnstein. I stopped and put him over my shoulder. I found that I could move faster. The noise of pursuit grew. When I saw the gates opening just thirty paces from us I hurried. Arne Four Toes and Siggi threw a long plank across the ditch,

"Hrólfr, get across!"

Ulf's voice told me that the scout was protecting my back! Normally I would have run across the wooden board but I was tired and Gunnstein was a dead weight. I almost overbalanced in the middle.

"Hurry, Hrólfr! You can make it."

Siggi's words gave me confidence and I leapt the last three steps. Arne took me and Gunnstein and pulled us through the gates. Ulf bundled into the back of me knocking Gunnstein and me to the ground. As the bridge was withdrawn and the gates were slammed shut Siggi's face appeared above me. "You came close to Valhalla then Hrólfr! Is the Jarl's brother dead or alive?"

Ulf said, "He fell when we attacked the drekar. He hurt his leg but his head struck a piece of metal on the ship. It was only in the last few hundred paces that he passed out. It is good that Hrólfr is stronger now!"

The Jarl held a hand out to help me to my feet. "I owe you my brother's life now Hrólfr. Beorn, see to my brother!"

"Where is Alf the Silent?"

Ulf pointed to the east. There was the slightest of glows. "He is in Valhalla but we gave him a dragon ship to carry him on his way, Siggi. They have but one drekar left and they have lost many men. We have slain almost twenty. We saw their dead in the ditch. Perhaps they will leave."

Beorn picked up Gunnstein and carried him to the hall. The Jarl shook his head. He pointed to a line of bodies. "We have lost too. One more attack would have seen him over the walls. We wondered why they did not come again when darkness fell. They suddenly withdrew from the walls. Thank you for your attack. It has bought us time." He turned to Siggi, "What do you think, old friend, will they come again this night?"

"Which ships did you destroy?"

"Not the one with the serpent's head. The ones with the dragon prows."

"Then one will be the ship of Harald Black Teeth; Eagle's ***Heart'***. He will not be happy and I think there will be harsh words this night. We have a night to prepare." He put his arms around Ulf and me. "Come, these two heroes need food and we need to plan, Jarl Gunnar."

I saw the Eriksson brothers. They looked older and both bore wounds. They smiled and waved as we passed. I searched for other familiar faces and wondered how many of the old crew lay beneath their cloaks by the hall. I ate while Ulf told them of our efforts outside the walls. Siggi nodded his approval. "Your bow was a good purchase."

"It was, Siggi, but it now lies beyond the walls. I fear I have dropped it."

Arne Four Toes smiled, "It paid for Gunnstein's life. It is *wyrd*. Besides we may find it when we rid our home of these raiders."

"How?"

The wound to his brother and the loss of such old friends as Ulf Squint Eye had made the Jarl doubt himself. That was not good. In some crews that would mean another would take the Jarl's place. Ours was a different crew. I still do not know what made it different. The only explanation I could think of was that we had served with the Dragonheart. His crew served through loyalty rather than hopes of reward.

Siggi shook his head, "We have sat behind these walls long enough, Jarl. It will not take them long to decide to use fire against us. I am only surprised they have not done so already."

"That is because they think we have vast quantities of treasure and they are buried but Black Teeth wishes the Jarl and Hrólfr here, dead. The loss of his ship may well make him angry enough to attack and to use fire regardless of what Hermund the Bent wishes."

"But have we enough to attack them?"

"Ulf, where is their camp?" As ever it was the calm mind of Siggi which plotted our course.

"They are close to the farmhouse in the dell sheltered from the north winds. They have many small fires and are spread out."

Siggi thumped the table making me start. "Then we attack them. We use a shield wall and approach silently. If they are spread out, then we take them piecemeal."

We all looked at the Jarl. Our faces told him that we could do this and that we wished to try. If we were to die, then better to throw the bones and take a chance than wait for a fiery death. He nodded, "Aye then."

Siggi turned to me, "You have done much, Hrólfr, and each man within these walls owes you but I would ask one more sacrifice from you."

They all looked at me now. I nodded, "I am oathsworn, Siggi, and I will do whatever is asked of me."

"I would have you be Hrólfr the Horseman. Take Dream Strider and when we attack I would have you charge from the west. If we attack just as dawn breaks, then you will approach from the darkness. We have all heard Dream Strider's hooves as they pound on the turf. It sounds like death is approaching."

"But I will be alone! What can one man do?"

"You will be a man on a horse and they will not know that you are alone. You shout as though you lead a whole army." I nodded. Siggi put his hand on my shoulder. "I do not ask that you become a berserker. Just distract them and then look after yourself."

Ulf laughed, "I have fought with this one enough times to know that you are spitting in the wind Siggi but I like the plan. Hrólfr the Horseman can do this and we will tell the tale this winter when we recall how we destroyed three drekar crews!"

"Then I had best go prepare my horse. He will be ready to ride!"

Once outside I found Rurik One Ear and Erik One Hand waiting for me. I could not keep the smile from my face. They were both alive. "Come, we have to prepare my horse."

Rurik looked at me quizzically, "Your horse?"

"I am to charge our enemies!"

"Alone?"

"I will have Alf the Silent and the spirits of the other dead warriors with me. Do not worry I do not fear this. I will be on my horse and I have seen their camp. The Jarl intends to attack them and end this!"

As we walked to Dream Strider's stall I told them of the last few days. Erik suddenly became excited, "I will join you later! I have something to do!"

Dream Strider was pleased to see me. I could see that he was well fed and watered. He stamped his hoof. He was ready. We saddled him and Erik returned with Bagsecg. He carried my mail.

"It is not totally finished, Hrólfr but Erik told me what you intended. I could not let you ride out knowing that this might be the mail that would save you. It is not oiled and it still needs the mail for your arms but it will do. Come let us try it on."

I had just donned it when Siggi came in. "We are taking out some of the palisades at the rear of the wall. We will use them to make a bridge for you and then you can leave without their sentries and scouts spotting you." He noticed the mail and nodded his approval. "A warrior at last! May the Allfather be with you today! Leave whenever you are ready."

"How will I know when to attack?"

Siggi laughed, "Do not worry; you will know!"

I put on my helmet and Erik fastened my wolf cloak around my shoulders. I did not need it to hide me but I knew that it would bring me luck. I touched my horse amulet and hung my shield and helmet from my saddle.

Arne handed me a spear, "Use this like those Moors we saw near Bourde."

I took it and led Dream Strider towards the rear wall. The Eriksson brothers were just finishing laying the two wooden posts they had taken from the wall across the ditch. I walked ahead of Dream Strider. Nipper tried to follow. I shouted, "Stay!" Reluctant he did so. I led Dream Strider to the bridge and I spoke to him all the way. I did not want him to fear the drop into the corpse-filled ditch. Once on solid ground, I watched as the two posts were replaced. Erik's wave seemed final. I mounted my horse and rode north and west. I intended to ride around the island and avoid any contact with the enemy. I needed to achieve surprise. As I neared the cave I heard skittering in the undergrowth. I readied my spear but as Dream Strider did not react I was not worried. I came across one of the men we had slain the other day. The foxes and the rats had been at his body. Nature would soon eliminate all traces of our battles. I was familiar with this part of the island. I rode confidently. I used my ears and watched Dream Strider. He would let me know of any danger. By the time I had turned and headed east towards the haunted farmhouse I saw false dawn in the distance. I resisted the urge to hurry. I still had time. As a precaution, I hung my shield from my left arm. It was then I realised that if I was to use my shield properly from the back of a horse I needed a different bit and longer reins. I would use some of my coins to have Bagsecg make me one. For the present, I would have to adapt quickly. I donned my helmet and fastened the leather thongs beneath my chin.

I knew that I was nearing their camp when I smelled the wood smoke. I reined in on the rise just a couple of thousand paces from the camp. The trees and bushes afforded me cover. I decided to wait. I did not want to warn the enemy of the approach of our shield wall. I could picture the clan as they prepared. The Jarl, Siggi, Arne and the warriors with mail byrnies would be in the front two ranks. A forest of spears would protect them. At the rear would be the younger warriors; the ones who had no mail. They would fill the gaps when the ones at the front fell. Shields would be held above the heads of those at the front. I knew that if the enemy had a warning they would form their own shield wall and ours might fail. Siggi's plan relied upon surprise. And so, I waited.

There was the hint of dawn now. The sky seemed a shade or two lighter than it had been. I thought I caught a movement to my right and ahead of me. I took a chance and kicked Dream Strider on. He was ready and looked around almost as though he was saying, *'What is keeping you?'*

I had not travelled more than four hundred paces when I heard a roar and a shout of, "Raven Wing!"

The attack had begun. I held my spear so that I could thrust with it. I had to keep my enemies at bay. I heard, even with my helmet about my ears, the sound of consternation in the enemy camp. Men had been asleep. Fuelled no doubt by beer. They would not be wearing armour and they would not know from which direction came the danger. I kept a steady pace with Dream Strider. There was a long area of turf before their camp and I wanted his hooves to drum rhythmically. It was an easy way to ride. And then I saw the wedge. It had burst through the outlying men and was heading, like a large, moving machine, towards the main camp and Hermund the Bent. Harald Black Teeth was trying to organise a shield wall but men had been asleep and had not had time to put on their mail. Had they done so it would be have been a long day. Mailed men against mailed men take a long time to die.

The half-formed shield wall met Siggi and the Jarl. There was a loud crash and cries. Although the enemy wall was breached it had slowed down the wedge. Warriors tried to flood around the side. I was less than five hundred paces away and I saw one or two warriors look around as they heard the thunder of hooves. It was time to play my part. I shouted as I waved my spear forward, "Warriors of the Wolf, ride on! Let us slaughter our foes! On Warriors of the Wolf!"

I was not sure if the enemy heard all of my words, it did not matter. The first ray of sunlight glinted off my helmet and spearhead. The four who were less than forty paces from me turned and ran. I kicked Dream Strider and he leapt forward. I pulled back my arm and thrust my spear into the back of the slowest of the four. As I passed his dying body I pulled out my spear. I had little time to react for the next one half turned. I rammed my spear into his mouth. As he fell back the spear was almost torn free. Others had witnessed my charge and the death of the two men. More men began to flee towards the single drekar which lay just a half-mile away. These were not oathsworn. These were men who looked to make an easy killing and quick profit. With only one ship left the weaker would seek shelter there.

A warrior, braver than the rest, turned to face me. He had a shield and a sword. I feinted, as though I was going to throw my spear and when he lifted his shield I rammed my spear through his mail and into his stomach. His dying hands clutched the spear and it was torn from my grip. I drew Heart of Ice. I swung it to my left as a warrior turned to try to strike at Dream Strider. My horse's bared teeth made him flinch and my sword hacked across his throat. I swung it to my right and hit a fleeing warrior across the back of his neck. He too fell dead.

I was aware that there were many men fleeing before me and that the battle was to my right. I reined in Dream Strider and turned. The two lines were now facing each other. Although evenly matched I had to intervene. I was behind the enemy lines. Any warrior in a shield wall fears being attacked from the rear. I played on that fear. I rode to within fifty paces and stopped. I had learned how to make Dream Strider rear and I pulled back on the reins and stood in the stirrups.

"Harald Black Teeth! Today you die! The Wolf Warriors are coming!" I played on the fact that Jarl Dragonheart and his Ulfheonar were feared. They were not here but I was known to be their friend. I galloped towards them. Some broke immediately and ran to my left and right to avoid what they thought was a column of warriors. The light was behind me now and as I approached those at the rear I pulled back on Dream Strider's reins. He reared again. I swung my sword at a helmet to my right as his hooves smashed into two men before him. I twisted his reins so that my sword faced those on my right. I could see Siggi and the Jarl furiously fighting with Hermund the Bent and his few oathsworn. I had free rein to hack at men who were busy fighting the Raven Clan.

It was too much for Harald Black Teeth and I saw him stab forward to strike Knut Eriksson in the face and, as he fell, he shouted, "Back to the drekar! There will be another day!"

I could not allow that. I turned Dream Strider's head around. Harald Black Teeth still had oathsworn. Two of them turned to face me. As one hacked at my left leg I swung my sword and hit the other in the face. The blow to my leg hurt but the mail held. The Weird Sisters had decided that I had had enough luck for one day and the dying man fell into Dream Strider. My horse lost its footing and he fell upon the man who had hit my leg. My horse's body crushed the warrior. As I fell I kicked my feet from my stirrup and rolled clear. Dream Strider rose and, frightened, galloped north.

I ran after Harald Black Teeth. I was young and I did not tire easily. I began to catch him up as we neared the farmhouse. Ahead I could see, in dawn's early light, the first of those who had fled wading out to the drekar which was now moored less than thirty paces from the shore.

Harald's oathsworn were dead and he was alone. Perhaps he heard me as I pounded across the turf after him for he turned with a snarl, "You whelp! I will have the pleasure of killing you first!"

A year ago, I would have been terrified of this man who made my life on Ljoðhús such a misery but I had changed. "I do not fear a man with breath which smells like a pig's arse and who runs while his men still die for him!"

He swung his axe at me. I may have been overconfident for I met it with my shield and did not angle it enough. I felt my arm shiver and Harald Black Teeth laughed, "You do not have Siggi White Hair to watch you now!"

That was it! I had to use the lessons Siggi had taught me; use my speed and use my head. Be like my sword and be ice. I feinted with my sword and he laughed, "Boy! I wish I had more time to kill you slowly!"

He swung his arm around to end it with a massive blow to my head. He swung diagonally so that if it missed my head it would still strike my weakened arm and shoulder. I would die. I leapt forward and smashed my shield into his face. It hurt my arm and I was numb from the shoulder down but he only hit my shoulder with his hand. He stumbled backwards with blood pouring from his nose. His nasal was bent and he spat out two of his famously black teeth. I laughed. "Now you are the Bent and you have no black teeth!"

He became angry and swung his axe wildly. I had all the time in the world to step back and then, as the axe head flashed before my face I stepped in and hacked at his knee with my sword. His byrnie stopped short of his knee and I not only drew blood but shards of bone shone on my sword. I was ice personified. I did not allow him time to react. I spun around and brought my sword behind his right knee. My sword slashed through his tendons. He sank to the ground. I stepped over him and put my weight on his right hand which held his axe still.

"You faced me as a man and I will let you keep your weapon. When I see you in Valhalla, move aside! Hrólfr the Horseman will remember you and your treachery!" I plunged my sword into his throat. He seemed to cough and choke. His eyes stared lifelessly at the sky. My demon was gone.

I turned and heard a shout behind me. I saw the Jarl raise Hermund the Bent's head high. We had won. The enemy was defeated. Even as I watched the last three survivors shed their mail and swam out to the last drekar which, with just ten oars manned, headed north. There they would tell the world that the island of the Raven Wing Clan was a dangerous place to go. As I looked up I saw Dream Strider wandering towards me.

He had survived. He did not limp and I thanked the gods. I would be a horseman still.

Epilogue

We had many dead to bury. Olaf would not be alone. Einar Einarsson and Thorir Thorsen were among the fifteen warriors who died. Others had wounds. Knut did not die but he lost his eye. He became Knut One Eye. We all had warrior bands to boast of our bravery. When next we fought our enemies would know who we were.

We had great quantities of mail and weapons. Ran gave us back more when a storm a few days later brought in the mailed, bloated corpses which had drowned trying to get to their ship. Few of our warriors were now without mail. We tended our wounds and we sang songs of the battle.

The Jarl rewarded me with a small jewel-encrusted dagger he had taken from Hermund the Bent. His brother gave me a spare set of mail. The greatest reward was the song they sang of me. The Weird Sisters had shown me favour and I was now accepted as a warrior of the Raven Wing Clan.

The horseman came through darkest night
He rode towards the dawning light
With fiery steed and thrusting spear
Hrólfr the Horseman brought great fear
Slaughtering all he breached their line
Of warriors slain there were nine
Hrólfr the Horseman with gleaming blade
Hrólfr the Horseman all enemies slayed
With mighty axe Black Teeth stood
Angry and filled with hot blood
Hrólfr the Horseman with gleaming blade
Hrólfr the Horseman all enemies slayed
Ice cold Hrólfr with Heart of Ice
Swung his arm and made it slice
Hrólfr the Horseman with gleaming blade
Hrólfr the Horseman all enemies slayed
In two strokes the Jarl was felled
Hrólfr's sword nobly held
Hrólfr the Horseman with gleaming blade
Hrólfr the Horseman all enemies slayed
                    The End

Glossary

Afon Hafron- River Severn in Welsh
Alt Clut- Dumbarton Castle on the Clyde
Andecavis- Angers in Anjou
Balley Chashtal -Castleton (Isle of Man)
Bebbanburgh- Bamburgh Castle, Northumbria. Also known as Din Guardi in the ancient tongue
Beck- a stream
Blót – a blood sacrifice made by a jarl
Blue Sea/Middle Sea- The Mediterranean
Bondi- Viking farmers who fight
Bourde- Bordeaux
Bjarnarøy –Great Bernera (Bear Island)
Byrnie- a mail or leather shirt reaching down to the knees
Caerlleon- Welsh for Chester
Caestir - Chester (old English)
Casnewydd –Newport, Wales
Cephas- Greek for Simon Peter (St. Peter)
Chape- the tip of a scabbard
Charlemagne- Holy Roman Emperor at the end of the 8th and beginning of the 9th centuries
Cherestanc- Garstang (Lancashire)
Corn Walum or Om Walum- Cornwall
Cymri- Welsh
Cymru- Wales
Cyninges-tūn – Coniston. It means the estate of the king (Cumbria)
Dùn Èideann –Edinburgh (Gaelic)
Din Guardi- Bamburgh castle
Drekar- a Dragon ship (a Viking warship)
Duboglassio –Douglas, Isle of Man
Dyrøy –Jura (Inner Hebrides)
Dyflin- Old Norse for Dublin
Ein-mánuðr- middle of March to the middle of April
Eoforwic- Saxon for York
Faro Bregancio- Corunna (Spain)

Ferneberga -Farnborough (Hampshire)
Fey- having second sight
Firkin- a barrel containing eight gallons (usually beer)
Fret-a sea mist
Frankia- France and part of Germany
Fyrd-the Saxon levy
Gaill- Irish for foreigners
Galdramenn- wizard
Glaesum –amber
Gleawecastre- Gloucester
Gói- the end of February to the middle of March
Grenewic- Greenwich
Haesta- Hastings
Hamwic -Southampton
Haughs- small hills in Norse (As in Tarn Hows)
Heels- when a ship leans to one side under the pressure of the wind
Hel - Queen of Niflheim, the Norse underworld.
Herkumbl- a mark on the front of a helmet denoting the clan of a Viking warrior
Here Wic- Harwich
Hetaereiarch – Byzantine general
Hí- Iona (Gaelic)
Hjáp - Shap- Cumbria (Norse for stone circle)
Hoggs or Hogging- when the pressure of the wind causes the stern or the bow to droop
Hrams-a – Ramsey, Isle of Man
Hywel ap Rhodri Molwynog- King of Gwynedd 814-825
Icaunis- a British river god
Issicauna- Gaulish for the lower Seine
Itouna- River Eden Cumbria
Jarl- Norse earl or lord
Joro-goddess of the earth
kjerringa - Old Woman- the solid block in which the mast rested
Knarr- a merchant ship or a coastal vessel
Kyrtle-woven top
Leathes Water- Thirlmere

Ljoðhús- Lewis
Legacaestir- Anglo-Saxon for Chester
Liger- Loire
Lochlannach – Irish for Northerners (Vikings)
Lothuwistoft- Lowestoft
Louis the Pious- King of the Franks and son of Charlemagne
Lundenwic - London
Maeresea- River Mersey
Mammceaster- Manchester
Manau/Mann – The Isle of Man(n) (Saxon)
Marcia Hispanic- Spanish Marches (the land around Barcelona)
Mast fish- two large racks on a ship for the mast
Melita- Malta
Midden - a place where they dumped human waste
Miklagård - Constantinople
Leudes- Imperial officer (a local leader in the Carolingian Empire. They became Counts a century after this.
Njörðr- God of the sea
Nithing- A man without honour (Saxon)
Odin - The "All Father" God of war, also associated with wisdom, poetry, and magic (The ruler of the gods).
Olissipo- Lisbon
Orkneyjar-Orkney
Portucale- Porto
Portesmūða -Portsmouth
Condado Portucalense- the County of Portugal
Penrhudd – Penrith Cumbria
Pillars of Hercules- Straits of Gibraltar
Ran- Goddess of the sea
Roof rock- slate
Rinaz –The Rhine
Sabrina- Latin and Celtic for the River Severn. Also the name of a female Celtic deity
Saami- the people who live in what is now Northern Norway/Sweden
St. Cybi- Holyhead
Scree- loose rocks in a glacial valley

Seax – short sword
Sheerstrake- the uppermost strake in the hull
Sheet- a rope fastened to the lower corner of a sail
Shroud- a rope from the masthead to the hull amidships
Skeggox – an axe with a shorter beard on one side of the blade
South Folk- Suffolk
Stad- Norse settlement
Stays- ropes running from the mast-head to the bow
Stirap- stirrup
Strake- the wood on the side of a drekar
Suthriganaworc - Southwark (London)
Syllingar- Scilly Isles
Syllingar Insula- Scilly Isles
Tarn- small lake (Norse)
Temese- River Thames (also called the Tamese)
The Norns- The three sisters who weave webs of intrigue for men
Thing-Norse for a parliament or a debate (Tynwald)
Thor's day- Thursday
Threttanessa- a drekar with 13 oars on each side.
Thrall- slave
Tinea- Tyne
Trenail- a round wooden peg used to secure strakes
Tynwald- the Parliament on the Isle of Man
Úlfarrberg- Helvellyn
Úlfarrland- Cumbria
Úlfarr- Wolf Warrior
Úlfarrston- Ulverston
Ullr-Norse God of Hunting
Ulfheonar-an elite Norse warrior who wore a wolf skin over his armour
Vectis- The Isle of Wight
Volva- a witch or healing woman in Norse culture
Waeclinga Straet- Watling Street (A5)
Windlesore-Windsor
Waite- a Viking word for farm
Werham -Wareham (Dorset)

Wintan-caestre -Winchester
Withy- the mechanism connecting the steering board to the ship
Woden's day- Wednesday
Wyddfa-Snowdon
Wyrd- Fate
Yard- a timber from which the sail is suspended on a drekar
Ynys Môn-Anglesey

Historical note

My research encompasses not only books and the Internet but also TV. Time Team was a great source of information. I wish they would bring it back! I saw the wooden compass on the Dan Snow programme about the Vikings. It was used in modern times to sail from Denmark to Edinburgh and was only a couple of points out. Similarly, the construction of the temporary hall was copied from the settlement of Leif Eriksson in Newfoundland.

Stirrups began to be introduced in Europe during the 7th and 8th Centuries. By Charlemagne's time, there were widely used but only by nobles. It is said this was the true beginning of feudalism. It was the Vikings who introduced them to England. It was only in the time of Canute the Great that they were widespread. The use of stirrups enabled a rider to strike someone on the ground from the back of a horse and enabled the use of spears and later, lances.

The Vikings may seem cruel to us now. They enslaved women and children. Many of the women became their wives. The DNA of the people of Iceland shows that it was made up of a mixture of Norse and Danish males and Celtic females. These were the people who settled in Iceland, Greenland and Vinland. They did the same in England and, as we shall see, Normandy. They were different times and it would be wrong to judge them with our politically correct twenty-first-century eyes. This sort of behaviour still goes on in the world but with less justification.

The Vikings began to raid the Loire and the Seine from the middle of the 9th century. They were able to raid as far as Tours. Tours, Saumur and the monastery at Marmoutier were all raided and destroyed. As a result of the raids and the destruction, castles were built there during the latter part of the 9th century. There are many islands in the Loire and many tributaries. The Maine, which runs through Angers, is also a wide waterway. The lands seemed made for Viking raiders. They did not settle in Aquitaine but they did in Austrasia.

At this time, there were no Kings. There were clans. Each clan had a hersir or Jarl. A Hersir was more of a landlocked Viking while a Jarl usually had ship(s) at his command. Kings like Canute and Harald Hadrada were rare.

Hermund the Bent is an actual Viking name but I do not know why he was called Bent. It seemed appropriate for my villain. Harald Black Teeth is made up but the practice of filing marks in teeth to allow them to blacken and to make the warrior more frightening was common in Viking times.

Books used in the research
British Museum - 'Vikings- Life and Legends'
'Saxon, Norman and Viking' by Terence Wise (Osprey)
Ian Heath - 'The Vikings'. (Osprey)
Ian Heath- 'Byzantine Armies 668-1118 (Osprey)
David Nicholle- 'Romano-Byzantine Armies 4th-9th Century (Osprey)
Stephen Turnbull- 'The Walls of Constantinople AD 324-1453' (Osprey)
Keith Durham- 'Viking Longship' (Osprey)
Anglo-Danish Project- 'The Vikings in England'
The Varangian Guard- 988-1453 Raffael D'Amato
Saxon Viking and Norman- Terence Wise
The Walls of Constantinople AD 324-1453-Stephen Turnbull
Byzantine Armies- 886-1118- Ian Heath
The Age of Charlemagne-David Nicolle
The Normans- David Nicolle
Norman Knight AD 950-1204- Christopher Gravett
The Norman Conquest of the North- William A Kappelle
The Knight in History- Francis Gies
The Norman Achievement- Richard F Cassady
Knights- Constance Brittain Bouchard
Knight Templar 1120-1312 -Helen Nicholson

Griff Hosker
April 2016

Other books by Griff Hosker

If you enjoyed reading this book, then why not read another one by the author?

Ancient History

The Sword of Cartimandua Series
(Germania and Britannia 50 A.D. – 128 A.D.)
Ulpius Felix- Roman Warrior (prequel)
The Sword of Cartimandua
The Horse Warriors
Invasion Caledonia
Roman Retreat
Revolt of the Red Witch
Druid's Gold
Trajan's Hunters
The Last Frontier
Hero of Rome
Roman Hawk
Roman Treachery
Roman Wall
Roman Courage

The Wolf Warrior series
(Britain in the late 6th Century)
Saxon Dawn
Saxon Revenge
Saxon England
Saxon Blood
Saxon Slayer
Saxon Slaughter
Saxon Bane
Saxon Fall: Rise of the Warlord
Saxon Throne
Saxon Sword

Medieval History

The Dragon Heart Series
Viking Slave
Viking Warrior
Viking Jarl
Viking Kingdom
Viking Wolf
Viking War
Viking Sword
Viking Wrath
Viking Raid
Viking Legend
Viking Vengeance
Viking Dragon
Viking Treasure
Viking Enemy
Viking Witch
Viking Blood
Viking Weregeld
Viking Storm
Viking Warband
Viking Shadow
Viking Legacy
Viking Clan
Viking Bravery

The Norman Genesis Series
Hrolf the Viking
Horseman
The Battle for a Home
Revenge of the Franks
The Land of the Northmen
Ragnvald Hrolfsson
Brothers in Blood
Lord of Rouen
Drekar in the Seine
Duke of Normandy
The Duke and the King

Danelaw

Hrolf the Viking

(England and Denmark in the 11th Century)
Dragon Sword
Oathsword
Bloodsword
Danish Sword

New World Series
Blood on the Blade
Across the Seas
The Savage Wilderness
The Bear and the Wolf
Erik The Navigator
Erik's Clan

The Vengeance Trail

The Reconquista Chronicles
Castilian Knight
El Campeador
The Lord of Valencia

The Aelfraed Series
(Britain and Byzantium 1050 A.D. - 1085 A.D.)
Housecarl
Outlaw
Varangian

The Anarchy Series England 1120-1180
English Knight
Knight of the Empress
Northern Knight
Baron of the North
Earl
King Henry's Champion
The King is Dead
Warlord of the North
Enemy at the Gate
The Fallen Crown
Warlord's War
Kingmaker
Henry II

Hrolf the Viking

Crusader
The Welsh Marches
Irish War
Poisonous Plots
The Princes' Revolt
Earl Marshal
The Perfect Knight

**Border Knight
1182-1300**
Sword for Hire
Return of the Knight
Baron's War
Magna Carta
Welsh Wars
Henry III
The Bloody Border
Baron's Crusade
Sentinel of the North
War in the West
Debt of Honour
The Blood of the Warlord
The Fettered King

**Sir John Hawkwood Series
France and Italy 1339- 1387**
Crécy: The Age of the Archer
Man At Arms
The White Company
Leader of Men
Tuscan Warlord

Lord Edward's Archer
Lord Edward's Archer
King in Waiting
An Archer's Crusade
Targets of Treachery
The Great Cause
Wallace's War

**Struggle for a Crown
1360- 1485**

Hrolf the Viking

Blood on the Crown
To Murder a King
The Throne
King Henry IV
The Road to Agincourt
St Crispin's Day
The Battle for France
The Last Knight
Queen's Knight

Tales from the Sword I
(Short stories from the Medieval period)

Tudor Warrior series
England and Scotland in the late 14th and early 15th century
Tudor Warrior
Tudor Spy

Conquistador
England and America in the 16th Century
Conquistador
The English Adventurer

Modern History

The Napoleonic Horseman Series
Chasseur à Cheval
Napoleon's Guard
British Light Dragoon
Soldier Spy
1808: The Road to Coruña
Talavera
The Lines of Torres Vedras
Bloody Badajoz
The Road to France
Waterloo

The Lucky Jack American Civil War series
Rebel Raiders
Confederate Rangers
The Road to Gettysburg

Hrolf the Viking

Soldier of the Queen series
Soldier of the Queen
Redcoat's Rifle

The British Ace Series
1914
1915 Fokker Scourge
1916 Angels over the Somme
1917 Eagles Fall
1918 We will remember them
From Arctic Snow to Desert Sand
Wings over Persia

**Combined Operations series
1940-1945**
Commando
Raider
Behind Enemy Lines
Dieppe
Toehold in Europe
Sword Beach
Breakout
The Battle for Antwerp
King Tiger
Beyond the Rhine
Korea
Korean Winter

Tales from the Sword II
(Short stories from the Modern period)

Other Books
Great Granny's Ghost (Aimed at 9-14-year-old young people)

For more information on all of the books then please visit the author's website at www.griffhosker.com where there is a link to contact him or visit his Facebook page: GriffHosker at Sword Books

Printed in Great Britain
by Amazon